S. E. B. Whitlock

REBIRTH

SHANTIR SAGA

BOOK 1

Life is a song—sing it.

Life is a game—play it.

Life is a challenge—meet it.

Life is a dream—realize it.

Life is a sacrifice—offer it.

Life is love—enjoy it.

Sai Baba

TABLE OF CONTENTS

CHAPTER 1

THE GREAT LIE

The old man's voice was hoarse and low. As he spoke, the boy at his feet hung on every word. He had heard this tale a thousand times but he never tired of it. It was the tale of his people, the story of their suffering and perseverance. Most importantly, it was a tale of hope. Hope that one day it would be better and that they would, in some distant future, regain their honor and rightful place in the world. As the fire crackled in the dark room, fighting back the cold of winter, the old man continued his tale.

"The Great Father created seven children. Each was created in order from greatest to least and given a gift of Himself. The first of these children was Hadriah. He was strong and powerful beyond the others, and their power could not touch him. Then the Great Father also gave them the world. The eldest, our beloved Hadriah, was given dominion over the world and instead of ruling it alone, which was his right, he portioned parts of it to his siblings, keeping the lion's share for himself of course. His brothers and sisters grew greedy and begged him for more. Naturally, he refused." The old man stopped his story to take a drink from the crooked glass on the table.

THE GREAT LIE

The boy watched and waited patiently for the story to continue. When the old man had finished his drink, he asked the boy, "Why did mighty Hadriah refuse?" He watched the boy's face light up. He knew the child had the answer to his question because he had been teaching him for all ten years of his life.

"Because only toil, suffering, and victory in battle can increase one's worth!" the boy stated clearly, his voice strong and vibrant against the fire and wind. The old man smiled, his teeth all but missing behind his graying tattered beard.

"Correct. They had done nothing to deserve more than what they had already been so generously given. But that did not stop their greed. They then pleaded to their father. He told them that only the eldest had the right to divide the world as he wished. The selfish six twisted his words to mean that by killing the Mighty Hadriah, they could control the world. In an act of cowardice, they stole into his bed chambers while he slept and savagely beat and bound him. Then with no remorse at their actions, they tossed him into the abyss. He was not given the chance to defend his honor in a fair fight. For this reason, he felt the Great Father give him hope. This hope he shared with his evil siblings as he drifted into darkness. One day his shantir would return to the world. This vessel would cleanse the world of their taint, restoring the rightful order of things. And when each of their shantirs had been cast out, He would return from the darkness."

The boy sat patiently on the hard, cold floor, watching as the old man stared into the fire. After a few minutes the boy ventured a question. The tale always ended here but he had to know.

"What happened then?" The old man found the child's face in the fire glow. He cleared his throat and started again.

"Well, after Hadriah was gone, the Great Father was very upset. The six tricked him with false repentance and He forgave his dubious children. Having lost his eldest son, he named Luniah, the greediest of them all, Mighty Hadriah's successor. She redivided the world, but fearing Hadriah's fate, catered to the desires of her younger brothers and sisters. Always the diplomat, she deceived them into believing they got the part of the world they wanted. Her final act of insult was to move Hadriah's beloved creations, our ancestors, from their homes of plenty and warmth to this jagged and bitter cold island." Again the old man's gaze fell to the fire. He and his people shared so much with the flame. The heat of their rage had burned within them since the day their beloved Hadriah's shantir was ripped from them. They longed to destroy the six kingdoms as the flame devoured everything it touched.

Lost in his thoughts, the old man was startled by the child's voice, even stronger and clearer than before. "But we have beaten them. They thought to destroy Hadriah's legacy, but we have held it in our hearts. They thought we would die here, but we have lived. We have tamed the seas, and our ingenuity and strength have provided us with machines to work the land. We have Hadriah's strength still, and one day very soon we shall lay them below our feet as they always should have been." His face shown like a star in the dim light. The old man would never tell the child, but he loved him very much. Of all the man-children in the kingdom, this one above all embodied all Hadriah had been. The old man fought back his growing hope. For many years he had taught and trained hopefuls just as his father had done and his father before him. Since the beginning, they had prepared possible vessels hoping that their God would return to them. This boy, already a head taller than his peers and strong as an ox, at only age ten, was most promising.

"That is absolutely right lad. Now, off to bed. We have hard work in the morning and training before lunch. You will need much rest." The boy leapt to his feet and disappeared into the dark of the room. His footsteps on the ladder could be heard as he climbed to his bedchamber in the crawlspace. The old man's eyes returned to the fire. In silence he issued a simple prayer. "Rikard deserves your shantir, Hadriah. Do not neglect us any further."

Panting, the old man leaned on his walking stick. The morning was colder than usual, and the fog rolling in from the sea made the mountain pass more dangerous than ever.

"Shall I carry you?" the boy, now a young man,

strutted back into view. Though only six years later, he could easily be mistaken for a seasoned man of twenty. He had grown ever taller and stronger than any man in the village.

"Absolutely not! A man must forge his own way. I will get there in my own time." The old man saw the enormous form of Rikard disappear once again into the fog. They had taken this trip every morning since the day he turned sixteen. Up the dormant volcano to the shattered temple at its peak. Every day he had waited and prayed that the shantir would be bestowed. Today was the last chance. Tomorrow Rikard would be seventeen, and he would need to focus on the other hopefuls, all far less impressive than the young man hidden ahead of him in the clouds.

"One more time," he had not given up hope yet. The shantir passes at some point during the sixteenth year. In the other kingdoms, where the vessel already holds the shantir, they need only perform the right of shantinox and the new vessel is filled. They do this traditionally on the sixteenth birthday, but it can be performed at any time that year. For his kingdom of Hadrir, it was different. No vessel of Hadriah had ever existed. No shantinox had ever been performed. Each day of his considerable life, he had ventured up the mountain with the line of hopefuls in tow, only to return the same way unrewarded. This year had been different, just as the year of Rikard's birth. A strange plague had swept the island kingdom that year. All male children in womb or conceived perished prior to birth.

THE GREAT LIE

Only Rikard had survived. This was the first sign that Rikard could be the one. His physical stature and ability were the second. But all meant nothing, if today went as the previous days had.

As the old man crested the peak, the fog cleared. No weather ever touched their shattered temple. His ancestors had erected it when the world began, but the devious six had shattered it almost immediately. His people had found resolve in this insult and refused to rebuild it. It was perfect the way it was. Both a show of their strength and devotion to Hadriah, and a testament to the undying hatred of, and for, the Six. There the boy stood, in his place beside the overturned altar. As the old man made his way across the sanctuary, weaving between boulders and stone ruins, something amazing happened. A red glow began to emanate from the altar's broken bowl at Rikard's feet. The old man froze. For eighty six years, he had brought hopefuls here; and for eighty six years, he had waited for something to happen. In all that time, he had never known what it would look like. This was more terrifying and wonderful than he ever could have imagined. The red glow became a red mist, and the red mist began to climb into the air around Rikard's feet. Instinctively, he went to take a step back, but the old man frantically shouted for him to stay still.

The mist enveloped him, swirling around him faster and faster until he was the center of a great crimson tornado. The walls of the funnel began to shrink. As the mist touched him, a sharp burning sensation filled his skin. He fought the cry of pain in his throat. The mist covered him, penetrated him. The pain was so intense, Rikard fell to one knee, but never did he cry out. Just when he thought he might lose consciousness, the pain vanished. It was replaced by a tingling sensation. His whole body shimmered for a moment and then it was done. Despite these remarkable events, all seemed calm and normal again. But that was not the case. The old man fell to his knees, tears of joy streaming down his face and dripping from his tattered gray beard.

Rikard rose to his feet. He could feel the new strength within him...and new rage. Though he had always hated the six kingdoms for their neglect and treachery, his hatred was now much deeper. It stretched beyond time and space and was all encompassing.

"My Vessel, what do you command?" The old man's eyes took him in with pride and fear. Rikard stepped toward the old man who had taught him so well for all these years and placed a heavy hand on his shoulder.

"Now we prepare for war." He glanced down at the face of his teacher, smiled at him and then, in a single, smooth motion, snapped his neck. He lifted his body and carried him to the altar. As he placed his shriveled corpse upon the altar, he whispered into the old man's unhearing ears. "I am sorry, my friend. But we need all we can gather for the strong and battle ready. The old are no longer of value. I will remember you always. Rest in the bosom of Hadriah, my beloved teacher." He gazed one last time at the old man's frozen expression of admiration.

THE GREAT LIE

He then turned and strode back down the mountain path alone. He had a kingdom to rally, an army to train, powers to master, and, most importantly, six kingdoms to destroy.

CHAPTER 2
THE FIRST BLOW

Rikard looked down at his army. As he watched the bustle below him, he was carried back to the day he descended the mountain alone. An elder had asked him where the old man had gotten off to. Rikard had flatly told him of the old man's death and how that fate must befall all who would be unable to fight in the upcoming war. The elder had taken the news badly. He ordered Rikard seized as a murderer. Rikard's new found strength proved to be too much for the men who attempted to capture or kill him. When the fighting stopped Rikard stood unscathed amid nine dead and six wounded. He knew they needed proof of his shantir, that alone would end this farce. He strode to the nearest machine, weighing well over twenty men, and lifted it into the air. He remembered fondly the gasp that had silenced the crowd. The cries of joy and the prayers and thanks that began to echo from the kneeling spectators. From that moment, he was never again questioned or challenged. His word was law and they eagerly obeyed.

His army and his people were one and the same.

THE FIRST BLOW

Their numbers were few, but their weapons and strength were great. He was not sure what they would face when they made landfall in a short time, but he was sure they were ready for it. It took nearly three years to carve a fighting force from the starving and overworked rabble that had been his kingdom. His first act had been to harrow the island of all over the age of thirty five. The resources needed to maintain them would be needed to nourish and support his army. Next he had inspected all children under the age of six. If they were malformed or sickly, they too were sacrificed. All able bodies over the age of six, men and women (not with child) were to be trained. His entire nation would become a fighting force, one great army.

Rikard had also commissioned new machines. They already had machines to help them in what few fields they planted, machines to help them in the mines where all the useful metals and coal were found, and machines that helped them traverse expanses of land more quickly than even the lightest foot could hope to. Now he needed machines that could not only carry passengers and move swiftly, but inflict great damage upon building and flesh. He wanted machines of war. Resources were hard fought so any machine that was not needed was repurposed. All metal now went to creating ships that could transport not only the soldiers, but the machines as well. The first great obstacle in this battle for dominance was the sea. They had fished it for over a thousand years, but never had they attempted to cross it.

Soon they would set sail. The great ships were nearly complete. He only waited on word from his spies. He had sent several fishing boats carrying a handful of people each to attempt the crossing. If they succeeded, they were to scour the shore for a landing spot that would be secret. This was imperative because he wanted Lylunir to fall first. This meant crossing over an entire kingdom and then the mountains undetected. One of the boats had washed ashore only days later, empty and half filled with water. After two weeks people began to find pieces of another washed up on the rocky beach. In both cases, all the men on board had been lost. It had been nearly two months now. His patience was growing thin and soon he would be forced to set sail without word. As he stared, lost in thought, a sound hit his ears. A horn. No, not *a* horn, *the* horn. The sentry, tasked with watching for the sailors' return, his horn was sounding.

In one motion, Rikard flung himself over the rail before him. Landing sturdily on his feet from the three story jump, he turned and bounded toward the shore. As he rounded the corner, his eyes met a sight that filled him with pride. The small vessel bobbed above the waves. At least one head was visible in the mist. As it drew closer to the shore another came into view. When the boat was only a few feet out, one of the men jumped into the water and began tugging the small boat toward the growing crowd. Rikard rushed to him. He looked exhausted. His clothes reeked of his stench and his hair had gone untended for some time. He fell to his knees before his king. Eyes toward the ground he managed to say, "My Vessel, we have succeeded." From his robe he pulled an object. It was metal, but it glittered like sun on the water. He held it up to his king. As Rikard's fingers encased the flat, round object the man fainted at his feet.

"Carry them to my throne room. Nurse them to health. I must know where this came from. What he held in his hand resembled a plate, but was much too small for that use. What he could not know, was that he held a small golden disc that had been a child's play toy. The land they had reached was a land of wealth and beauty. It took three days for the men to come around. The first to wake was the man who had been unconscious in the boat when his companion had tugged it ashore. He told his king of the perilous journey across the sea and how they had nearly starved to death before they saw the great continent. They had traveled down the shore, keeping a great distance between it and the boat. By night they ventured onto the land in search of food. The land was dry and barren.

The only sustenance they found were large rock like fruits that fell from tall, thin trees. As he spoke, the awe, and amazement he must have felt at the time came through his voice to the small crowd listening to his tale. The only trees Hadrir had were small and gnarled. They bore no fruit and were even useless for burning. To imagine trees that grew tall and provided food boiled within Rikard. Truly they were neglected by the Six if their peoples had such wonders. He told them how they found the object that now hung around their king's muscled neck, how they traveled so far south that the land began to change, how It grew green, of the fields where food was grown. Then he told Rikard of the mountains, the great mountains that separated one land from another. Beyond the mountains were great cliffs. So he and his compatriots believed that if the army made landfall at the very edge of these mountains, the ships would be hidden from view and they could hike along the edge of the cliffs unseen.

Rikard heard these words and seized them. It was time. They now knew not only that crossing the sea could be done, but where to make landfall. "Make sure they are strong enough for the journey. They will guide us." With these words, Rikard prepared himself to begin his life's purpose. In less than a week, they would be sailing toward his destiny.

Pol sat in his throne gazing out at his kingdom. He communed with Tuniah's shantir within him, embracing the power of his god as his eyes traversed the expanse of his busy kingdom, from the cold of the north, through the mines, to the fields to the south. He smiled at the honest toil below him. His throne sat high against the cliff wall. Almost stretching to the top. From here he could see all the way to the sea. As his gaze neared the edge of his domain, he sat straighter in his chair. There, along the southern most edge, were ships unlike any he had ever seen. In his youth he had traveled to each of the kingdoms, as was tradition, so that as a vessel he would feel connected to the other kingdoms and picture them always in his mind. These ships were made of a dark metal and bigger than any he had ever seen. Out of them poured not only men, but women and children and large contraptions.

Lylunir was known for its contraptions. Some produced light using the special stones native to each kingdom. Others helped in preparing food or harvesting in the fields. But these machines were different. They appeared frightening. Pol felt an uneasiness growing with in him. He had to know what they wanted, but caution prevented him from simply walking up to them and asking. They were so near to the cliffs now. He searched the cliff side above them for a suitable outcropping and upon finding one, bent space. Now hidden above them on the small ledge, he stayed as still and quiet as possible. If they were friendly, he would return to the castle and make a grand entrance followed by a procession of gifts and food. If not, he feared what they might do to him if he were discovered. The bustle below made discerning individual voices impossible but he gleaned bits and pieces here and there. They were well organized and had strange names for each of their caravan of machines. The men themselves were strange to look at. Their skin was a dark reddish brown, the color of bronze before the weather has taken it. Their hair was a similar shade of brown, but it was their eyes he noticed most. The color they held was very familiar to him, the color of gold.

As he lay there studying them, their color, their dress, and most importantly, the odd swords hung from their uniforms, a crashing behind him caught his ear. Turning as silently as possible, he saw a machine returning through the woods. He had not seen this one before and ventured a guess that it had been the first to be unloaded, sent off on exploration. There were two men inside the contraption. Each bore a great lever in their hands and were making circular motions with them, driving the massive machine forward. The machine moved more swiftly than anything he had ever seen. Trees in its path fell as if unattached to the ground. When it came to a stop, a large man, taller and stronger than any man Pol had seen before, walked toward it. One of the men jumped out of the machine and knelt before the big man.

"My king, there are two enormous flat lifts, like the ones in the mines. Below each is a huge carving of doors. Around each door are symbols."

"Does one have images of suns or stars?" The big man gazed into the distance. Pol held his breath. He knew the answer before he heard it.

"Yes, my Lord, the farthest bears those symbols." As the soldier's eyes fell to the ground, the gargantuan above him smiled.

"Then that is our destination. Load the Caravans!" At his word, all manner of people around him became a fury of motion. Hundreds, if not thousands, of people disappeared into the bellies of the machines. Pol's heart froze. Lylunir, they were headed to Lylunir, the seat of everything in the Six kingdoms. Gazing back to his throne, space bent again and he stood safe, for now, in his sanctuary. As fast as he could, he summoned a runner to him. There was a secret path down from the rear of his throne room, one that would lead his messenger into Lylunir. Imparting a message of fear, he sent him to Marina and Marcus, the royal family of the Kingdom of Light.

Again he gazed to the south. The army had already disappeared. Frantically he scanned the cliff base. When he finally found them, they were approaching the lift. The runner would not be fast enough. These invaders crossed an expanse that would take a rider on a swift horse at least three hours, in less than half of one hour. The runner would not make it. In a panic he called for his birds. He scrawled a warning to each Vessel, alerting them that there was a danger they had never experienced rolling through their world. The note urged them to destroy their lifts and destroy what they could of their footpaths over the cliff walls. As soon as the army had vanished, he dispatched a small contingent of guards to disable his lifts. Hoping his message would reach its destination in time, he also ordered the path down behind the throne destroyed.

Marcus and Marina Lyonus stood on their balcony and gazed down at the happy faces and lovely decorations covering the square below. The Festival of Life was in full swing and it was a great day. Marcus turned his head to look at his wife. She beamed in the sunlight, almost glowing. Her pale skin shone like a star as her black hair moved freely with the breeze. His eyes drifted down to her neck, to her shoulder, and then down her arm that rested across her enlarged abdomen. She was caring his child. His queen, Lylunir's beloved vessel, was about to bear the next vessel. All else seemed trivial compared to the love he felt for his queen and his unborn daughter. He knew it would be a girl. He knew she would be his only child. But above all else, he knew he would love her more than life itself; in fact, he already did.

Marina turned to see her husband smiling at her. She blushed and smiled back. "My king, why do you smile at me so?" Her eyes, like the purest amethysts, sparkled.

"Just remembering the day we met. I was terrified. An arranged marriage to the vessel was the most frightening thing I could have ever possibly imagined. Now I look back and think how foolish I was. What was there to be afraid of? Certainly not you, the most beautiful and kind woman I have ever known. I love you, my sweet Marina. Please know I always will." His eyes filled with tears. She placed her hand on his and drew him close, kissing him softly.

"And I love you, my husband." As she pulled away slightly she wobbled on her feet. This pregnancy had been long and she, and her body, was growing weary with it. Soon it would be finished, and she would hold her daughter in her arms. Marcus had noticed her stagger. He wrapped his strong arms around her for support. With a final wave to their citizens below, he helped her back into their bed chamber. This is where the birth would happen, just as it was where her birth had happened and her mother's before her. Over one thousand years of her mothers had been born in this castle, in this room, in this very bed, since the world began.

Another pair of arms rushed to help support the weakened queen. These arms were soft and gentle, matched with a smile and a loving heart. Lerna, her midwife, had been there at her birth. A woman of near sixty, she had provided her care to the royal family of Lylunir for most of her life. Her dark skin and white hair reminded them always of the world beyond the Mountains. She was a priestess of Ziah, born and raised in Zailia to the west. She had been a gift from the Vessel of that kingdom to Marina's mother after a disaster had hit her nation. Lylunir had come to her aid, along with many of the other kingdoms and, in gratitude; accomplished healers were given to the courts of each. Lerna had proven invaluable to Lylunir. Each day brought the sick and wounded of Lylunir to her feet to be mended. She, of course, was not the Vessel of Ziah, but she knew much about herbs and techniques that could both cure illness and alleviate pain.

With their help, Marina was lowered into her bed. "It won't be long now." Lerna said as she pulled the covers over Marina's legs. She turned to Marcus. "I will need a few things; I feel the baby comes tonight, tomorrow at the latest." With this statement she led him from the chamber, spouting a list of items and herbs she would require. As the door closed, Marcus turned and hurried down the hallway, repeating the list in his head—so much to do. He passed the guard at the end of the hallway without seeing him, too lost in thought for even a simple hello. The guard chuckled softly, remembering how he had been the same when each of his children were born.

Marcus imparted the list to the palace butler and he hurried away calling all manner of servants to him, giving each a portion of the list. Marcus settled into his throne. Despite the events unfolding up the stairs, life as usual was happening around him and decisions had to be made. Audiences began and business as usual rolled on for the merchant kingdom.

As night approached, hourly updates were brought to Marcus from his wife's bed chamber. Her water had broken. Her contractions were intensifying. Everything was on the verge. As Marcus was readying to rush to his wife's side, he heard a great commotion outside the throne room. He walked toward the door and when he had nearly reached it a man burst through it. His skin tone and hair told Marcus that he was from Tunaeshir. The bird had arrived over an hour ago, but it had gotten lost in the multitude of well-wishes coming in time for the birth of the princess. The man doubled over himself, breathing heavily. Sweat poured from his body and his clothes were soaked through. Between his pants Marcus heard words. Listening closely he made out the words "army", "unknown", "from the sea", "coming here", "evil", "dangerous", and "run". As the man finished his shattered statements he collapsed. He had run from the throne room of Tunaeshir to deliver this broken message and had given his last breath to impart it. But before Marcus could interpret it, another body burst through the doors. This was one of his palace guards. He too was breathing heavily and on his face was written terror.

"My king! Invaders! They come over the mountains! They are coming for you! You must protect our Vessel!" As the soldier finished he glanced down at the body on the floor. "They must have come over the mountains from Tunaeshir. The warning has arrived too late." The soldier bent down, lifted the lifeless, small, soaked body into his arms and carried him to the nearest table, laying him down, out of the way.

"Who are these invaders? Where do they come from? Can they be reasoned with?" Marcus' head was swimming. No kingdom had ever been attacked before, at least not by other people. There have been disasters that have caused panic and suffering to be sure, but never something like this.

"I do not believe so, my lord. They kill all in their path. They travel in great contraptions shrouded in steel and iron. Only an hour ago, they descended the Great Lift; and already they are at the central city walls. They will be upon us in moments. We have no army to defeat them. Please, you have no time, take our Vessel, our queen, and flee this place!" The soldier finished his heartfelt plea as twenty or so other guards filed into the room. "We will hold them as long as we can." The guards bowed to their king, then turned to bar the great doors. Outside, the sounds of screams began to grow louder. He heard the crashing and crackling of breaking trees and stone walls. All at once, thoughts of his queen and daughter filled his mind. He turned and fled up the stairs praying she would be alert enough to shroud herself and escape this nightmare.

CHAPTER 3
A LIFE FOR A LIFE

Marcus reached the landing outside his bed chambers. Steadying himself, he swung the door wide. His wife lay in the bed, her legs propped up on pillows. Sweat beaded and ran down her face. Her eyes were red and her hair, always so perfect, was now tousled and tangled around her shoulders. Lerna was leaning over her holding her hand, whispering things into her ear. When she noticed Marcus standing in the door she called out for him to leave. He ignored her and strode, with urgent purpose, to the bed.

"Can you enter the shade, my love?" Her face almost didn't register his statement. "Answer me! Can you enter the shade? I need you to enter the shade! Right now!" Marina let out a cry of pain as another contraction hit her. She was far too caught up in the events befalling her to entertain such a silly and pointless notion. Then she looked him in the face. She didn't see the face of her husband, but the face of a man gripped by crippling fear. Terror was painted there, thick and urgent.

"No, not right now. Why? What's wrong?" Lerna

looked up from the queen, hearing the confusion and urgency in her voice, to find the same terror on Marcus' face that Marina had.

"She cannot muster that level of concentration as long as she is birthing. Perhaps an hour or so after it is done she will have the strength. Why do you need her to do this so badly?" Lerna's voice was growing stern. Her job was to bring this child safely into this world. All else would have to wait its turn. Marcus' answer shook her to the core.

"We are being assaulted. An army is coming, coming for you and the baby no doubt. "Lerna blinked. This wasn't possible.

"That's impossible. There has never been a war between the kingdoms. Every Vessel has diplomats here at this very moment to welcome the princess. They would never endanger their own. It's just...not possible..." Her voice trailed off. Her mind raced—back to her childhood, all the lessons she had learned, the history of the kingdoms. Nothing. Nothing explained what was happening.

"These men that come, they are not from the kingdoms. The messenger from Tunaeshir called them strangers." Lerna's face changed. An old legend floated to the front of her memory. A bedtime story concerning a seventh race, the followers of a cast down and forgotten god. Marcus touched Lerna's arm. She was mumbling to herself. She looked up from her thoughts. Tears were filling her eyes.

"It was all true. They do exist." Her eyes fell again to the bed. Marina let out another cry of pain. This snapped Lerna out of her stunned daze. "It doesn't matter right now. This baby is all the matters."

"Who exists, Lerna?! Who are they? What do you mean it DOESN'T MATTER?! My wife and child are in danger, of course it matters!" Marcus felt rage growing inside him. How could she care so little for the destruction rolling toward them like a rogue wave on the ocean?

"Calm yourself, my king." Her eyes met his. Fear coursed through them, but they calmed Marcus all the same. "Nothing can happen until this baby comes. Our queen cannot be moved, nor can she shade herself or anyone else. Therefore, the baby must come first."

Marcus, his voice calmer than it had been since he entered the room moments ago, asked, "Then what can I do?" He gazed down at his wife. Pain stretched across her face as yet another contraction bared down upon her. Lerna's voice was soft again, but there was an urgency to it this time.

"Guard the door. Buy us as much time as you can. As soon as the baby is delivered and she is able, we will depart into the shade. You have my word." This was a heavy request, but one Marcus had always been willing to pay. He walked around the bed and leaned in, kissing his lovely wife on the forehead.

"I love you, Marina." Looking to Lerna, he said, "Make sure she and my daughter are safe. Tell them every day that I love them, always." With that he turned and strode to the door. He was willing to die for his family and now would be his chance. Reaching the door, he looked back one final time. "Bar the door as best you can." He swung the door closed behind him. Once on the other side, Marcus readied himself. He could hear Lerna bracing the door with whatever was at her disposal, all the while coaxing his beloved wife to breathe, just keep breathing. Below he heard shouts from the guards. The throne room doors were being beaten to splinters. The heavy thuds rattled the ground of the second floor landing where he stood. Suddenly, there was an enormous crash, followed by loud gasps and stunned cries—then the clashing of swords. Amongst the cries of soldiers feeling the sting of another man's steel, he could hear the cries of pain emanating from behind him.

The shouts were growing louder before and behind him. Shadows began to move on the stairwell. He stood poised, not really sure what he would be able to do unarmed as he was. He was fairly good with a blade. Every possible suitor to the Vessel was trained in a number of arts such as table manners and diplomacy and combat, not for situations such as these, but for the wilds. There were things in the forests that frightened even the most hardened man. He would, as a husband, have need of these skills if they ever confronted one of these creatures. Never had he thought his first real combat would be unarmed against another man.

The shadows grew smaller and more defined. In the

bluish white light of the illuminators lining the hallway, they resembled the beasts of the forests. As the figures came into view, he relaxed a bit. His own guards were rushing up the stairs. He stood up straight, out of the combat crouch he had been holding and then immediately regretted it. The men were in shambles. There were three of them. All were bleeding, and only one still wore his helmet. One of the non-helmeted men bore two swords, though one was certainly an enemy's. It had a straight blade and looked to be rusty and heavier that a Lylunian blade, which were arched and made of silver. Making eye contact with the soldier, Marcus motioned for the sword. Tossing it to his king, the soldier simply said, "It's heavier, Your Majesty. Be careful."

The soldiers turned and backed their way to their king. Forming a short wall before him, they readied themselves. Marcus did not need to ask. These men were poised and ready for battle. The invaders would soon be upon them. Another scream come from behind the door. The soldiers turned to stare at the carved wood, and then at their king. He could see their fear. "We will protect them, won't we?" The guards steadied themselves. Yes, yes, they would. More shadows on the stairs. They grew smaller and more sharp as their creators drew closer. The end of a blade matching the one Marcus held in his hand came into view. Now begins the fight of his life.

The Hadrian soldiers rushed up the stairs. There were at least five in the clump before them. For a moment the two groups stood frozen sizing each other up. Marcus could not be mistaken and the leader of the Hadrians, known as a brakbark, sneered. "Your Majesty. How good to meet you. And where is your lovely wife?" Instinctively, all four men moved a hair closer to the door behind them. "Ah, then, through you we must go." With this he and his men began to progress forward. The guards and Marcus returned their pace. The helmeted guard swung first. The Brakbark narrowly avoided the swing, but countered with one of his own. His blade dug into the guards' thigh, causing him to lower his center of gravity. Raising his blade, the Brakbark swung again. Before the blade could find its destination in the soldier's neck, another blade blocked its path. It had begun.

In the narrow hallway, the nine men battled. The first to take a fatal wound was the helmeted soldier. His leg betrayed him and without his full balance, he toppled to the ground. It was here he died; the Brakbark's sword plunged into his heart. The next two to fall were Hadrian. But the Brakbark answered in kind, killing the two remaining guards with one long stroke, slicing the last almost all the way through. As their bodies fell to the hallway floor, he looked up at Marcus. He had fared well in the fight so far, claiming the first Hadrian. Again the sneer crossed his face as he lifted his blade. His swing was met. Marcus was a strong man. Tall and muscled. He trained for several hours every day with his sword, not because he needed to, but because it was good exercise. He had grown quite good with a blade over the last eighteen years in the palace. The sword in his hand may have been foreign, but he couldn't help admiring it. The shape and weight of it made it more deadly. The more he used it, the more deadly he became with it. Blow for blow, Marcus held his ground. A violent clash left the Brakbark off balance. Marcus capitalized, spearing him through the gut. As the Brakbark slid off his sword Marcus heard another scream from the door behind him. This one was different, deeper and more intense. It was followed by a different kind of cry, a soft higher pitch cry. The cry of a baby. His child, his daughter, was born. Staring down at the man bleeding to death on the floor, new vigor raced through him. The fear in his face was replaced with determination. His child was born. He had succeeded. Soon she and his wife would be safely in the shade, departing this terrible place.

Lifting his blade, he let out a cry and charged into the two remaining men. He quickly dispatched one who was still frozen from the death of his general. The second countered swing after swing. The two men exchanged blow after blow, each time narrowly avoiding the other man's blade. The Hadrian swung his blade, as it collided with Marcus', he lost his footing. Marcus quickly spun and ran his blade through the soldier to the hilt. This drew the other man to within inches of Marcus. A mistake. The solider drew a dagger from inside his cuirass and plunged it into Marcus' chest. Marcus felt more than just the wound. There was an unnatural burning that accompanied it. All at once he knew. It was not rust on the blade, but poison. They did not need to do anything more than wound to kill. As the burning began to flood his body, he stepped back from the soldier, the dagger still planted in his chest. The man's body slid to the floor, Marcus' sword firmly lodged through it.

Marcus fell against the door—only silence within. He had succeeded. His wife and daughter were safe. As the light around him began to fade into the burning, another shadow appeared on the stairwell. This one did not grow smaller as the others had but larger. Higher and higher it spread up the wall until its owner came into view. He was the largest man Marcus had ever seen. Standing nearly seven and a half feet tall, and thick like slabs of stone, Rikard loomed over him. Descending to one knee, he pulled the dagger from Marcus's chest. His voice was calm as he leaned closer to him. "Your Majesty," was all he said before running the dagger across Marcus's exposed throat.

CHAPTER 4
OUT OF CHAOS

Lerna cradled the newborn, still covered in her mother's blood. The baby cried and writhed with her new life. Lerna could not enjoy this moment. The birth had been breech, and Marina was bleeding very badly. The sounds of fighting and death were echoing in from the hallway and outside screams rose from the fire-licked houses. All the world was chaos, and this chamber was no different. She set the baby down on the blanket laid out at the bottom of the bed and quickly wiped some of the blood off her face. Marina lay still, breathing and moaning quietly. When Lerna finished wrapping the baby, she lifted her into her arms and turned toward Marina. But her plans of handing the baby to her mother faded quickly. Marina was slipping away more quickly than she had anticipated. Lerna knew the birth had left her weak and that the bleeding would be difficult to stop, but she had not expected this. Her queen lay dying in front of her. Marina's eyes dimmed. She stared at the small child in Lerna's arms. Then her eyes fell away. Behind Lerna a shadow formed. A tunnel out of the castle. Lerna turned and peered into the black. She had traversed such passages through the shade many times, but never without the light of Marina to guide her path. Turning back to the queen she started to speak.

"Come on. We have to get you up. Take your baby, while I try to stop the bleeding. We have..." Marina's hand touched her lips, her fingertips like ice to her face. Marina smiled gently as her hand fell to rest on the baby's head. A small glimmer of light flickered and then faded in the infants eyes.

"Her name is Kai, Kailandra Marina Lyonus. Take good care of her. I...we are counting on you to protect her, Lerna. Now go. You haven't much time." Marina's arm fell away as she finished. Her strength had left her. As her arm hit the bed, a cry drew their eyes to the door. Through the furniture piled against it they heard a cry that could not be mistaken. Marcus's voice screamed in pain. The thud against the door that followed plunged through Marina. She turned back to Lerna. "Go! Now! Take her to Forrenfar. Brannon will take care of you both. Go!" Lerna pulled the baby close to her chest. Tears streamed down her face. She took one last look at her queen, the woman she had brought into the world in this very room. Turning away from the blood soaked bed, she ran to the shadow. As she entered the darkness, it closed in behind her. The only direction now was forward.

Marina watched the gateway close. The pain of her body subsided to relief. At least her child would be safe. She had passed the shantir. It would lie dormant for sixteen years, but at least it would live on. Loud bashing could now be heard. The chamber door shuddered more violently with each new blow. When it finally it gave way, the furniture that had been propped against it scattered across the floor, splintering to bits under the force of the final blow. A man's abnormally large figure stood in the doorway. As he took a step into the room, past the shattered door, now barely hanging onto the frame by its bottom hinge, Marina took in his face. It the bluish light, his reddish brown skin took on a demonic quality. This coupled with his golden glowing eyes gave him the most terrifying silhouette she had ever seen. Her eyes cast down from his face. As she tried to focus on the hallway behind him, she noticed the lump he was dragging. No, not a lump. Marcus. His lifeless body hung by the shoulder from the gargantuan's grip. Her eyes filled with what little tears she had left.

Rikard surveyed the room, finding only the woman, lying in a pool of blood within. Unceremoniously, he dropped the corpse of her king and took several more steps into the room. His voice cold and fierce split the silence. "Your Majesty, where is your child?" His eyes took in the scene again. There were only a few places to hide. He moved swiftly to the balcony, but found nothing. Marina watched in sombre silence as he crossed the room to the dressing rooms, throwing open the doors and quickly searching them. "I said where is she! I know you have birthed. Allow me to send you hence with your ENTIRE family." With his hand, he motioned to her dead king as he finished his demand. His smile was hollow and cold, and she could hear the rage deepening in his voice.

Marina had no strength left. Her eyes fell closed. Death was upon her. She made one final prayer to her goddess to watch over her little Kai, and then she was gone. Rikard crossed quickly to the bed. Seizing the cold, drained body, he demanded again. Shaking her lifeless frame again he insisted, but it was too late. Never again would her voice be heard. She had managed to escape his justice. He had planned to make her suffer, to relish her cries to her goddess before he struck her down. She was to die only after witnessing her family, her people, slaughtered before her. Not only had she escaped his revenge, but so had her child.

He let her body fall back to the bed. Consumed by his rage he didn't notice as several of his soldiers entered the room behind him. It wasn't until one of them ventured to touch his arm that he realized their presence. "What?" His voice was harsh and hot with anger. The soldier that had dared to touch him backed away slightly. He had bad news to deliver.

"Sir...I mean, my lord, the lifts, they are burning." Rikard spun around to face the soldier so swiftly that the soldier fell backward onto the ground.

Rikard took a step toward him. Looming over him, he said again, his tone even more frightening than when last he spoke, "WHAT?! What do you mean burning?!" Rushing to the balcony he glared around him. Beyond the smoke rising from the burning houses, far in the distance he could just make out the line of the cliff wall that formed the boundary between kingdoms. As his gaze moved along the ridge he could see them clearly, like stars in the night sky. Fires atop the cliffs. Though they were hundreds of miles from the cliffs, the light of the fires could not be mistaken. "How did they know?" He slammed his fist on the balcony rail so firmly that it crumbled beneath the blow, raining debris on the square below.

"And..." The soldier began but realized that perhaps the rest of his news should wait. Rikard waited a split second for the rest and when no further words came, he turned again to look at the soldier.

"Yes and...?" His face had grown hard and though the soldier feared his reaction to the news, the idea of refusing his request frightened him even more.

"The engineers say that we cannot leave this place. Without the lifts we cannot get out. We cannot get into the other kingdoms. We are trapped here." Rikard's fist again flew. This time it found the side of the poor soldier's head. His skull shattered like a soft rock hit by a large hammer. Rikard stood fuming. This had not gone as planned. Not only did his revenge fall short, but the child escaped and he was trapped, unable to continue his march across the kingdoms. Clearing his mind, he focused on the one thing that had gone as planned. He now stood in Lylunir. He had brought his people from their dark, cold, harsh island to this metropolis of plenty. He would find a way across the walls around him. And if he was trapped, so, too, was the child. He would find her as well. But in the meantime, his people would live as they always should have, like citizens of the six kingdoms.

Lerna raced through the darkness. Before her, she could see the light of the end. The shadowy tunnel was leading her out of the castle, but she wasn't sure how far it would take her. Clutching the infant in her arms, she prayed for her queen, and prayed for herself, that her goddess would grant her the strength and wisdom to fulfill the final wishes of her queen. As she neared the end, she realized she had a hard road ahead of her. Outside the shade where she was safely hidden lay the streets of the central city. Lylunir was a great kingdom of urban centers and trade. There were cities of trade arching out from each of the monumental lifts that brought goods for trade each day. Not far from them were the Great Gates, enormous and intricate carvings of doors into the cliff face. The cliffs were over a mile thick, but these gates did not open to a passage. Instead they were symbolic of the kingdom that lay just beyond the wall. They bore images of those lands and their people. Each generation there was a great gathering. Each nation's Vessel, their family and their court, would enter Lylunir through these Great Gates, opened not by muscle but by the power of shadow. Tunnels, much like the one she was in, would open, allowing the amazing processionals to enter.

Her heart felt hard in her chest. The city of trade with Forrenfar lay far to the east, where it surrounded the lift to the land of animal tenders. That was her destination, her quest. Between her and her goal lay at least three hundred miles of road, leading out of the Central City, through the forests and farmland in the "in-between", and then the walls and streets of the City of Beasts. Alone, on foot, and caring a cold hungry infant, she dreaded the journey. Despite her fear she stepped out of the shadow and into the chaos. She would never reach her goal if she didn't start. Around her, people raced past. Fire and smoke surrounded the street on every side. Chaos closed in on her. Determined to succeed, she ducked her head and began running, bending and weaving around the throngs of people filling the streets in shock and terror. Between the cries of pain and fear she could hear voices barking orders and threats. Screams of anguish and death echoed around her. The army of the enemy was entering homes and dragging citizens from their beds and hearths into the streets. Most were being herded into lines, marching toward the castle. Others were simply slaughtered on the spot. Under her feet the paving stones became slippery with blood.

Lerna bent her head and blocked out the world. If something blocked her path, she diverted down a side street or clambered over whatever it was. Only once in this mad dash did she truly realize what was going on around her. When she was climbing over a particularly strange road block she had taken the time to truly look down. She realized it was a mother and child clinging to each other in what would be their last embrace. The sight of their dead, frozen faces stopped her cold for a moment. She screamed and stumbled backward, almost dropping her precious cargo. This sensation alone snapped her out of what could surely have evolved into crippling shock. Regaining her feet she turned instead down a side ally and hurried away from the tragic scene. Never again would she question what was in her path.

Lerna didn't know how long she had been running. It was not until she could feel the blood filling her shoes that she again looked at the world around her. While people were still moving quickly through the streets, no homes here were on fire. And, while the sound of panic and fright could still be heard, no screams of pain or images of murder where to be found. She was almost to the wall. Even at her quick pace she could not have crossed the city in less than three and a half hours. It had seemed like minutes. She allowed herself a moment to rest and instantly regretted it. Her body betrayed her. Aches and injuries began to scream at her from each limb and every muscle. Her feet were in so much pain she could barely stand now. At least the baby in her arms was sleeping peacefully. Lerna searched the area around her for a place to rest for a while. The wall was just ahead. Streaming out of it were small huddled family groups carrying little more than rucksacks. She fell in line with them. She wanted to call out to a man on horseback ahead of her. Call to him for aid. A swifter ride to the City of Beasts for his infant princess. But fear stayed her tongue. Anonymity was little Kai's only defense right now, and she would cling to it dearly.

Once outside the walls, Lerna broke away from the caravan. Her body, in its aged and weary state, could no longer carry her and the baby. A short distance off the road she found a small hollow. In it was an abandoned barn and burned farmhouse. "Perfect." She muttered. This place had burned last winter. She knew she didn't have long to rest but she needed whatever she could get. She remembered a small stream near the city walls. As soon as she woke she would find it. The baby would also need food soon. Perhaps she could fall in with the refugees again in a few hours and beg some milk off one of the travelers. Kindness was common here and even in this time of uncertainty, she felt confident that someone would help her.

Lerna settled down in the rear corner of the barn, behind what was left of a humble wheat harvest. Cradling the baby, she began to sing, a simple lullaby she had sung so many years ago to another young queen. Too afraid to sing words, she hummed the simple tune over and over again until sleep came to her weary body.

CHAPTER 5

BREAD AND MILK

Lerna's dreams were frightening, chased through the streets by a nameless mass carrying her baby queen. The mass was lashing out at her with arms made of dead citizens and blood. Fire echoed from its mouth as it called her by name. She tripped over the mother and child, hitting the ground hard. Kai began to cry. She rolled over onto her back and glared up at the beast of death bearing down on her. His face was fierce and his eyes glowed with an eerie yellow light. The baby continued to scream—so loud. Her cries were so loud.

Lerna's eyes fluttered open. Soft light filtered in from the holes in the barn walls. Kai was indeed screaming. Her grip had loosened in the night, and the baby now lay in her lap. There was an unnatural chill to the air. Their queen had always ensured the sun's warmth fell on the whole of her kingdom each day. It was late fall on Plaettan, and without her, the cold came fast. Lerna pulled the baby close to her, sharing what little warmth she had with the cold and hungry child. She would need much if she was to make it to her destination. When Kai's cries quieted down a bit, Lerna struggled to her feet. Much of the fatigue of last night was gone, but not all. Her shredded feet ached, and her arms and shoulders were sore from the weight of the baby during her frantic flight.

Sighing, she made her way to the barn door. Cautiously, she gazed out into the morning. The processional out of the city continued. Only now there were wagons intermixed with those on foot. Kai's cries grew louder. First the princess would need to be cleaned. Lerna walked out of the barn, away from the road. Crossing between the barn and the remains of the burned home, she found the river, though now no more than a creek. Its flow was seasonal due to the dams built along its course for irrigation in the in-between. She crouched on the bank and peered at her reflection in the water. Lerna was an older woman, but her beauty had never faded. To look upon herself now shocked her. Her face was dirty, and her hair was a mess with twigs, straw and soot. Blood was also prevalent on her hands and clothes. She cringed thinking of all the bodies she must have crawled over last night. The image of the mother and child came back to her again, stopping her cold.

"No." Talking to herself seemed to work. The image retreated, and her purpose returned to her. After gently setting Kai aside, Lerna began cleaning herself in the warm water. Though the morning was chilly, the water still ran with the warmth of the previous day. After tending to her face and hair, she unwrapped the baby. The baby's pale white skin almost had a glow to it. Dried blood from the birth could still be seen, cracked and flaky on her flesh. Lerna had not had time to properly wash her when she entered the world. Ripping a piece of the blanket away, she dipped it in the water and began to try and wipe the tragedy from the innocent child.

It took nearly half an hour to clean the baby properly. Once she was satisfied Kai was clean, she bundled the hungry baby back into a swaddle. Now for food. Lerna's stomach turned at the thought of food. All the blood she had sent down stream had robbed her of her appetite, but the baby needed to eat. Holding Kai close to her again, Lerna rose to her feet and made her way back to the road. The caravan still filed out of the city. Lerna fell in line and began looking for families with small babies as they were more likely to have milk. Strangely, she found none. The youngest child she found was almost four years old. For over an hour she walked, peeking into wagons and asking people on horseback, but no one responded.

After almost half the morning Lerna learned the reason for the baby-less procession. Checkpoints set up along the road leading to the gate. The soldiers had seized each and every infant child and slaughtered them on the spot. If parents or onlookers interfered, they too met with the blade. Lerna's blood turned cold. They were killing infants. Her grip on Kai tightened. The man who had answered her question noticed the small bundle in her arms for the first time. Fear crept across his face. His wagon came to a stop just ahead of where Lerna stood, still frozen with the thought of so many dead babies.

Babies who died simply because Kai lived. The man jumped down from his seat and rushed around the horses to Lerna. He took her by the shoulders and with a gentle push snapped her out of her daze.

"You can't be caught with that." His eyes glanced down at the baby. "Come." The pressure on her shoulders nudged her forward. Gently, he guided her to the back of his carriage. Lerna looked up at the small carved wooden door then looked back at the man. He nodded slightly. Turning back to the door, Lerna's trembling hand grasped the door knob and twisted. With her head down she stepped up into the tiny doorway. Climbing inside Lerna found a woman in all manner of distress. As she climbed in beside her, Lerna's instincts and training kicked in. The woman was obviously grief stricken, but it was the non-emotional signs Lerna found that pulled at her. The woman's abdomen was large and swollen and from the look of her clothing and bedding her water had broken some time ago. So, Lerna thought as she took in the wagon's interior, babies were killed, but pregnant women were allowed to leave unharmed. Pushing that thought aside, Lerna set Kai down gently and moved to the woman's side. The wagon began to move again, but not for long. The man pulled the wagon to the side of the road and then joined the unfolding scene. "She went into labor in the panic. It's been almost sixteen hours. Can you help her?" His eyes were red from hours of fighting tears.

Lerna gazed at him for a moment. "Yes I think I can. I need all the blankets and water you can spare." As she finished, she caught sight of his hand. Burned into the top was a strange symbol. The wound looked fresh and growing with infection. She reached for it but he instinctively pulled his hand away.

"Worry with her first. Answer me truthfully, Lerna Zailian, can she be delivered?" His eyes were pleading. He knew her name, at least the one given to her when she came to Lylunir. He probably knew a great deal more about her. It took only one cry from the woman to snap Lerna out of her stunned silence.

"I will do all I can." With her words satisfying his need, he turned and crawled out of the carriage. She heard him moving on the top of the wagon. Soon, he returned with several blankets and containers of water. "I need you to assist me. Can you do that?"

"Willam, my name is Willam. Yes, I will. Put the baby up there, that way she won't get hurt." He motioned to a shelf at the front, just behind the driver's bench. Lerna placed Kai there and began to deliver her second baby in twelve hours. Hopefully this birth would go better than the last one.

It took almost two hours. Screaming and breathing and cries emanated from the wagon on the side of the road. Lerna's voice remained calm and steady through the whole ordeal, though the same could not be said for Willam and Reesa, his wife. When the baby finally came, a boy, the parents were so exhausted they could not even name him. Lerna used the remaining water to clean him.

BREAD AND MILK

After swaddling him in the smallest blanket Willam had fetched, she gave him to his mother who lay almost unconscious on the wet blankets.

"We need to get these wet things out of here. Your job is not finished Willam, help me." Together they slid the wet things from beneath Reesa. While Willam hauled them out of the carriage and folded them, Lerna helped Reesa change into a new gown. "Can you nurse?" Lerna asked as Reesa cuddled her baby.

"I think so. Does the girl need milk, too?" Reesa's eyes moved to the small shelf. Lerna had almost forgotten Kai. She had lain still and quiet throughout the entire thing, unnatural for a baby in even the best circumstances. Lerna felt her mouth hang open. Of course Kai needed milk. The poor infant had not eaten yet, but to ask a woman who had just given birth to nurse a strange baby had seemed like too big a request. And now it was being offered freely.

"Y..yes. Are you sure it wouldn't be too much?" Lerna's heart was about to burst. To find milk was one thing but to actually get to suckle was another entirely. Breast milk was healthiest for a newborn, and she knew it.

"Of course." Reesa's smile, though tired, was warm and caring. While cradling her new son in one arm, she reached up the other toward Lerna. Lerna lifted Kai down from the shelf and placed her gingerly into Reesa's arm, pulling her into her chest, Lerna helped Kai find the nipple. The starving princess needed no further motivation and began immediately to nurse. Reesa smiled and leaned her head back. Within seconds she had drifted off to sleep, both hungry babies feeding from her. As Lerna made ready to crawl out of the wagon to tell Willam they could move on, she saw the same angry symbol. It was embossed on the back of Reesa's hand, the one holding the swaddled form of her son, burned into the flesh like a livestock brand.

As she climbed out of the wagon she was met by Willam. "They are fine. All three are resting now. I have questions, as I am sure you do as well, but I think it best that we get moving before we discuss them." Lerna's words caught him as he was about to speak. Instead, he closed his mouth and motioned her to the front of the wagon. She climbed aboard, and he slid in beside her. With a flick of the reins, they were moving again. Once they had returned to the flow of refugees, Lerna turned to him. Her eyes fixed on the brand. "What is that?" Her simple question took him almost five minutes to answer. When he did answer, she could hear the pain in his voice.

"The soldiers at the check points. They took all the babies, killed them...." Willam swallowed hard. He choked on these words. After another few moments of silence he spoke again. "Those who were expecting, as we, were branded with this. Those who had no children or had babies that were...they were branded as well, but it was different. A different symbol." His eyes began to turn red with tears again. Lerna knew he was replaying the scene again and again in his head. Desperate to free him from this hell, she asked a different question.

"How do you know my name?" his turned to face her. She had tried to hide the panic in her voice, but he had heard it none the less.

"Because you saved my life once. No one ever forgets something like that." He must have seen the confusion on her face because he continued to explain. "I don't doubt you can't remember. It was many years ago when I was just a boy. I am from the City of Grain, to the southeast. When I was about three, I came down with red fever. I was so ill with it my parents brought me to the court of our Vessel to see the royal healer. You sat with me and cared for me for almost a week. You saved my life. My parents told me the story many times in my childhood, and I can still see your face in my dreams."

Lerna remembered the boy, almost twenty eight years ago now. She had almost lost him. She had even discussed taking him over the cliffs to Zailia once or twice to see her Vessel for help, but he began to improve. Until last night, he was her toughest patient. Her eyes filled with tears, to be remembered so fondly after so long. "Then you must know..." Her face went cold. The thought of poor Kai and all the infants killed in her place chilled her to the bone.

"That you carry our princess? That our young vessel lies just behind us, suckling from my wife? No, I don't know that, and neither will anyone else." He gave a weary smile, turned his eyes back to the road, and hitched the team of sturdy horses a bit faster. For the first time since Marcus had burst into the royal chamber, bearing grave news of an invasion, she felt at ease. She knew it wouldn't last, but for now she could relax a bit. Willam handed her a hunk of bread from a bag beside him. At first Lerna doubted she would be able to eat, but as she bit into it she found her hunger. Only bread made from the grain of Akiliree tasted so good. Remembering he was from the City of Grain, she decided he was most likely a merchant there, bringing his wares to the Festival of Life. This wagon was most likely his goods cart. As she ate the delicious bread, she imagined a past without the invaders. A version of history that saw Kai brought out onto the balcony for the joyful crowd to see. Cheers would have echoed throughout the streets, and Willam would have made a fortune peddling his delicious wares to the elated citizens. Life might have been perfect. But it wasn't. The queen was dead, the king with her, and the princess was in mortal danger from an army that was already searching for her, wielding the most barbaric of tactics.

CHAPTER 6

CROSSROADS

The wagon jolted as a stone rolled under its wheel. Lerna's body jerked forward, hurling her mind back to reality. The thoughts of the world as it should be had given her the best of dreams. She shuddered as her eyes took in the world around her now, dark and hidden. She turned her face toward Willam. He was still sitting next to her, reins in hand, coaxing the team of horses to keep moving. His head was bent low from his shoulders and his eyes were heavy with wanted sleep.

"How long was I asleep?" Her question startled him a bit. He had not noticed her stirring beside him. He turned to meet her gaze; but when she saw the exhaustion in his face, she did not wait for his answer. She took the reins from his weak grip and steered the team to the side of the road. There were very few travelers with them now on the road. They had crossed out of the farmland and into the fruit orchards. As early as tomorrow, they would be at the eastern crossroads continuing at this rate. Once the wagon had stopped, she placed her hand on his face. He struggled to resist her studying gaze, but his strength had left him hours ago. "Sleep," was all she said.

"No, I can keep going...really..I can.." He could not even muster the strength to finish his thought. Smiling slightly, he nodded and climbed down from the driver's bench. When his feet hit the ground, he turned once more to Lerna. "If you reach the crossroads before dawn, just wait there." He waited for her nod, then disappeared around the side of the cart. Lerna waited for the door at the rear to open and close and all the commotion within to die down. Willam made two soft thumps against the wall just behind her when he was settled. Flicking the reins, she pulled the wagon back onto the road and continued on. Willam had said she could reach the crossroads before dawn. This statement puzzled her. Time had seemed to blur in the last two days, and she did not know exactly where she and her companions were in relation to the central city or even what time it was. Her mind felt clearer now than it had in days. As she drove through the darkness, her thoughts focused on the invaders. She had only had seconds to think on them before the queen's birthing had pulled her back. Now, in the silent dark of the road, she had all the time she needed to remember. She struggled to pinpoint the old tale from her youth that the news of the strangers had called up in the royal chambers only yesterday.

She remembered her mentor telling her an old legend, the story of a seventh race, created by the fallen god. A race that was not destroyed (out of pity) when the tyrant, Hadriah, was thrown into the abyss. Luniah had left them to themselves, in her eyes they did not deserve to share their god's fate. Her mentor told her stories of sailors seeing an island far from the northern shore where noises of life could be heard from a distance. No one had ever ventured close enough to the island to actually see people or make a foot print. It appeared to be desolate and barren to the eyes, a volcanic island that most thought appeared after the earthquake nearly 800 years ago. Lerna replayed her mentor's words in her head. Descriptions of the people were vague, but one thing was certain, if these invaders were not of the kingdoms, this was the only explanation.

The sound of the wheels rolling over the gravel lulled Lerna into a strange state of a waking sleep. Her eyes glazed over as her mind searched her memories, her lessons, for any instructions that might aid her now. Images of Kai sleeping in her arms, crying on the river bank, suckling at Reesa's breast intermingled with her thoughts. Lerna opened her eyes again. The dark road still lay before her. The trees grew closer to the road now than when she and Willam had traded places. Lerna's thoughts of Kai had caused panic to well in her chest. Where was she to go, how would she get there and what was to become of the kingdom if she left? All these questions flooded her mind, and for a moment she felt overwhelmed. Tears began to swell in the corners of her eyes, and she felt her hands and knees tremble. Before her emotions over-washed her, her queen's voice echoed in her ears. 'Take her to Forrenfar. Brannon will take care of you both.' Forrenfar, the kingdom of animal keepers.

At the crossroads, she would need to turn north. The City of Beasts lay two day's journey from the crossroads on foot while Akiliree, Willam and Reesa's destination, was equidistant to the east. They would have to part ways. The idea of leaving her only friends in this time of peril fought against every instinct. For a moment she fantasized that maybe they could accompany Willam and Reesa home, live in obscurity with them, hidden in plain sight from the usurper who sought Kai even now. The thought of Kai growing up in her homeland, surrounded by her people brought a smile to Lerna's face, but it quickly faded. Willam's knowledge of her rushed forward in her mind. He would surely not be the only citizen who knew her face. She could not count on the silence of every voice who knew her. Eventually someone would reveal them, or the usurper himself would search the city and find them. Reesa might be able to claim Kai as her own, but Lerna bore no mark. No brand to signify she had already been questioned.

Lerna's eyes fell to her lap. In the pale blue light of the illuminator hanging from the corner of the wagon, she could see her dress. Though it had seen better days, she could not help but appreciate the intricacy and delicate nature of its details. The royal symbol was embossed in the center of her bodice. Before now, it had been a thing of pride to bear the crest on her person. She was a member of the royal court of Lylunir; though not her kingdom of birth, it was her home. Now the crest would surely draw unwanted attention. She would need a change of clothes, and soon. Fear crept into her mind. What if they had already set checkpoints at the city gates of each of the trade centers? What if there were soldiers waiting at the crossroads to slaughter more babies of unmarked parents? What if they were watching her right now, planning their attack as soon as she revealed the location of the princess they searched for? The dark of the road and silence of the forest began to play tricks on Lerna's mind. She started to hear whispering all around her. The cry of a bird was the call for reinforcements, and the rustle of branches in the wind became the footsteps of infantry surrounding her. Panic filled her again, as it had so many times in the last days.

Ahead of her in the darkness, farther along the road, a small light came into view. She stared into the darkness trying to decide whether the light represented salvation or damnation for her small band of travelers. She did not stop the team, but slowed their pace. If indeed the light were held by the enemy, they had already seen hers as well. She dare not stop or turn away for fear of the suspicion it would cause. Quickly she looked about her on the bench. Under her was a rough spun dark wool blanket. Lifting her body slightly she pulled the blanket round about her, pulling it over her hair, and using it to hide the bulk of her garment. The nearer she drew to the light, the more her chest tightened. Had she come all this way only to be found so easily, walking right into the enemy's hands?

She was about to call out to Willam when she noticed something curious about the light causing her palpitations; it did not move. Not once since she noticed it had the small light shifted position in any way. Her mind cleared a bit. She began to calm her body and look at the light, not as a panicked fugitive, but as the scholar she was. Now she saw the truth of it. Standing at least fifteen feet from the ground, and glowing white as her hair, stood the crossroads marker. In her daze of thought and memory she had traveled almost six hours and now approached the crossroads. She hitched the team back to their original pace. The light from the marker showed an empty expanse where the three roads diverged. No guards, no checkpoints. As she reached the marker, she pulled the team straight across into the small hollow that lay beyond. Lurching the team to a stop, Lerna took the lantern from the side of the wagon and descended. Her legs felt wobbly under her and the ache in her feet returned. She stretched beside the wagon for a time, then walked up to the horses. When she placed her hand on the neck of the horse closest to her the flesh was hot, and the coat was drenched. The team had not had a rest in nearly a day and a half now. If they did not get one soon, they would expire and then all their plans would end.

She took the lantern and moved into the hollow. She found what she was looking for only a short distance ahead. A stream ran beside the grassy expanse. This would be perfect. Lerna returned to the team and placed the lantern on the ground. She began fumbling her way through the rigging that held them to the wagon. Though it took her some time, she managed to free them of the hitch. Using one of the straps she had unfastened incorrectly, she fashioned leads for each horse. Leaving the illuminator on the ground next to the cart, she led the team to the banks of the small creek. She bound the lead of each horse to low hanging branches along the water's edge, ensuring that each could reach the water and a small stretch of grass around them. Satisfied that the horses were taken care of, she returned to the wagon and retrieved the lantern from the ground. Lerna climbed back into the driver's seat and pulled the rough wool blanket high around her shoulders. The first soft glow of dawn began to creep in around her. She sat in silence and watched as the darkness gave way to views in gray of the hollow ahead of her. Slowly, color returned to the world. The chill of the morning, now far more acute than she could remember, did not seem to phase the blooms on the cherry and apple trees that surrounded their small wagon. She could see the horses now, reaching into the limbs to which they were fastened and pulling green fruit from their branches, drinking the cold, clear water of the brook beside them. She closed her eyes and listened to the stirrings of the early rising animals. Squirrels and birds of all kinds were waking around her. The orchards seemed oblivious to the tragedy befalling their owners. Lerna prayed the flames that had consumed much of the City of Light did not make it to this beautiful place.

She had almost fallen asleep when the sounds of life

began behind her. She heard shuffling and whispers. Reesa'a soft voice mixed with Willam's deep tones. Occasionally she heard the coo of a baby. Soon, the door at the rear opened and closed. She did not stir but opened her eyes. Willam's footsteps moved along the side of the wagon. When she felt he was almost to her she said in a clam and deliberate voice, "I need a brand."

His steps ceased, then started again. She felt the wagon lean a bit as he pulled himself into the seat beside her. His silence spoke volumes to his answer, but she would insist. Clearing her throat she said again, "I need a brand. I will never make it through a checkpoint without one, and I have far to go yet." She sat forward and looked at him. His eyes were focused out into the hollow. He did not answer her but simply nodded. "Can you do this for me?" She studied his face. He looked older than he had yesterday, wearied and tired.

"On one condition," he looked at her. His stern expression had taken a solemn, contemplative turn.

"Yes?" She braced herself. She had made up her mind not to stay with them. She would part ways here at the crossroads and attempt to reach the City of Beasts before the invaders had time to fully search there.

Willam cleared his throat and, with conviction in his voice, said, "You will wake me before you unhitch my team again." The seriousness in his voice was too much for Lerna. She could not hold in the burst of laughter that now streamed from her. Willam smiled as she cackled hysterically. All the nervous energy she had built up inside her heart for the last few days came rushing out. As tears began to stream down her face, she calmed herself and looked at Willam, still smiling at her lunacy.

"Of course." They sat beside each other laughing for a bit longer. When both had finished their reverie, Lerna discovered that Willam's youth had returned to him, as had hers.

"Shall we eat first? Reesa said she was starving when I left her." Willam turned and jumped down from the bench. From the ground, he began digging in the bags and barrels that lined the sides of the small wagon. Lerna clambered down beside him. When she reached his side, he began handing her all manner of food, eggs, a hunk of salted meat, and jars of milk. Lastly, he pulled a large loaf of that delicious bread wrapped in baker's cloth. "We shall fill our bellies before we deal with unpleasantness."

Lerna nodded. Her stomach surged with desire as she carried the wealth in her arms. She followed Willam a short distance into the hollow where he took the blanket from her shoulders and laid it out over the ground. She placed the other food items beside the bread on the blanket and began helping him gather wood for a fire. As they worked on their simple task the morning brightened around them. Once the fire was started, Willam fetched a few pans from the top of the wagon and Lerna crawled through the small door to check on Reesa. She was much livelier this morning. She was sitting up in the bed cradling the two babies in her arms. Her smile beamed up from her lovely youthful face. Lerna had no difficulty seeing the reason for Willam's choice in wives. As Lerna drew closer to her, Reesa began to stir, shifting the infants in her arms so that she could swing her legs over the side of the small bed.

"No, you should stay in bed, child. You have been through too much to go walking around just yet." Lerna's voice was earnest, but Reesa dismissed the warning offhandedly.

"Nonsense. I feel fine; and if I spend one more minute in this carriage, I will lose what little mind I have left. I demand fresh air, and so do these babies." Lerna could not argue with her smile. Reesa held her son up to Lerna. "Arn. His name is Arn. We decided that this morning." Reesa pushed herself up a bit further. Lerna motioned for Kai.

"I will take them out so that you can get dressed." Reesa passed her the second baby and Lerna quickly turned and retreated from the wagon. Willam met her outside the door. After pushing it closed behind her, he took his son into his arms. He and Lerna carried the small bundles to the blanket. The smell of food cooking filled the hollow. Reesa joined them quickly and together they spent breakfast exchanging information about their pasts and sharing the wonderful meal Willam had prepared.

The joyful morning could not last forever and, as noon approached, Lerna took on a more serious mood. Her time was waning. She had two day's journey on foot ahead of her, and she could wait no longer. She rose from the blanket, taking care not to disturb the sleeping children at her side. As she moved away from the group, Willam called after her.

"Where are you going?"

Looking back, her face solemn, she said, "To gather what herbs I can. I mean to bind our brands before we part. Yours are already growing with infection." Her eyes lingered on Willam's face. For a moment he looked as if he would protest, but instead only nodded.

As he began to rise as well, Reesa asked, "What do you mean 'our brands'? You didn't suffer that terrible humiliation, Lerna." Her eyes moved from Willam to Lerna and back again. Her face grew red with panic. "No. You can't mean to perform such an abomination on her. She does not deserve such insult, Willam. You can't..." His hand reached the side of her face before her thought could finish.

"She will never pass a check point with Kai without one. It's the only way to be sure Kai is safe." Reesa pulled her face from his hand. He could see the anger growing in her eyes.

"It's NOT the only way! She and Kai can come home with us! We can keep them safe!" Her voice cracked and tears slipped down her cheeks. She reached out her branded hand and placed it lightly on the sleeping form of Kai. Her body began to quiver with sobs.

"I have to take her to Forrenfar." Lerna's words brought even more desperation to Reesa's face.

"Forrenfar? But why?" Lerna returned to the blanket. Settling down again next to Reesa, she too placed a light hand on Kai.

"Because that was the last thing our Vessel requested of me." Lerna met Reesa's gaze. "She made me swear it, and I must keep my word." Reesa'a anger gave way to sadness. She knew there was no disputing something like this. Her eyes filled even fuller with tears and the sobs now came freely from her. Lerna wrapped her in a soft hug, and Reesa let out her tears into Lerna's soft white hair. They sat this way for several minutes, Willam had cleared away the pans from breakfast before Reesa pulled away suddenly.

"What about the great lifts?" Her face had become red and puffy from crying, but Lerna sensed that calm had come to her.

"What about them?" Lerna was not prepared for Reesa's answer.

"They burned the night of the invasion. All of them. Willam saw them as we were packing our rooms to leave." Lerna felt her heart drop. Hopelessness licked at her. Without the lifts she was trapped. Imprisoned with an army that wanted her and Kai, her only purpose for living now, lying dead at the point of their swords. Frantically she looked to Willam. His face was stern as he took up a small piece of metal he had pulled from the cart.

"Burned? Surely you are mistaken." Her voice cracked. The panic of the last days swept back through her. The uncertainty and doubt that had almost driven her mad in the night returned to gnaw on her plans.

"Afraid not. I saw the fires in the distance along the

cliff wall. But there is another way." He lowered himself back onto the blanket and began to bend the small piece of metal. As he worked he spoke again. "There is still the old trade path. It hasn't been used in centuries, but for the most part it should still be intact. Most people have forgotten about them. I only remember because I used to play on the ancient path to Akiliree as a child. They are narrow and difficult, but if you mean to cross the wall, they are your only chance. My only fear is that in some places the path has given way to cliffs. Will you be able to cross such expanses on your own?" Lerna knew he was about to offer himself to assist her. She would hear none of it. He had a wife and baby to take care of, not to mention getting them safely back to the City of Grain.

Lerna shook her head. "I will manage. Now.." She rose back to her feet. "I still need those herbs." She turned and walked quickly to the hollows edge. As she picked the small white flowers necessary to bind their wounds, she tried desperately to remember her childhood playing. Zailia is a mountainous kingdom. Their cities, towns and monasteries are built on and in the mountain sides. She spent the better part of her youth scaling regions even the rams feared to attempt. Though many years had passed since then, she was still in spry condition. Surely she could muster enough of her youth to bridge the small gaps where time had ruined the path. When she returned to the blanket, she found a somber couple sitting by the fire. Willam had finished his makeshift brand and now held it in the flames. It needed to be red hot if her brand was to look as fierce as theirs. She set about binding the wounds on their hands. Reesa's came first. When Lerna had finished, Reesa requested to return to the wagon with the children. She did not wish to see what was about to happen. Lerna helped her inside with the young ones and returned to Willam. After binding his hand, he pulled the brand from the fire. Though not red hot, the metal had begun to glow a bit.

"This should be good enough," he said as he turned toward her. Lerna rolled up her sleeve and place her hand flat on the ground. The herbs and cloth to bind her wound waited close by for the deed to be done. Taking a stick in her teeth she closed her eyes tight and waited for the pain. Willam took a deep breath and, before he lost his nerve, placed the scorching metal on her dark flesh. Lerna's muffled scream torn through him, but he held fast, rocking the design back and forth, ensuring a complete brand. After several seconds, he lifted the odious piece of metal from her hand and tossed it aside. Lerna's scream died away, and she leaned heavily on her other arm. She almost lost consciousness from the pain but managed to pull herself around. The smell was foul, and she quickly applied the herb paste to her fresh brand. Almost instantly the pain lessened. She took a look at the angry mark, now permanently affixed to her flesh. It was different from the one Willam and Reesa bore upon themselves. She looked up at Willam, confused.

He must have sensed her thoughts. "It's the one they gave people who had no children, or had one ... Anyway,

CROSSROADS

I figured you could pass for a nursemaid for Kai. No guard would be fool enough to believe you are her mother." Through her pain, Lerna smiled. He was quite right. She was a stark opposite to the Lylunirian peoples. She could never pass for Kai's mother. After binding her hand, Lerna left the fire and headed to the creek, where she washed her face in the cold water. Crouched at the water's edge, she noticed her gown again. The crest of Lylunir, embroidered in silver thread, glittered in the warm sunlight. She would need several things before she departed Willam and Reesa, one of which would be another dress.

CHAPTER 7
BATTLE PLAN

Rikard sat uneasily in the small throne. His hips pushed at the arms, making them pop and crackle; and his head and shoulders stood tall above the high back, obscuring the gold embossed carving of a crown emanating light from all directions. By any other measure, it was a large chair, painstakingly carved from a single trunk of walnut centuries ago. There had been two, but one lay in ruin on the floor, a casualty of last night's battle. Rikard was certain that this had been the king's throne; and, though Marcus was not a small man, he was a child by comparison to Rikard. He did not want to cast it aside however. His whole life had been led to this. He had grown up dreaming of the day he would sit in this very room, in this very chair, triumphant. He sat, listening to the throne groan and creak under his weight as his generals reported the day's events. For hours Brakbarks filed in one at a time to report on casualties, prisoner counts, and the status of the search for the missing infant princess. With each report of failure, Rikard grew more impatient. He had sent his troops to each of the large gates out of the city as soon as the castle had been taken. A checkpoint was to be set up and any child that could not walk on its own was to be killed. He had pulled two of the iron letters from one of the war wagons and twisted them with his bare hands into their symbols for "lost" and "empty". His final instructions were to brand every adult that passed the checkpoint. Those that had a child killed or had no children at all were to be labeled as empty. If any women came to the gate heavy with child they and their husbands were to be labeled lost. This way, if they passed through another checkpoint the guards would know if they had been checked.

He had hoped that whoever took the child would have pleaded for the life of the princess at one of the checkpoints as she fled the city; and he would have had the pleasure of killing the infant himself. Some small consolation for the queen's uncooperative death. But hours passed. Reports of hundreds of deaths from the checkpoints echoed in the sanctuary. Rikard's head grew heavy. Daylight had come and gone as he sat in this ever shrinking chair. His failing mood was also drowned in the smell of the flesh from royal guards, whose bodies were piled high in the far corner of the room. The king and queen still lay crumpled on the floor of the chamber upstairs. Suddenly, he lifted his head. Perhaps they hadn't left the city, or tried to cross the checkpoint as a mother and child; and she was already dead. Both of these thoughts gave him hope. He rose to his feet, interrupting the Brakbark giving his report. Rikard crossed the large room quickly and pulled open the large carved wooden doors. With a gruff bellow, he summoned every Brakbark in the castle grounds to him.

It took nearly an hour for the generals to gather in the throne room. Rikard paced angrily before them waiting for the heavy doors to close. "We have taken the City of Light!" He paused as the cheers from the gathered rang out in the sanctuary. "Yes, yes, we have accomplished much since our landing. But one thing remains undone. The princess still lives. There are many places in this city where something as small as a child could be hidden. As of now, the gates out will be sealed. Every building, alleyway, and park is to be searched thoroughly. The remaining citizens will be brought back here to join those captured in the siege. Find her. Bring her to me alive." Rikard paused. He could tell from the looks exchanged throughout the crowd that many doubted they would be able to find the child. He stretched to his fullest height, expanding his chest. He was a mountain of a man and puffed up in this way he was even more formidable. He gazed into the crowd, identifying one of the mumblers. Extending his huge arm, Rikard pointed his strong fingers at him. "You. Rise. Say what is in your mind." The soldier hesitated. Fear crept into his eyes. Slowly he rose to his feet.

"My Lord?" The fear in his voice brought a smirk to Rikard's face. He ruled his people this way. If they were afraid of him they would obey his every word.

"Speak your mind." Rikard watched as the soldier

swallowed. His gaze scanned the room, but found no support. Every other brakbark's eyes were cast to the ground or the ceiling or the walls, but none met his gaze. "SPEAK!" Knowing that Rikard had little in the way of patience, this demand was his last chance at life.

"My Lord, I only thought that maybe she may have made it out of the city before we set up the checkpoints. Perhaps we should send forces into the other cities. Like the city we traveled through at the base of the lift. If she made it out of here alive, surely she would head to one of them. They would hide her; she is their princess." Rikard took in the man's words. Though he raged at his impertinence, the man had a point. It was hours before the checkpoints had been ordered. Maybe she had escaped in the arms of a soldier or, more likely, a midwife or maid. The soldier's suggestion repeated in his head. Rikard's posture loosened a bit.

"Perhaps you're right. What was your name? Karnus, was it?" Rikard paused. He knew the names of every Brakbark in his command because he had chosen them personally to lead. He waited for Karnus to nod and then continued. "There is a good chance she escaped the city. Very well, you will create a battalion for each city, including this one. You will handle the search of each and every city. After all, she can't get out of Lylunir any more than we can." Rikard smiled as the shocked Brakbark nodded in confusion. He glanced around him and with a shaking finger, he pointed to five generals about the room. They rose and followed him out into the courtyard.

"Those who remain, you will organize the prisoners. Separate the men from the women and children. Set up a section of the city to relocate them into. Then, you will find homes, nice ones, for all of our people. We may be here a while and I intend for us to live as they have for all this time. They shall know what it was like to have little and want for much." With that he swung his great arm toward the door. His generals, who had been sitting all around him on the floor, rose to their feet and frantically made their way from the room.

Rikard returned to his tiny throne. He stood in front of the intricately carved chair. It was beautiful and befitting a king, but its size and material was not suited to him. Perhaps it was the queen's throne and the king's lay in the heap by the wall. He stood in thought for several minutes before crying out, "Where are my engineers?" Within moments, the sounds of people entering the room made him turn. Six of his engineers filled in, silent and solemn. They looked tired, as did all of the men. The brightest men his kingdom had to offer approached and stood in front of him. "First, I need a new throne. This infernal chair is too small. But I like the look of it. You," pointing at the smallest of the men before him, "You will be responsible for creating this." The man bowed and quickly skirted past his king to the chair. He began studying and measuring the throne. Rikard watched for a moment and then, satisfied with the engineers efforts, turned back to the remaining five. "The rest of you are tasked with getting us out of Lylunir." Silence fell in the usurped sanctuary. Behind Rikard, the engineer working with the throne smiled to himself. His task was at least possible. The five men glanced at each other. As their eyes traveled from one to another in soundless dismay, Rikard grew impatient. "Well, any ideas?" The urgency in his voice compelled the men to speak.

One of the men cleared his throat. "Why don't we carve out a path up the cliffs and down the other side?"

Another quickly dismissed this. "No, no, we would lose too much on the climb, the cliffs are too steep and the rocks too soft to hold the machines. We would slide off to our deaths before reaching the top. We could instead rebuild the lifts." Rikard's face pinched at the memory of the contraptions that now lay as little more than smoldering ruins in the distant cities. For a moment consensus seemed to circulate in the room. Mumbled agreement and nodding of heads prevailed until one man shook his head in resolute disagreement.

"Did any of you bother to study the lift as we were riding it? I did, it was astounding. Made of great trees of hard wood. One thing I am certain of now that we have been here a while is that those trees did not come from Lylunir. The only trees we have seen here are small and thin, designed, it would seem, to bear fruit and incapable of baring substantial weight. It would take thousands of trees to rebuild one of the lifts, trees that do not grow here." The trees of Lylunir neither grew tall enough nor had strong enough timber to manage the lift they had come in on. The nods of consensus were now nods of dismissal. After a long pause of thought, yet another engineer spoke up.

"What if we dig through the cliffs? Create tunnels into the other kingdoms? Hadrians are practiced miners; it would be no small feat, and would take years, but it would work." Rikard stopped for a moment and thought on this suggestion. It was true that his people had spent years digging into the earth, but they had none of their machines for such work.

"We could repurpose the machines into diggers. But we would not be able to change them back once we reached the other side and crossing the kingdoms on foot would be no small task. Also, I feel the other realms will not be so easily taken as Lylunir. They obviously know we are here, they burned their lifts to keep us out. We will need all our people in fighting condition. I will not have them exhausted in this labor, not when we came here to escape such toil. No, digging through would take far too much from us." Again silence fell in the room. The men mumbled to each other debating other possible strategies. Slicing through the silence came a different voice.

"Why not use the slaves?" Rikard looked into the growing darkness of the chamber. His eyes were followed by the five men who sat before him and the one behind, who had been busying himself with designs for his Vessel's new throne. The sun had gone down several hours ago. Though the strange rocks had begun to glow, there were still shadows in the rear of the sanctuary.

"Come forward." Rikard's voice was tinged with

anger and curiosity. From the back for the room footsteps could be heard. Into the pale blue light of one of the stones stepped a woman. Though she was on the small side for a Hadrian, she bore the uniform of a soldier. "What are you doing in here? I sent for no soldiers." Rikard's eyes moved over the woman; she could be no more than eighteen years old. Her uniform bore the splatters and scars of battle, and she had hurriedly bandaged wounds on both her thigh and abdomen. Her hair was wild and curly, held loosely back from her face with what he decided were small daggers. His anger left him. He stared at her, entranced. He thought hard to remember her, surely he had seen her many times. Practicing in the yard, training in the rings. How could he not remember such a beautiful creature. "Use the slaves?" The engineers were grumbling amongst themselves. Rikard could hear the frustration in their voices. She was not meant to be here. She was not an engineer, how dare she intrude on this meeting? Rikard looked down at his men, he could see the insult in their eyes, so he asked again. "Use the slaves? What slaves, girl?"

"My name is Tawni." She took several determined steps toward her king. She showed no fear. When she had reached the line of engineers, all struck dumb by her show of impertinence, she spoke again. "These white skins we have herded into cages, are they not now our slaves? Why not break their backs against the cliffs. Let them dig our tunnels. It may take longer, they aren't nearly the specimens we are; but our backs would remain strong and our machines of war unchanged. Would that not solve our problem?" The strength and confidence in her voice intrigued Rikard. Since the day on the mountain just over three years ago, his only desire was to reach the kingdoms and lay them beneath his feet; but this girl stirred something different within him.

"Tawni, is it, how long have you been there in the back?" Rikard moved toward her. The engineers scattered like scared children to flee his path, but as he drew closer to her she moved closer to him.

"I came in with the Brakbarks. I thought I could help." Her voice cracked slightly. Rikard was now only inches from her. He towered over her as her father had done when she was but a child. She held his gaze in her own and stood her ground. He could kill her with a single halfhearted swing of his hand. But it did not come. Instead his face spread wide with a smile. She had impressed him.

"You have helped me, Tawni, very much." Rikard took her by the arm and led her to the front of the room. "Men, make ready the slaves. As soon as the cities are ours we will begin digging. Tawni, you will remain here. My personal counsel." Rikard turned to the engineer tasked with his throne. Brushing him aside, he lifted Tawni like a doll and placed her into the throne. It fit her perfectly. "Good, it's yours." Turning to the engineer, "I trust you will work quickly?"

Terrified, the engineer only nodded. Turning from his king, the man fled the throne room. Rikard waved his large arm at the other engineers. They, too, quickly clambered to their feet and fled. Rikard stood over Tawni and studied her. She seemed to feel at home in the small throne. "What do you advise I do next, Royal Counselor, Tawni?" A proud smile spread across her face. Looking about the room, her eyes fell upon the rotting bodies in the corner.

"I would advise my King and Vessel to burn those."

"And the ones up stairs? What of those?" Rikard lifted a quizzical eyebrow. He wanted to do something dramatic with the dead royals littering the floor above them. Tawni thought for a minute and then met his eyes.

"Put them on display in the courtyard. Let them rot where all people can see them. Show them that their precious Vessel fell easily by your hand, and that they have no hope." Rikard's chest swelled with pride. He had found a woman worthy of him. Tawni would soon be more   than   just   his   counsel.

CHAPTER 8
THE CLIMB

The clop of the horse's hooves was all Lerna could hear now. For hours she had sat on the blankets atop this horse. Despite the monotony, she was extremely grateful for it. When she had left Willam and Reesa at night fall, Willam had insisted she take the smallest horse in his four-horse team for her journey. They would have more than enough to pull the wagon home, and she could reach the City of Beasts in half the time. She had ridden at a fast walk all night long, stopping only briefly to relieve herself, change Kai, and for both of them to eat a bit. Willam had been even more generous with his food. Under her riding blanket was draped a heavily laden saddle bag. It held everything she would need to successfully complete her cliff crossing. He had packed her several loaves of that marvelous bread and six bottles of milk for Kai. She could eat almost four times from one of them. In the other side, one could find herbs she had gathered in case of injury along with some bandaging and rope. There were several small cans of oil and a flint for starting a fire. Reesa had dressed Lerna in her smallest dress, though it was still cut for a woman with child, it fit her well enough. They had burned her court dress. She had cried as the silver crest turned to ashes in the flames.

Lerna pulled the blankets around her a bit closer. She was wrapped in no less than eight shawls and blankets. The one closest to her had been tied around her in a sling to hold Kai. Another had been tied deliberately to hide her hair. The rest were slung around her waist or across her shoulders. Though she was rather hot inside all these layers, she knew that the cliff pass would be bitter cold and that the nights were chilly enough here on the ground. As she tugged and twisted, Kai began to cry. It was nearly noon, perhaps she was hungry. Lerna steered the horse off the road and a short distance into the woods. This stretch was still wild. Though the trees were fruit bearers, this was no orchard. The closer she drew to the City of Beasts the more wild the land had become. There were stories of strange animals and even monsters in these woods. She stopped the horse just out of eye-shot of the road. If someone came by, they would not be able to see her; but it also put her into the dark of the forest. This was her third stop like this on her journey, and so far she had seen little more than a squirrel and a few blue birds; but the stories told day after day by travelers were hard to block out, especially when some of them were true.

Forrenfar held creatures that the other realms did not. It is true that every realm held beasts: cats, dogs, birds, rabbits and the like. Small creatures. Each realm also had a small assortment of domestic food animals suited to their particular terrain. Lerna had grown up with mountain rams but had never seen a cow until she had been given to Lylunir. Each kingdom had what was necessary for them to live healthy lives, but not Forrenfar. That kingdom held not only the common animals of the world, but also an assortment of fantastic and terrifying creatures. Each sprang inexorably from the imagination of their God, beasts like the Antelox, a huge field creature the size of a small house with antlers like branches in a tree. These antlers were used to build homes in place of wood, or at least that's what Lerna had heard, because they wouldn't burn as wood does. Just one of their skins could cover an entire family in long winter coats, and their meat was sweeter that even that of a deer, Lerna's favorite meal and a delicacy in Lylunir. The Draconus, or dragon in the common tongue, was rumored to have gone extinct. A large reptile with feathers and wings like a bird, it had been seen many times along the mountains in the northern most territory of Forrenfar for centuries. Another of these fearful creatures was the Wolvari. This creature was not unlike a dog, but a thousand times more savage and ten times as large. It had great tusks protruding from its upper jaw and spikes along the ridge of its back. While its back legs were rather short, its chest and front haunches were massive, giving it the appearance of a battering ram. Many years ago travelers began referring to the creature as a worg because it looked like the bastard spawn of a wolf, a wart hog, and an ox.

The worg is the creature Lerna most feared in these

woods. There was now a small wild population of these creatures in the forests surrounding the City of Beasts. A traveling menagerie had once roamed Lylunir, bringing these animal wonders into each city for the population to gaze at in amazement. When they were returning to the city of Beasts, to send the weary creatures home, the wagon carrying three worgs overturned and the creatures escaped into the darkness. Since then there had been no traveling animal shows, and the roads around the animal city were feared, especially at night.

Lerna worked quickly, feeding Kai and changing her wrapping. When the princess was full, clean and sound asleep against her chest, Lerna reached into the saddle bag and grabbed the last of the first loaf of bread. She sat on a small mossy knoll and watched her horse graze on the green fruit hanging low in the trees. At first she thought the sounds she heard were simply animal noises from the forest behind her, but as they grew louder, she knew they were man made. Fear crept into her heart again. From the road behind the trees came the sound of many feet and heavy wagon wheels. There was no mistaking this sound. No refugees would walk in this manner, and no wagon she had ever heard groaned and growled as this one did. She had to know for sure. She pulled Kai from her sling and placed her on the ground, then she tied the horse far enough away that she didn't have to fear it trampling the sleeping princess.

Slowly and silently, Lerna crept though the trees toward the road. The closer she drew the louder the procession became. Soon, she felt little fear for a broken twig or a rustle of leaves, no one could hear such small sounds over the den of this caravan. Behind the largest tree she could find, she took in the army on the road. They moved slowly, as most were on foot. The one vehicle they had, moved behind them unaided by horses. The men looked tired and worn from walking. Lerna thought to herself that it looked as if they had marched in this fashion from the City of Light without stopping. As she watched the men pass she began to count. Five men in a row, at least fifteen rows, that's...sixty five men. That's not so bad. Just then, a cry rang out from the top of the massive vehicle now directly in front of her. A large young man stood on the vehicle's nose and bellowed to the men to take a short break. The side of the wagon opened and nearly twenty men and women piled out, each carrying a water jug and a little food. The soldiers from the rows crowded around the wagon getting what refreshment they could from the people that had been inside. Lerna's heart fell when she heard a similar cry further back. Chancing a glance, she strained to see behind the machine in front of her. More lines of men and at least one more of those machines lay off in the distance behind it, not sixty five, not even ninety. There were at least two hundred men and two of these massive war machines in this procession, and they were headed toward her destination.

Frantically, she made her way back to her horse and Kai, still asleep on the moss. She lifted the princess into her sling and freed the horse from its tree. Walking quickly she led the horse parallel to the road through the forest. After nearly ten minutes, she ventured closer to the road. She could see the army, still resting behind her. Up ahead there was a small curve. If she could get to the other side, she could mount up and ride hard for the city gates. Maybe she could warn them, give them a fighting chance, something the besieged City of Light had not had. She pulled the horse along in the trees by the road side. Just before the curve, she pulled herself on the horse.

As she landed on the blankets atop his back, the horse let out a loud whinny. Terrified, Lerna turned in her makeshift saddle. Sure enough, one of the men had heard the sound. He stood at the front of the crowd staring at her . She was a good three hundred yards from him, but she could tell from his face and pointed finger that he had discovered her and was alerting his fellows. Lerna did not hesitate any longer. She dug her heels hard into the horse's sides, and he jumped into a full run. Pulling her body close to his, she cradled Kai as best she could. The horse flew down the road, cutting curves and jumping the occasional fallen tree. For nearly two hours, Lerna maintained this insane pace, only giving it up when it was clear the horse might give out if she didn't stop.

She slowed to a walk. The processional of soldiers had been moving very slowly when she had watched it on the road, perhaps she had left them far behind her. Though, when she had seen them, they had no quarry fleeing before them to chase. Maybe now their pace had quickened. She walked along at a normal gate through the darkening forest. Dusk was creeping in on her. The forest was far more frightening now, knowing that behind her on the road, drawing ever closer to her, were soldiers bent on her death. She stared at the small baby on her chest. Tears rolled from her eyes as she remembered little Kai's mother's face. Poor Marina. She had been like a daughter to Lerna. Now she was gone. She had loved Marcus like a son, and he was gone too. Only Kai remained, little helpless Kai.

The sound behind her roused her from her thoughts. Crashing and shouts came from the forest. She turned on her perch to look into the woods. Through the trees she could see distant flames. She realized almost immediately what the machines were for. Instead of following her at her breakneck pace through the curving and twisting wooded road, they had simply cut their way straight through it. They would be upon her in mere moments.

"NO!" Lerna's cries were met with shouts. She turned back to the road and again kicked the horse into a full run. The horse grudgingly obeyed. They sped down the road; she could not cut through the forest as her pursuers had. Two turns later she discovered she did not have to. There, across a bridge, were the heavy stone gates of the City of Beasts. The whole city resembled a creature's cage. Iron bars and stone walls encompassed the smallest city in Lylunir. Lerna crouched low over her horse and headed straight for the gates. Behind her she heard the machines break free of the forest out onto the road—so close to her now. She did not look back but kicked the horse to quicken pace. As she crested the bridge, she felt a sharp pain in her calf. She glanced down to see the shaft of an arrow protruding from her lower leg. No matter, she turned back to the gates. As she drew closer, men began to appear, standing in the opening. They stared at the incredible scene unfolding before their eyes. A woman raced toward them pursued by all manner of strange people and contraptions. Lerna began to call out to them.

"Ready the gates! They mean you harm! Ready the gates!" She yelled this over and over again until she saw the men begin to act. As she passed below the large stone arch, a great metal clad wooden door slammed to the ground behind her. The sound, and shaking of the ground, frightened her horse. It reared onto its hind legs, sending her, the baby, and all the blankets tumbling to the ground. Once freed of its burden, the horse bolted at a speed she had not seen it use into the crowd, away from her. All manner of men now crowded around her. In the topple from the horse, Kai had been awakened and was now crying; and the shawl hiding her hair had slipped down and hung loosely from her shoulders. She lay on the ground surrounded by curious and frightened faces. Finally, one of them spoke to her.

"What is going on here?" The older gentleman, dressed well by any standards, extended an arm to help Lerna to her feet. As she struggled to stand, a sharp pain reminded her of the arrow in her leg. Leaning on the man, she reached down and unceremoniously yanked the projectile from her flesh. As it tore from her, a cry accompanied it, both from her and the crowd about her. She had no time for pain, no time for sympathy or questions.

"They have killed your king, your Vessel; they mean to kill your princess." Lerna motioned to the crying babe bound to her chest. "I need to get over the cliffs into Forrenfar, and you need to defend your city, though I fear both maybe hopeless." Lerna struggled to put weight on her injured leg. The wound had an unnatural burn to it. She realized it must have been poisoned. She pushed that to the back of her mind. She would deal with that as soon as she and Kai were on the ancient trade path.

The old gentleman spoke again, "But my lady, the lift has burned. There is no way to Forrenfar." Behind him men had already begun to fortify the gate and gather what little weapons they could together; arming themselves for the coming battle. Lerna could not help but see them as children preparing to fight giants.

"I was told of an ancient path, weathered by time and forgotten by most, which leads up and over the cliffs. Do you know of such a trail?" The old man looked doubtful before her. She began to lose hope, if she could not find the path in time all would be lost. Just then, a young voice came from the street in front of her. All eyes turned to the boy of no more than ten who stood there, looking up at them.

"I know that path, it's in our yard, but it's hard to

climb, and a short way up it gets very narrow and slippery." The boy was looking straight at Lerna. His face was solemn, showing no sign of foolish childhood.

"Go home, boy, tell all you pass to hide. Go, now, this is no place for you." The old man's voice was sincere in its concern, as well as its doubt to the boy's story. Still the boy stared at Lerna. Behind her she heard the first shuddering crash against the gate. The machine bashed against the metal clad hard wood. It would hold for a time, but that machine would be the victor. She had no time to debate.

"No it's true, I can take you there! Follow me!" He moved forward and took Lerna's hand. He tugged on it, and she could see the truth in his eyes. She bent down and lifted the saddlebag into her hand, throwing it over one shoulder. The boy did the same and grabbed the rest of the blankets. Despite the protest from the gentleman, Lerna found herself being led quickly through the streets by the small boy. Panic had erupted in the City of Beasts. All sorts of people flooded into the avenues and alleys around her. Cries, of panic and fear, came to her from every direction. First their Great Lift was set ablaze from the other side, and now invaders were attempting to breech their city walls. The boy wove through the throngs of people, careful not to let his grip on Lerna slip away. Lerna did her best to follow him. The pain in her leg was growing steadily worse, but she did her best to ignore it. Twice along their path a person had bumped the wound, sending an uncontrollable cry shooting from her. Each time she fought the tears, nodded to the boy and continued on in silent agony.

Finally, the boy led her through the front door of a small row house. Through the living rooms and out the back they went, not another soul in sight. As she passed through the rear door, Lerna caught sight of the cliff wall. Only feet from the back of the row of small homes rose the unnatural boundary between the two kingdoms. "It's here!" The boy released her hands and ran to a small group of trees at the corner of the yard. Lerna followed him, forcing her way through the bramble, she found herself standing at the base of what was, at some point, a narrow, steep path up the cliff. She followed the path with her eyes. Time had worn the trail thin, mere feet in some places. As she stared up the small path she felt the boy laying the blankets around her shoulders. He pulled the saddle bag from her and began tying it around her waist with its straps. She tore her eyes from the treacherous climb ahead of her to watch him. Not once did he hesitate. She had found the most steadfast man in all of the city, and he was no more than ten. She smiled in spite of everything as she watched the boy tying the knot.

"Now, it gets pretty cold up there this time of year, so don't leave the blankets, no matter how heavy they get. About a mile and a half along the path, there is a section that has fallen down. Maybe twenty or so feet are missing. You will need to climb the distance to reach the rest of the path, but that's the worst spot like that, at least on this side. Don't tell my mother, but I have been all the way to the top before. It will take you the better part of a day to reach the top, then a little while to cross the top, then down the other side of course. You should be able to make it by tomorrow evening if you don't stop for long." As the boy finished his instructions he took a step back to admire his work. There Lerna stood, bundled expertly in the blankets, the saddle bag tied securely about her middle. He then looked her in the face. His eyes were so much older than the boy he was.

"Thank you. What is your name, young man?" Lerna placed a hand on his shoulder. She was absolutely astonished by him. So old and intelligent for his age.

"My name is Baron, ma'am. And you best be going before they get here. It will take you an hour before you will be out of sight." With his final advice imparted, he turned and ran into his home, calling for his mother. Lerna listened for a moment to him barking directions to her to keep her safe, just as he had for Lerna. Then everything got quiet. Turning back to the steep path ahead of her, she began to climb.

Each step shot pain up her leg, but she had no time to stop. Baron had told it would take an hour of climbing before she was invisible to the people below. As she scaled the path, more and more of the city came into view below her. After only a few minutes, she could see over the top of Baron's modest home into the street beyond. A few minutes more and she could see half the city, still frantic, people running through the streets and barricading intersections. After another ten minutes, the gate came into view, at least what was left of it. Not long before she had caught sight of it the machine must have burst through violently. She could just barely see the flashes of light as swords met swords. They were still fighting at the gate. She knew that soon the hundreds of soldiers would overpower the few men that guarded the gate. Soon houses like Baron's would burn, and many of the faces she had seen in the streets would lie dead in the very places she had passed them. She whispered a heartfelt prayer for Baron and his mother, and the old gentleman at the gate.

It wasn't long after the sight of the broken gate that smoke came to her nose. They had started burning. Though the flames were only near the gate, the smell of burning wood was heavy and thick in the air. She covered her nose and mouth as best she could with her sleeve and leaned against the cliff wall—just a bit further. She began coughing from the acrid smoke. During one of the convulsive coughs, her wounded leg betrayed her. She fell forward onto the narrow path, barely catching her weight before she crushed her passenger. Rolling onto her side, she lay for a moment blinded by the smoke and the pain. She would need to stop soon, or she would not make it. It had been nearly an hour since she had been shot with the poisoned arrow. The burning in her flesh had been growing steadily worse from the moment she had pulled the weapon free.

Struggling to her feet she pressed on, up the path. After a few more minutes she felt the air grow lighter.

THE CLIMB

The smoke was far less thick here. She had crossed some invisible line that the smoke could not. The dark of night was upon her now but she dare not light a flame. The pain in her calf had become too much to ignore. She leaned against the cold of the cliff wall and slid down, her rear landing fiercely on the rocky ground. Breathing heavily, she dug in the bag for the small illuminator stone and case that Willam had packed for her. It wouldn't be much light, but it should be enough for her to see her wound. Finding the special stone, she dropped it into the glass cylinder in the case. Instantly a small light illuminated her face. She lowered the case quickly and set it on the ground next to her. In the small circular glow, she pulled the tattered dress away from her blood soaked leg.

The wound was far worse than Lerna had expected. The flesh around it had already drained of its dark natural color. The black of her skin had been replaced by an eerie pale green. The wound was quite swollen and pus had already started to form along its corners. She had never heard of a poison that worked this fast. She dug in the saddle bag again, pulling out the herbs she had collected. She sorted through the different flowers and roots until she found the blanch root she sought. The small blue flower eased pain and drew out infection, it was her first choice for any type of poisonous bite or sting. She placed the small bitter flower in her mouth and chewed it for a moment, then applied the paste to the wound. The instant the herb hit the wound pain shot through her body. She tensed her jaw and even covered her mouth with her hand for fear of crying out. Within seconds, the pain subsided. While the burning was lessened, it did not completely subside. Lerna's face furrowed. This had not stopped the poison entirely, but at least she could walk again. She issued another prayer to her goddess that if the poison meant to take her life to at least let her make it to Forrenfar first. She bandaged the weeping puncture and returned the herbs and illuminator to the saddlebag. Kai stirred against her, and Lerna heard the rumbling of her own stomach. Reaching into the other side of the saddlebag she retrieved a bit of bread for her and milk for Kai. In the dark, they sat together eating.

The light from below was growing brighter through the layer of smoke. The City of Beasts was burning. Every home, every tree, was being licked by flame. Lerna's prayer for Baron issued again from her lips. Such a crafty and intelligent young man would surely have a way to escape this peril. At least that's what she repeated to herself over and over again as she watched the glimpses of light dance below her. Once Kai stopped eating and fell again to sleep, Lerna rose to her feet. In the dark she could barely see anything in front of her. With her back pressed against the cliff side, she moved forward up the path, using her foot to test the ground in front of her before she applied her weight. Baron's warnings of missing path sections had not fallen on deaf ears, especially since she had heard the same warning from Willam only the day before. For well over an hour she continued on this way. Exhausted and terrified, she pressed on up the narrow and slippery path.

Loose rocks occasionally gave way under her feet, and she would feel the tingling sensation of falling before she would catch herself along the cliff wall. In the dark, she could not tell how wide the trail was at any given moment, but she knew from the way the breeze would stir just in front of her toes and climb up her body that mere inches separated her from nothingness. In the darkness, her leg began to ache again. The wind grew colder. She knew she needed to stop soon. She continued until she could no longer feel the wind licking her ankles. Certain that the path was a bit wider here, she slid down the wall. Pulling a blanket free of her shoulder, she drew it up over her chest and snuggled in as best she could against the cold rock wall. The wind whistled in the stones above her head, but here, hunkered to the ground, she was free of it. Kai's steady breathing lulled Lerna into a troubled, light sleep.

CHAPTER 9

DECENT INTO FORRENFAR

The pain in her leg roused her. Lerna opened her eyes to a gray world. She sat, leaned against the cliff wall where she had stopped hours earlier, surrounded by a thick mist. Kai wiggled slightly against her chest. Though the baby was not crying, she was wide wake. Lerna went to push herself a bit more upright and was met with searing pain. Now the burning of her calf was almost all the way up her leg to her hip. Shifting a bit, she pushed the blanket off to the side and lifted her skirt. In the misty light of breaking day, the wound looked ten times worse than it had in the faint light of the illuminator. Greenish tendrils were creeping their way up her leg just below the fading flesh. Her entire left leg was a good bit larger than her right now, swollen from the infection. She reached into the bag and drew out her herbs again. This time she used an assortment of infection fighters and pain killers. After chewing them a bit, she pressed the mush into the open wound. She barely contained the scream that followed, but as it had last night, the pain, for the most part, subsided.

DECENT INTO FORRENFAR

She packed up her wares and returned the blanket to her shoulders. After feeding Kai, she struggled to her feet. Once standing, pressed against the cliff side, she scanned her surroundings. The mist obscured everything in front of her. She had no way of telling how high she had climbed, or the condition of the gate city below her. To her left and right the mist obscured anything beyond fifty feet, though she wished it had obscured more. The section of the path she had chosen for rest in the dark was indeed wider than the previous one. It stood nearly three feet wide, from wall to ledge, and had a few small pathetic looking bushes growing along its ridge. "That explains the lack of wind, I guess." Lerna muttered to herself. On the cliff side, the only other sounds were faint wind whistles in the distance; and she feared she might go mad in the silence and pain, especially as she thought about the section she had come through in the dark. Though she knew the path had been narrow, she was not prepared to see the truth. In the pitch dark of the night, she had sidled along on a ledge that looked to be only a foot or so wide, in some places even less. The thought of her and the baby being so close to the edge made her stomach turn. All the times her feet had slipped on lose stones and she had caught herself on the cliff side, how close she had been to death, made her glad she had not eaten with Kai.

As bad as the path behind had been, it was still preferable to the path ahead. She had stopped only feet from the large gap in the path Baron had warned her of. His words rang true, the gap was about twenty or so feet and luckily this section was relatively flat, unlike the steep climb from earlier. Lerna stood facing the gap, scanning the wall for suitable foot and hand holds. She had climbed cliffs this steep in her youth and the longer she stood looking at the face, the stronger her confidence became. There were an abundance of crags and inch-or-so wide ledges between where she stood and where she wanted to stand. After nearly ten minutes of planning, tracing out her crossing hold by hold, she set about preparing herself. She would not be able to keep Kai in front of her. Gingerly, she removed the bundled princess and all the blankets from her. Keeping a few loose blankets for Kai, she took the rest and tied them to the saddle bag around her waist. It was still securely fastened. After checking to make sure it was still snug with it new weight, she set about tying Kai to her back. Though the sling had worked wonderfully thus far for securing Kai, hands free, to her body, Lerna was leery of dangling the small princess from her back this far off the ground as she scaled the cliff wall gap. Using the extra blankets she had kept out, she fashioned extra support for the princess. When she was sure that Kai was safe, Lerna inched to the edge of the path and turned to face the wall.

She reached up to the holds that would start her trek. As she pulled her weight off the ground, her arms wobbled a bit. She tensed her body. Perhaps she should have eaten something, but the unease in her stomach reminded her that she would still have had an empty stomach now even if she had eaten with Kai. She placed her toes on the small ridges. She had expected her leg to protest, and it did not disappoint. After a moment, the pain settled a bit. She reached for the next hold. As her fingers wrapped around the small ledge, she slid her body inches across the gap. Inch by inch she moved her body. As she reached for the next hold, her left leg began to shake. She pulled back and put more of her weight on her wounded leg. As much as it hurt her, she needed that leg to make it across the gap. After a few moments the shaking stopped, and she began again. Lerna now hung only inches from the far ledge. Moving one last hand hold over she reached out her wounded leg to the edge of the path. She felt the stone under her toes. Relieved that her climb was almost over, she smiled slightly and eased her weight down onto her foot.

Less than a second later, she found herself swinging from one hand, hanging over the abyss hidden within the gray mist. The path had given way under her weight. Foot after foot crumbled down in slow motion, widening the gap another fifteen feet. Her body tingled as she swung loosely from her precarious grip. For a moment she thought she was falling, deep into the nothingness below her. When her fingers began to ache, she realized she had not fallen. She was still clinging to the wall, still alive, still carrying Kai. She pushed against the wall with her right foot, spinning again to face the cliff, her free hand found another hold. She clung to the cliff, breathing heavily. Leaning against the cold dark stone, she clenched her eyes shut. She pressed her forehead against the stone wall and tried to steady her breathing.

Opening her eyes, she leaned back slightly and tried to find new holds along the cliff face in front of her. Her arms were beginning to quiver, and her leg was growing weaker. She could feel the wound beginning to ooze blood; it ran down her ankle and into her shoe. Gritting her teeth against the burn, she reached for the next hold, then the next. As she moved to each successive untested hold, the rock under her fingers grew sharper and harder to reach. The cliff was becoming more sheer than anything she had ever scaled as a child. Her age was betraying her, not to mention the poison working its way into her torso. She forced herself to continue, repeating in her head one more, just one more. As she reached her left arm for a ledge farther from her than the ones before it, the grip of her right hand failed her. She clung desperately to the new hold. The sharp rock sliced her fingers almost clean to the bone. A scream escaped her. Tears began to stream down her face, and hopelessness crept into her heart. She tried desperately to find a foothold, but none surfaced. Frantically, she groped blindly for a hold for her right hand. Finding one, she looked ahead to the ledge. She was only a few feet from the path. She had to keep going, but the pain was too much. Her grip was failing her, and her body was too weak to continue.

Bracing herself as best she could, she rocked from hand to hand. With what little strength she still had, she did the one thing she could think to do. With her momentum up as high as possible, Lerna flung herself toward the ledge. She held her eyes shut until she felt the stone edge dig into her hips. Her knees slammed into the newly revealed rock below the ledge her body now teetered on. She pulled with her arms and kicked with her feet against the stone, hoisting herself further up and onto the path. As her hips cleared the ledge and the majority of her body now lay safely on solid ground, she allowed her arms to go limp. Pain overwhelmed her. Her left hand was bleeding badly, her right as well, her knees were battered and torn, and the wound in her calf was now oozing something not unlike slime. Her whole body ached and burned. The poison was taking hold. She tried to slow her breathing, her heart rate, slow the poison. As her body calmed, her ears suddenly began working again. Kai had been screaming since the path had fallen from under her feet. Only now, lying in a growing pool of her own blood, did she hear those screams.

Kai's frightened cries gave her purpose. She fought back the pain and began to move again. Pulling herself toward the cliff wall, away from the ledge, she began removing the blankets that held the little princess to her back. Careful not to drop the child, she brought her around to her lap. Lerna held her for a moment, cooing and comforting the small screaming babe. After a few moments, Kai calmed. Lerna set her aside and began to bandage her battered and torn body. Then she changed Kai and rocked her to sleep. Returning the baby to the sling about her chest, Lerna sat for a moment and confronted her own mortality. The poison was creeping steadily toward her heart. She probably only had hours left. She could not afford to let the pain slow her down any longer. She prayed one last time to her goddess for strength and climbed to her feet. The path she was now on was wide, and after a bit it turned steep once more. Into the white mist, she walked. Gritting her teeth against the ache she could do nothing about.

She walked on for an hour or so before the mist started to clear. Once she emerged on the other side, she took a moment to look back. Realizing only then that it hadn't been a mist, but a layer of clouds. On the other side of the white fluffy blanket, the sun was blinding and the air was cold. Pulling several blankets from her saddle bag belt, she bundled herself and the baby against the chill and pressed on. Walking along the path, higher and higher, she lost track of time. Her mind cleared of everything but the path. She studied every stone, every edge of the ancient trade route, imagining the treacherous trek with horses and wagons in tow.

She did not look up from the ground until the cliff wall beside her disappeared. She had reached the top. It was not what she had expected. She knew the wall was over a mile thick at the base; but here on top she could see all the way across the large, flat expanse. She stood in awe at the edge of what looked to be a plain of stone. To her left, far off in the distance, she could just make out the charred remains of what must have been the Great Lift. She thought for a moment she would go to it. Maybe only the Lylunir side had been set ablaze. She scanned the horizon again. She could see the place where the Forrenfar lift should have been, but found nothing. No lift, no debris, nothing. Gone. Every stick had fallen away.

Her eyes turned back to the edge across from her. Logically, she expected that the start of the path down would be there, directly across the expanse. Slowly, she began to make her way across the ridge. The light was growing softer. It was past noon, and she needed to make it down before night fall. She had to find someone to whom she could entrust her mission. Thoughts of direction and possible villages clouded her mind, and she did not notice the slight lip on the hard stone ground. Catching her toe, she tumbled forward. Just barely managing to roll her body enough that her shoulder, not her chest, hit the rock below her. Kai again began to scream. Lerna lay for a moment. What if she were to die here, on top of this massive cliff wall? The princess would last no more than a day before freezing to death. Then all of it, the fear, the pain, the tragic losses, would have been for nothing. Anger began to well up inside her. Until now she had felt only panic and urgency. Now rage coursed within her. How dare they! How dare they threaten the life of such innocence. How dare they kill the king and queen of such a peaceful and happy kingdom. How dare they insult the Six by killing one of their blessed Vessels. The anger gave her new determination. Kai would live, not because she was a baby, not even because Marina had asked Lerna with her dying breath to save her child, but because these invaders, this usurper, must be defeated. Kai would do this. Somehow, Lerna knew it in her heart. She could almost see the battle, feel the rush of victory, and see the towering madman fall.

Filled with new purpose, she rose again to her feet. One foot in front of the other, she crossed the top of the wall. Reaching the other side she stood, exceedingly close to the edge, and looked straight down. The same cloud layer lay several hundred yards below her. Her eyes scanned for the start of the path but found nothing. Undaunted, she looked to the side. First to the right and then to the left and back again. With each pass her eyes went lower and lower down the cliff face. Finally she found it. At some point since its abandonment the first fifty or sixty feet of the path had fallen away. The new start of the path lay to her right about forty feet down. Yesterday she would have spent hours trying to decide how to reach the ledge below her, but not today. As if driven by another's will, Lerna began shedding blankets. She also shed the saddlebag. From it she pulled the length of rope Willam had given her. A short distance from where she was she found a large stone and lashed the rope to it. She flung it over the side and watched as it unfurled against the cliff side. The end licked the air just above the path. She returned to the saddle bag and pulled one last bottle of milk from its depths, tucking it into the sling with Kai. Then, without a moment's pause or second thought, took hold of the rope and began lowering herself down, Kai strapped snuggly to her chest.

DECENT INTO FORRENFAR

When she finally let herself drop to the ground, her leg gave way. Her bloody fingers dug into the wall, no time to hurt. She pulled herself back upright and, leaning against the side, began to limp down the path. The Forrenfar side had apparently fared much better in the centuries since its last use. The sections that had fallen away were mere feet. Lerna jumped most of them. Only once did she need to climb on the wall for a short distance. All the while her face and heart grew colder. The burn of the poison had given way to a dizzying nausea. As she crossed out of the cloud cover, tree tops met her eyes. For the first time since the rage hit, she stopped moving. Her eyes focused for a moment of the wonder of Forrenfar, the Gigantic trees, for which all manner of craftsman traded, spread before her in wondrous glory. She was still hundreds of feet above the ground, and yet, here were trees. Perhaps they were the reason the path had not fallen to ruin. They had stood here longer than the path itself, guarding the cliff from the weather and time. Kai shifted against her, pulling her back to reality. She became aware of tears sliding down her face.

The rage had gone. It had come when she needed it most, and now that the hardest part of the journey had passed, it left her. She continued on. With each pained step her pace slowed. The trees gave way to a field. It stretched for what looked like miles. She heard laughter. It was faint but unmistakable—a child's laughter. She quickened her steps. A child meant a parent, an adult, a savior for Kai and another guardian to whom she could entrust her care. Lerna looked up from the path to find the source of the giggling. As she caught sight of the small boy she called out to him, and his face turned up to her. As she started to call out to him again, her feet failed her. She tumbled head first over herself. As her back came down on the edge of the path, the stone gave way. In a cloud of dust and rocks, she slid down the cliff side to the ground. As the light faded from her eyes the face of the small boy, no more than three, was the last thing she saw. She slipped out of consciousness listening to Kai's screams fading into silence.

CHAPTER 10

OCCUPATION BEGINS

The old man's head hung low over his lap. His thin graying hair cemented to the sides of his face, caked with blood, a mottled mixture of dry and fresh. The flames of the torches all round him sent bands of yellow light across his torn and broken body. His wrists and ankles were tied to the large rock he was sitting on. For nearly two days he had been kept like this. His once stylish, expensive, and well-made clothes hung loosely from his body, stained with his blood and torn from the weapons used on him.

"I'll ask once more...who was she?!?" The brakbark circling around him tightened his grip on the leather strap in his hand and gritted his teeth. The siege on the City of Beasts had taken him almost a day to complete, and even now most of its citizens were unaccounted for. Many had fled somehow from the walled city that as far as he could tell only had one gate. The first day of questioning the man who had tried to bargain with him for the safety of his town focused on how his people had escaped and where they had gone; but the man had been unresponsive, choosing silence to speech. When the brakbark had asked about the woman they had shot as she entered town, the old man's body had tensed and his eyes darted around the holding area for a split second, as if looking for the mystery woman. This changed the course of the questioning. From that moment on, every blow, every cut, had been in an effort to discover this mystery woman; but the old man was proving tougher than expected. Blow after blow, he held his silence. Even now he stared quietly at his knees in response to the latest inquiry. The brakbark raised the strap and brought it down hard across the man's shoulders. The strap, already wet and thick with blood, tore through the fine weave of the shirt and into the flesh. The end of the strap licked the man's left ear, sending a small piece of it into the air. The bit of flesh hit the brakbark on the cheek. The old man groaned a bit, but remained silent.

"I *WILL* KILL YOU OLD MAN!! NOW TELL ME WHAT I WANT TO KNOW!!" The brakbark had rushed the old man, placed his hands on the old man's shoulders and shaken him violently as he threatened the almost dead man's meager life. The gentleman's head rolled up onto his shoulder, and his eyes met the soldier's. There was little left of him now. The brakbark's voice softened a bit. "I can end this. I can let you go peacefully into the arms of your goddess if only you would tell me." He paused, the old man held his gaze of a moment then returned his eyes to his lap. In a rage, the brakbark balled up his fist and landed a furious punch on the side of the man's head, then another. He was raising his hand for yet another when a voice behind him stayed his hand.

"What can he tell us if he's dead?" The firm and deep voice of his vessel was unmistakable. The brakbark froze, his arm still twisted across his body, poised to strike. His eyes widened. As the color left his face, he turned to see his king standing behind him. A strange woman stood beside him, small and beautiful, her head held high with pride.

"My Lord! I was just softening his tongue. It seems to be made of stone." The brakbark bowed and backed several steps away from both the man and his king. Still bent low, he continued, "We cannot get a word out of him." Rikard stepped closer to the bloody pile of man sitting chained on the rock. The cobble stones of what just a few days ago had been a town square were almost black beneath his feet with the dried blood of people that had been questioned. They brought the few men from the gates that had survived the initial siege here, made them watch as they set the buildings on fire and dragged entire families from their homes. Some they simply killed; others were chained and led out of the square in long lines toward the gate. Once the square had been emptied, they set about clearing the rest of the town, intending on killing these men last, only after all their people had been led before them to either death or slavery, a final insult to their injury. But when the remaining sections of the city were searched, very few people had been found. It was as if the entire population of this metropolis lived only in the center, and that the row upon row of houses radiating out from it were vacant. The people had escaped. How became the mystery as the only gate had been heavily guarded from the instant it had been successfully breached. That is when the torturous interrogations had begun. Each man in turn found himself atop the great rock. Each man in turn had his blood splattered on his streets. Each man in turn said nothing—except for the old man. When he was first brought to the rock he tried to plead for the life of his people. His request was met with violence, and his sessions on the rock lasted longer and were generally more violent than the rest. Of the five men that had been captured, three were already dead. One died in the first interrogation. After that, they took to using the leather strap rather than their strong arms to coerce their prisoners. The other two had been sliced by foreign blades; and after eighteen hours of screaming, wrenching agony, they had died, green veins spreading out under every inch of their alabaster skin. These two were interrogated only once, until their wounds were discovered. Then the guards had tossed them aside, mumbling something about them being beyond reason now. The men had screamed and cried nonsense all through the night; only death brought silence to them. The old man had watched as the dead, one of them his son, were hauled a short distance and burned. Nobody was ever burned in the kingdoms. All who could afford it had their dead taken to Morghath, the kingdom of the South. There you could visit with their souls in the company of

OCCUPATION BEGINS

Mordiah's Vessel, who possessed his ability to commune with the dead. In this way, no one really died, unless their corpse were desecrated and destroyed, as he watched his son's become. From that moment until this one the old man had said nothing. His eyes had betrayed him when asked about Lerna, but not a word he had said.

The old man lifted his battered and bloody face so that he could see the leader capable of evoking such fear in his torturer. Rikard towered above him, a wall of a man. His face so far from the light of the torches that only the faintest of outlines could be seen of his features. The old man's head fell back to his lap. He had lost his strength. Rikard dropped to one knee and reached out a hand. With his strong fingers he lifted the man's head so that he had eye contact once again. In the smoothest and kindest voice Rikard could manage, he asked, "What is your name, elder?" Rikard held him steady, not loosing his gaze. For a moment the old man stayed silent. The Brakbark started to strike at him for his impudence, but Rikard lifted his free hand, stopping him. The old man whispered his name. "I'm sorry, elder, I did not hear it. Please.."

"Sander, Barrond Sander. I am governor of the City of Beasts, and I shall answer none of your questions." As Barrond finished his small speech, Rikard let his head fall from his fingers. In a rage, he swung his free arm at the bruised and bleeding Sander elder, slamming it against his arm tied along his side. Under the force, the bones within the appendage shattered. From the shoulder to the elbow, the old man's arm was now a sack filled with what looked to be rocks and sand. The sound of the shattering was accompanied by a muffled cry, pulled back in behind the old man's chattering teeth.

"My Lord, we have tried cruelty on him; allow me to try kindness." Tawni stepped forward and placed a hand on Rikard's inflamed flesh. The anger in him had sent his temperature soaring. At the cool caress of her fingers, he calmed. The brakbark watched in amazement as he stepped aside at this woman's request. Tawni bent low, placing her small bronze hands on the broken Barrond's knees. She whispered to him words of poison and filth, though no one but Barrond could hear her. She told him of his king and queen, rotting in the capitol. She told him of how his people would be ground to death against the wall behind them. She whispered of how the infants of every house would be slaughtered until the princess was found, and how he could stop all of it. All he had to do was tell them what they wanted to know. She leaned back and smiled at him. Barrond lifted his head slightly and found her gaze.

With what little he could muster he said in a soft mumble, "She was no one." His head fell back to his lap. Tawni did not get up. The tips of her fingers dug into the loose flesh of his knees. Again, she leaned in to whisper.

"Did that no one carry your princess?" Tawni made certain that her words were only hers and the old man's to hear. Still close to his face, she waited. Barrond did not lift his head this time. His breathing had become very shallow and his body began to go limp. He was dying.

As he fell into darkness, he whispered lightly into Tawni's greedy ear, "She is gone." With this last phrase, he slipped away. His body slumped on the rock. His eyes were open, but his soul was no longer within them. Tawni stood. As she backed away from the man the guards rushed over to him. Discovering he had gone, they set about unchaining his broken body. Tawni found her place beside her king. Rikard gazed down into her face and she met his eyes. With a velvet smile, she spoke to him.

"My Lord, you have nothing more to fret over with the princess." Rikard lifted an eyebrow. Tawni broke their gaze and watched as the old man's body was carried to the burning pile. "The princess did indeed make it here. But she is dead."

"He told you this?" Rikard turned Tawni's face back to his.

"His dying words were 'she is dead.' The hopelessness in his voice cannot be mistaken. He died knowing his people were doomed. She is dead." She smiled again into the face of her king. For a moment he studied her face. Then he returned her smile. He placed a hand on her elbow and led her away from the blood and darkness of the square, content that he would never again here word of a Lylunirian princess.

As they left the City of Beasts, he ordered the forests around the city searched. The remaining citizens would be found. The captured citizens were to be brought to the central city to see their beloved king and queen before they were sorted. He had plans to visit each of the seized outer cities, see the width and breath of his new kingdom for himself. Each of the trade cities gave him a small taste of what lay just beyond the wall, and he wanted to know the riches he would someday hold in his hands. Each would fall to him, he need only be patient.

CHAPTER 11
THE LETTER

Alon burst through the door of his small cabin home. Duncan, his three year old son, was close behind him holding a small glass jar of milk. Maga struggled to lift herself from her bed. Her strength was gone, aftermath of the tragedy that only days ago had robbed them of their second child. When Alon rounded the corner and appeared in the door way, Maga struggled to climb out of the bed. Though she had little power, she managed to pull herself into the chair sitting close to the bed, Alon's chair, where he had sat with her as she cried and moaned after the stillbirth. When Alon saw her trying to move herself, he began to protest; but Maga's concentration did not waiver. After a few seconds, she was uncomfortably seated in the large leather bound chair by the bedside. She shifted her weight a bit to relieve the strongest pain and motioned him to the bed. Alon crossed the room quickly and deposited the lifeless body into the soft mattress. Her flesh was black as soot, save for a strange paleness to her left side. Tiny spider web patterns in green were visible below the skin along her neck and left cheek. Her hair was as white as the clouds over head, and her clothes, too big for her, were torn and dirty. Accompanying her was the foul odor of rotting meat. As Alon began to pull his arms from under her, a small moan escaped the body.

"She's alive?" Maga's voice was thick with shock and grief. The poor creature laying before her looked as if she had been eaten by Wolvari and then cast back up again.

"That's not all." Alon's eyes met Maga's for a brief second then returned to the woman lying on the verge of death in his marital bed. His hands moved to the blanket wrapped about her chest. As he began tugging, the blanket moved beneath his hands, Maga's eyes widened. Alon lifted the edge of the blanket from under her shoulder and revealed the woman's surprise—a tiny baby. The baby was clearly not born of the woman who carried her. Her flesh was pale as new fallen snow, and her eyes were the color of lavender blooms. A small batch of coal black hair crested her small head. "She can't be more than a week old." Alon lifted the baby from the woman's chest. As he did, the woman's spirit returned to her; and with a weak hand, she reached for the baby. Her eyes struggled to open, and her face showed great pain and effort; but not a word did she say. Her mouth moved and small squeaks were barely audible, but nothing Alon and Maga could understand.

The woman fell back to the bed, her body racked with pain and exhaustion. Her eyes darted around the ceiling. Then, she turned her head. Her gaze found

THE LETTER

Maga's and for a moment they stared at each other. Then Maga noticed her hand moving. She watched for a moment as the woman's fingers did small loops in the air before she realized what it meant. "Quick! paper and writing stick, I think she wants to try and write something down!" Alon handed the small baby to Maga and bolted from the room. In the chamber outside, she could hear him shuffling and digging through drawers in the small desk near their fireplace. He returned moments later bearing the items requested. Alon placed the paper in her lap and struggled to line up the writing stick in her fingers as they moved. As he deposited the utensil in her grasp, the woman's focus on Maga was broken. Her eyes shifted to the paper in front of her; and with a shaking hand, she began to scrawl a letter. As she wrote her fingers trembled. Line after line she scribbled across the paper. Maga watched her as she wrote for nearly half an hour. Three sheets of paper later, and midway through a sentence, the woman's hand released the writing stick. It fell to the bed beside her. Her face again found Maga's. This time her eyes were filled with tears and sadness.

As Maga's stared at her, the woman's gaze drifted to the small infant in Maga's arms. Immediately, Maga extended the child toward her. Gingerly the woman placed a few of her weakened fingers on the child forehead and smiled. Then her face stiffened and contorted with pain. Her right hand moved quickly to her neck, struggling with the collar of the dress around it. Her fingers became frantic, digging at the rim of her garment.

Her teeth gritted and a small moan came from in her throat before her finger tips emerged with a thin wisp of chain. "Alon, come help her with this, will you?" Alon returned from the other room bearing bandages and hot water. He placed his load at the bottom of the bed and leaned over the poor woman. Her eyes streamed with tears as his hand clasped the thin silver chain. Her fingers brushed over his hand for a brief moment then fell again to her chest, limp and lifeless. Alon tugged gently at the chain. More and more of it he pulled from under her garment. After nearly a foot and a half of chain, a small medallion appeared, made of solid silver and in the shape of a crest. Alon lifted the small trinket from around the woman's neck, then retreated with it to the pale yellow illuminator on the bedside table. In the soft light, he turned the amulet over and over in his fingers. Finally he spoke.

"Maga...this...is the crest of Lylunir, the royal crest of Lylunir!" On one side, the crest bore the image of a moon encasing a sun. The other bore a lion head within a star. This crest had been seen several times by Alon on wagons and carriages as processionals came through the Great Gate, emerging through the unnatural shadow from the solid stone of the cliff wall. He pulled back to the woman's anxious face and asked, "Lylunir? You're from Lylunir?" The woman's weak head gave a slight nod. Alon's mind raced, trying to decide what to ask next. "This medallion, it's the royal crest, did you come from the capital? From the Vessel's court? But you are not

THE LETTER

Lylunirian, you're Zailian, right?" Again the woman's head moved in a nod. "Has something happened to Lylunir? To the Vessel there? Why have you come over the cliff and not through the Great Gate?" Alon's questions grew more and more frantic as they spilled form him. For the past few days everyone who lived within eye shot of the Great Lift had been in a panic. No word had come to them explaining why the lift had been set ablaze so suddenly. Now, dying in his bed, was a woman from Zailia bearing a child of Lylunir who had made the crossing on foot at the cost of what would surely be her life. In response to the questions that cascaded from Alon, the woman reached for the pages laying in her lap.

Her fingers brushed and poked them toward Alon. He lifted the scribbled pages from her. Her hand found his, and a slight squeeze told him that his answers were there. The woman released him and reached again for the small child. Maga leaned a bit closer. Her fingers brushed through the thin black curls atop the infant's head. A small smile crossed her face before she slipped into unconsciousness. Alon set the pages aside; his answers would have to wait. Though the woman seemed on the verge of death, he felt compelled to try and save her. First, he must find the source of the awful smell. As he began to check her for wounds, he noticed the green veins in her neck again. Her traced them down onto her shoulder and onto her chest. Pulling her sleeve back, he found them covering her left arm almost all the way down to the wrist. After giving a small glance to Maga, he began removing her dress. Using a sharp knife, he sliced through the fabric covering the ailing woman's chest. As her flesh was revealed, so, too, was the extent of the poison's work. Her entire left side lay pale and webbed in green. The pattern stretched across her heart, down her side, and licked at her belly button. As he continued to cut away the clothes, the veins became larger and more pronounced. He started to see the swelling in her flesh that her bulky garment had hidden from sight.

As he began to rip her skirt away, the smell became nearly unbearable. When the last of the fabric was pulled away, the bandage on her calf, soaked through with blood and oozing some other unnatural substance, came into view. Reaching for a blanket, Alon covered the woman's bare body and began unwrapping the wound. It took him nearly twenty minutes to uncover and clean the source of the infection, but once he had, he knew this woman had little time. The gash on her leg was rather small, or at least it had been at the time of its creation. He could tell that she had tried to treat it using blanch root and several other herbs that are known for their healing properties, but all they had seemed to do was slow the creep of what he was now positive was a poison. A trained hunter, Alon had learned young how to use poisons on big game. There were animals in his woods that could not be killed with a knife or arrow, but this poison was unlike anything he had ever seen.

As best he could, he bound her wound with fresh linen and burned her clothes and wrappings in the field.

THE LETTER

The woman never again regained consciousness. In a matter of hours, she was gone. Alon bound her body in the bed sheets and carried her out to the cold house. As he placed her corpse on the cold floor, he remembered the pages she had written. He had set them down in order to care for her wounds. After saying a short prayer to his god and her goddess, he returned to the house. Quickly he grabbed the pages and began to read them. The hand writing was erratic from the shaking of her hand, but he could tell from her penmanship that she was highly educated. Her thoughts were scattered and frantic. Sentences ended without conclusion, and her mind had bounced from one thought to another so frequently that it took him nearly an hour to decipher the letter. When he finished reading it, he sat down and transcribed the letter as best he could. He pieced together the broken time line and recreated her letter into a more coherent communication. As he finished, his eyes streamed with tears—Lerna, her name had been Lerna of Zailia. She had been the royal court healer of Lylunir. Through her scattered thoughts and broken images, he had learned many things. He knew now that the baby was Kai Lyonus, princess and Vessel to Lylunir, that he was to take her to Brannon, his Vessel and king, and that war had come to the kingdoms in the form of invaders from across the sea. He knew why the lifts had been burned, and he knew he had little time to waste.

He wiped the tears from his face, and sat in the quiet of his sleeping home. Maga had taken the baby with her and now slept with their son in his bed. The entire house was silent save Alon, sitting at his kitchen table, staring at a letter containing more tragedy that any one person deserved to see in a lifetime. He rose from the table and crossed to his bedroom door. Leaning against the frame, he gazed at the bared mattress that only an hour ago held the most honored healer in all of Lylunir. Reaching into his pocket, he pulled the small crest she had borne around her neck, wondering if she had received it the day she had become the royal healer, a token of their welcoming. Tears came again to his eyes. He stood in the door way sobbing for the poor, brave woman who gave her life for a baby. No, not just a baby, he thought, but for all of Plaettan. If she hadn't made it over the cliffs, they wouldn't know what was happening. they would have been as helpless as Lylunir had been. That poor woman had died trying to save everyone in the six kingdoms from suffering the fate of the Vessel and her king, of the hundreds of infants slain in her stead, of the multitude of citizens slaughtered in the siege.

From the other side of the house, he heard his wife's voice calling softly to him. He rubbed his face with his hands, trying to remove the tears from his cheeks. His wife had been through enough in the past few days; this tragedy could wait till morning. Crossing the room to the mirror, he inspected his well-tanned face. Maga had a way of seeing his true feelings on him. He would have to keep it dark in the room where she lay. His face was puffy and red, and his eyes were still heavy with tears. She would know in an instant that terrible things had happened while she slept.

When he heard her soft call again, he decided he could not hide it from her. He straightened himself as best he could and grabbed the illuminator from the table. This conversation would be hard, but it would have to happen sooner or later. With the light in hand, he crossed his simple home and opened the door to his son's bedroom. Maga had been waiting for him to open the door. As the light of the illuminator burst through the widening crack and flooded the room, she caught sight of his face. Sighing she lifted herself a bit higher on the bed, still cradling the pale infant in her arms, and said, "She's gone, isn't she?" All Alon could do was nod. For a moment he made eye contact with Maga but soon lost his nerve. When his eyes fell away from hers, Maga knew something was horribly wrong. She struggled to rise higher in the bed. "Tell me."

CHAPTER 12

BRANNON

Alon arranged the blankets in the wagon. The trip to Antlerbrooke, the capital city of Forrenfar and the seat of their Vessel, Brannon, was an eighteen hour journey. Maga would need a soft bed in order to make the trip without pain. He had not intended to take her with him, but she had insisted; and he had never been able to refuse her anything. She seemed in such good spirits this morning, and Alon knew it was because of Kai. Maga had fallen in love with the baby the moment she had held her in her arms. With the tragedy of the last few days weighing heavily on her, Alon was glad to see the spark of life return. The night the lift burned, Maga had been heavy into child birth. Their still born daughter had torn her asunder as she left Maga's body. The healer had barely saved Maga's life, though the news that Maga would never again bear children had threatened to kill her still. Confined to the bed, Maga had not eaten more than a morsel in three days, nor had she even had the energy to hold or care for their young son. The loss of her child, and all possible future children, had stolen her life away, and

Alon feared she was soon for the grave. Then Lerna fell into their world bringing Kai. Maga had almost completely come back to him over night. Her skin was no longer dull but had begun to glow. Her eyes had light, again, and her voice had cheer. She had even been able to nurse Kai in the night; her milk still quite full. While the joy of seeing his wife healing inside and out brought speed to his steps, he feared what would happen when the baby had to stay in the capital with Brannon.

When the makeshift bed was completed, he brushed these thoughts aside and hurried into the house to fetch his wife. Maga was the prize of his life. She had been much sought after and wooed by all the young men in their village. Alon had won her heart by showing her that he cared for her mind more than her beauty. Maga's beauty was somewhat less beauty and more novelty. Her father had been a Lylunirian merchant. He had fallen in love with her mother, the daughter of a craftsman, during a trade visit. Though cross kingdom marriages were not forbidden, they were very rare. Maga's father had moved to Forrenfar to marry her mother. Soon she was with child, and they were happy, until a tragic accident shortly before Maga was born tore her father from her life. Riding the lift with a cart of goods for trade, falling rocks spooked the horse. It had reared and kicked, sending Maga's poor father over the rail and to his death. All she really had of her father were a few Lylunirian physical traits and a finely crafted writing desk. She was thinner and smaller in frame than the common Forrenfarian

woman; and her skin was not the robust tan, but a pale
fair color that burned easily in the sun. Her hair was very
dark and her eyes, though they looked black in the sun,
shown with a purple hue at night. There was no mistaking
her mixed heritage.

Alon returned to the cart carrying his wife. Her face
grimaced as he walked, but not a sound of complaint did
she utter. She had insisted she could handle the journey
and to complain before it even began would be unseemly
at best. After placing her gingerly onto the bed he had
created, he returned to the house. He emerged several
minutes later with Kai in one arm and Duncan trotting
along by his side holding onto his fingers. He lifted the
small boy into the wagon, then climbed in after him. After
laying Kai into his wife's arms, he secured the last of their
cargo and found his place in the driver's seat. It was
nearly ten in the morning, and they had a long way to go.
He hitched his two wagon horses forward, and their trek
was underway. As he passed the outbuildings of their
ranch, his eyes lingered on the small mound of freshly
dug dirt behind the cold house. For a moment a lump
caught in his throat, then he hitched the team through the
gate, onto the road and out of sight of their small home
and Lerna's unmarked grave.

It was dusk, and soon the dark of night would be around
them. Their journey had been uneventful as Alon pulled
off the road into a small clearing. Maga had bound the
baby such that no passer-by could see Kai's uniqueness at

a glance, and they only stopped twice for food. There had been a lot of traffic on the road, more than normal, and Alon feared it was because of the same reason he now traveled. Something terrible was coming, and people were scared. He had planned to drive on into the night, stopping only when they had come through the city gates, after all they were only a few hours out; but Maga had insisted that they stop and make camp. He was sure her torn body could stand no more bumps from the road; but in truth, she wanted more time with the baby. Her attachment had grown fast, and she intended to spend as much time as possible with her little bundle before she would be forced to part with her. Alon set up their camp with the help of little Duncan, who followed him everywhere and was quite good at fetching tools. He lifted Maga from her bed and placed her in the tent with the baby; then he and Duncan cooked a small meal. Soon the whole family was snuggled together in the dark tent sleeping soundly—all except for Maga. She fell into a restless dream filled sleep, teetering between nightmare and fantasy. One moment Brannon would be telling her to keep the baby and raise it as her own; and in the next, the invaders of Lerna's broken letter would be waiting for them at Brannon's castle.

When morning came, Maga insisted on a full breakfast. Alon had protested at first; but when she had found the strength to cook, he caved. She had not been able to do more than lie still in days; and though she had to stay very still, leaned against a barrel by the fire to do it, she had cooked for them. Then, she insisted that they wait for full sun. By the time they got on the road, it was nearly noon. Alon drove on toward Antlerbrooke and by midafternoon, they were crossing through the stone walls into the capital city. Antlerbrooke was a strange sort of city. Like most in the kingdoms, the city was broken up into burroughs or sections, each with its own unique purpose or quality; but in Antlerbrooke, there was more definition. The city had started as nothing more than the home of the first Vessel along the banks of the Antler River. In the millennia and a half since those first days, the city grew up and out, encompassing the cluster of islands formed where seven rivers, creeks, and brooks joined into the Antler River on their quest eastward for the ocean. Each island had become its own little town within the city. Stone and wooden bridges were everywhere throughout the metropolis, crossing over waterways and small streams. Each island had its own name, based largely on the craft or trade that was shared by its inhabitants. There was Widdler's Haven where expert wood carvers made everything from children's' toys to large intricately carved murals that would grace a wealthy home's wall. Across a stone bridge was Hider's Wake, a collection of tanners and leather workers. Beyond the Wake was a small island called Crystal Den where trade goods from Tunaeshir and Lylunir could be found, fresh from traders returning from the wall. Island after island, Alon made his way through the crowded streets toward the castle in the center. He drew close to the gate, stopped the wagon, and waited for one of the guards to walk to the wagon.

"Hello, citizen, what brings you here this evening?" As he spoke, the nervous guard surveyed the contents of the wagon. Maga hid Kai from his gaze so he found only a small boy and an ailing woman on first glance. Returning his eyes to study Alon, he waited for his reply.

Alon cleared his throat and said, "We have urgent business with our Vessel." He watched the guard for a moment. When it became clear to Alon that the guard was about to send them away he added, "We bring news from Lylunir." With his hand, Alon motioned the guard back to the wagon. This time Maga pulled the blanket back, revealing the small Lylunirian child in her arms. The guard jumped back as if struck by a weapon. His reaction had alarmed the other guards who began to advance on the small cart. The sentry regained his poise and motioned the other guards back a bit. He eyed Alon suspiciously.

"How have you come by that child?" The guard's voice was hard and became full with fear, but his face showed more strength. Alon reached into his pocket and produced the amulet from Lerna's neck and the letter she penned before her death. The guard took one look at the amulet and stepped back from the wagon. He walked a bit up the path and motioned for Alon to proceed, then he turned and sprinted up the path toward the castle. Alon steered his wagon along the drive and right up to the castle doors. As he was pulling his team to a halt, the castle doors opened; and several men and women, including the guard, emerged. Then, as if his work were done, the guard quickly turned and headed back down the path to the gate. Alon jumped down from his bench, and the men began unhitching his team. When they were freed of the wagon, the men led the horses around the side of the castle and out of sight. Alon climbed into the back of the wagon and was soon joined by two of the women. One took Duncan into her arms and jumped down from the wagon while the other motioned for the baby. Despite Maga's small protest, Alon lift Kai and placed her into the woman's waiting arms, then he lifted Maga into his, and both he and the woman exited the bed of the wagon bearing their living cargo.

Once on the ground, the woman carrying Duncan said, "Please follow me." She turned and disappeared into the dark of the castle door, Alon close on her heels and the woman carrying Kai behind him. They were led through several chambers and down a wide corridor before they reached what was apparently their final destination. It was a small room by comparison to the ones they had just passed through, but it felt warmer and was better lit. In the middle of the room, busy hands were arranging furniture. Several chairs had been retrieved from around the room as well as one sleeping sofa. The woman holding Duncan motioned Alon toward the sofa, and he lowered Maga gingerly on to it. Then he followed directions to his own seat. The chair between his wife and him was now occupied by the woman holding Duncan in her lap. Lastly, the woman carrying Kai moved toward

Maga and placed the small baby back into her hungry arms.

In the bat of an eyelash, all the other people in the room were gone, save the young woman holding Duncan. In an uncomfortable silence, the small family sat in the cozy room and waited. For nearly fifteen minutes, they sat in an awkward stalemate listening to the far away sounds of castle life. Then voices began to grow in the hall. As they grew closer they grew louder, until through the door, came a young man and a dozen or so older men behind him. Alon rose to his feet quickly and bowed his head. Brannon smiled and took the empty chair next to Alon's. The men that had followed him formed a crescent shape behind him. "Sit please. I am anxious to speak with you. I was told you bear tidings from Lylunir." Brannon's voice was calm and deep. There was a sadness to him that made him seem older than his twenty years. Alon returned to his seat and fumbled in his pocket for the letter and medallion. He handed the latter to Brannon and began reading the broken letter of Lerna Zailian aloud. With each revelation of letter, the crescent of men gasped or mumbled. When he read that the king and queen were in all likelihood dead, moans of pain erupted form one of the crowd of counselors. When he finished, Alon fell silent and waited. Brannon looked stern as he turned the amulet in his fingers over and over again. "So, it is ill news you bear." Was all he said.

Alon shifted nervously in his seat. So many questions had come to him since he followed Duncan's cries to the unconscious woman in the field. "Our Vessel, what is to become of this child? Who was the woman who brought her here? Is it true that invaders have come to the kingdoms? Is that why the Great Lift was burned?" Alon's voice broke. He could not finish his long list of questions, no matter how urgently he wanted them answered. Brannon met his gaze. Seeing Alon's fear and confusion, he spoke again.

"Yes, invaders have come. I received a bird from Pol, Vessel of Tunaeshir, almost a week ago now, warning of strange men from the sea traveling at great speed in large machines of war. He warned us to burn our lift, so we did. As for the woman, Lerna, I would very much like to speak with her. Where is she?" Alon's eyes fell. From the pain on his face Brannon guessed the answer. "Oh...I see. Lerna of Zailia was the greatest healer I have ever known, aside from her Vessel of course. She was the personal court healer of Marina and Marcus, king and queen of Lylunir. It pains me greatly to know she has passed." Brannon bowed his head and said a silent prayer for the brave woman. When he finished, he stood and moved close to Maga. Kneeling down, he said softly, "May I see Kai?" Maga's face blushed hot. Brannon was not at all what she had imagined her Vessel would be like. She had envisioned a cold and stoic man who moved and spoke as if channeling another. That was all she could picture as a child when her teachers had tried to explain how the Vessel holds the spirit of their god within him. She imagined a puppet, controlled by invisible strings, not the strong, warm man kneeling before her. In his face, she saw the pain of loss. He had been married once, for a short time. His queen had fallen ill. All manner of healers were brought to Antlerbrooke, but to no avail. He had sent his bride on a journey to Zailia, to be healed by the Vessel of Life, but sadly his wife did not make it. She died along the road. It had been nearly two years since the queen had passed, and Brannon had not yet chosen another bride. As memory of his great loss mixed with the shock at his warmth and kindness, Maga quickly pulled back the wrappings to reveal the whole of Kai's small form. The men again gasped at this new development and then again fell silent. For a moment Brannon stared at the child; then a smile broke across his face. He could feel Maga staring at him. He lifted his eyes to hers, still wearing the slight smile.

Before she could stop herself, Maga asked, "Our Vessel, what brings a smile to your face?" She blushed immediately. Her eyes fell away from his; but the smile on his lips did not fade, nor did anger come to his eyes.

"All my life I have wondered if Lylunirian children are born bald as we are or whether they are born with that raven hair of theirs. I have my answer now; and please, won't you both call me Brannon." He returned to his seat and began again. "It would appear from Lerna's letter that the invaders wasted little time taking Lylunir for their own, and with no shortage of violence in the process. I fear that every kingdom lies in their path." Behind him the dozen men began to mumble to each other softly.

Brannon shifted uneasily his chair. "I need to consult my advisers before deciding our next steps. Please, you and your family will stay with me, here, until we decide what is to be done." With that, he rose to his feet. Alon followed his lead, bowing to his king. Brannon in turn bowed deeply to Maga and then left the room, followed closely by the men, now openly chatting about the evening's events. As soon as the Vessel had left the room, the servants returned. They cleared away the gathered furniture and showed the family upstairs to a small suite of rooms. Fresh linens had been placed on the beds, and food had been prepared and set out for them on a great carved table. Maga ate and fed Kai, then fell straight away into a deep sleep. Alon saw to Duncan and once his son was sleeping soundly, he climbed into bed beside Maga. The bed was strange and larger than his at home, but it was soft and warm and he found it much easier to fall asleep than he had expected.

As the family slept, Brannon and his advisers discussed through the night. They talked of an army to raise and defenses to build. While war preparations dominated the lengthy discussions, every time an adviser brought up Kai, Brannon would quickly change the subject. Thus the discussion continued all through the night. The next morning Brannon followed the breakfast trays into the family's suite. He sat with them and shared their bountiful breakfast. When the meal was finished, he suggested that the maid take Duncan to the garden to play for a while. Once the three-year-old was out of earshot, he laid out his conclusion regarding Kai to a nervous Alon and fearful Maga.

"I have decided that Forrenfar must prepare for war. We must raise an army and fortify our positions before this invasion finds a way past the wall. As you know, I have no wife." His voice broke a bit, flooded with the painful memory of his loss. Steadying himself, he continued, "and while I have many maids, I feel that what young Kai will need most is a loving mother and father. If I am preparing for war, I cannot provide this for her. I feel that perhaps the best and safest thing for me to decide is to leave her with you." Maga's excitement and joy could not be contained. As he finished his statement, she let out a small cry and hugged the sleeping baby closer to her. Tears of joy streamed down her face, and Brannon smiled. He had seen the love in Maga's eyes when she looked at the baby the evening before, and he had decided then and there that the best thing he could do was to leave her be. "I intend to send a small group of guards with you when you return home. She will be well hidden from prying eyes on your farm, unlike she would be here, raised in full view of the public. If she is ever in danger, you must be willing to move quickly and without argument. Are we in agreement?" Brannon's eyebrows raised, as he waited for a response. Maga simply nodded as she continued to cradle the baby and sob. Alon nodded, mumbling heartfelt thanks in the strongest voice he could muster. He, too, was in shock. Tears formed in his eyes. His life would never be the same. "Good. Alon, you and I have much to discuss before you venture home. Will you accompany me?" Brannon rose from his seat and bowed low to Maga as he moved away from the table. Alon followed him, bending down to kiss his wife's head before he left the room to meet with his Vessel.

CHAPTER 13

DECEIT

"Digging has started in the City of Gems, my Vessel." The soldier's words were soft, but in the great empty throne room, they echoed around him. Rikard scoffed a bit and then simply waved his hand. The soldier left quickly, trying not to give any reason to be called back. When they were alone again, Rikard rose from his throne. The engineer had done his duty. It was large enough to fit him well; and its design was exactly as Rikard had requested, though he hated sitting in it. Every day for the last year he had sat in that chair and listened to news. Good or bad, he had sat, not acted, not trained, but sat. He moved away from the chair and began to pace the room. Tawni remained in her throne. She was quite happy in hers.

"What upsets you, my King?" Her words were silk. He stopped pacing and turned to face her. When his eyes met hers, she stood and crossed the room to her king. Standing only inches from him she gazed into his face. He stared down at her for a moment before lifting her into the air. As he brought her higher, he kissed her. Fierce and strong were his kisses. Tawni wrapped her arms around his great neck and hung from his mouth like a greedy child. She returned his fierceness with her own as his arms encircled her in a hug that threatened to break her ribs. His hands slid across her back and into her hair. He enjoyed her body, her hair, her smell. After only weeks as his adviser, she had offered her body to him, and he had taken it hungrily. She had become his completely. Every day she graced the throne beside him, and every night she inhabited his bed. He had never felt for anyone the way he felt for her, save one old man so long ago now he struggled to remember his face. His hands moved down her shoulders, and his thumbs slid under her arms. Their lips parted, and her grip about his neck loosened. He lowered her again to the ground. As her feet touched the stone floor, he spoke to her.

"It has taken far too long. We should have been digging a year ago." He still held her close to him. His voice was no more than a whisper. She smiled up at him.

"It has started my Lord, which is all the matters now. We will dig our way through, and you will rain death upon all, I swear it." His frustration raged within him. Only three cities were now digging. The City of Beasts and the City of Death were proving to be most stubborn. Many of the citizens of these cities had fled into the forests at the first sign of siege. He had thought to send slaves from the other towns to start digging, but it seemed that there were too few of the white skins left now to spread them so thin. They were weak and soft, and it took ten of them to do what one of his own could. Tawni had advised him to establish his rule solidly before giving them tools that could be used as weapons, to wholly demoralize them and cement their slavery to him before setting them to their task. At first, this notion infuriated him. He had ordered the City of Gems to begin digging only a week after taking it. Hours after giving the slaves picks and digging tools, they had tried to kill the guards at their dig site. Three guards died before the rabble was brought under control. When the dust settled, nearly eighty slaves lay dead. Tawni did not gloat, but simply said again that they must be broken before they are put to work. After this setback, Rikard did as she advised. He ordered the cities broken into sections, one for the slaves, cold and uncomfortable, and one for his own people, comprised of the choicest homes. Food was rationed this way as well. His people chose first, and what was left was thrown to the starving pale skins.

After a few months, the three cities that were taken almost whole were starting to show signs that Tawni's plan was working. The slaves no longer rushed the gates when they opened to deliver food. Their bodies became thin and weak, and the light in their eyes was all but gone. Rikard had wanted to start digging again, but Tawni had insisted that all five cities needed to be ready before it started. His men were still searching the forests for the missing citizens. Every day more and more were found. She had convinced him that his soldiers needed to focus on one thing at a time and that it would be easier to plan his war when this kingdom was under his control completely. News soon began coming to him of his own people. In this new, rich land, they were flourishing. Every woman capable of bearing children, save Tawni, was with child. While this excited him, it also meant their fighting strength was half of what it had been when they had so ferociously come over the wall. This was yet another reason to slow his progress for a time.

Now, he stood in his throne room, over a year from the day it had become his, waiting for news that his war was finally starting again. The City of Beasts should be reporting in soon. As for the City of Death, he was not hopeful. They had found less than one hundred citizens in the city, though it stretched over a large portion of cold barren ground. Home after home they searched came up empty. Many looked as if they had never held a living soul. Some held only tables and chairs; others were devoid of any furniture. His own men had wanted to leave for fear of other worldly inhabitants. It had seemed as if there was not going to be a sizable enough slave population to dig through the cliff side until a large group of refugees were found in the forest almost three months ago. Nearly fifty were captured at once. They insisted that they were not from the City of Death, but that was where they were now. Soon even they would be broken.

His features softened a bit. Tawni pressed her face against his chest and was running her fingers across his abdomen; her gentle touch stirring primal needs within him. A slight smile crossed his face as his hands spread over her shoulder blades, pulling her closer to him. For a moment they stood, holding each other in the dim light. Rikard closed his eyes and enjoyed her caress. He had never known a woman before Tawni and she had been more than he had ever expected. He could feel the stirring of his loins against her body. His arms moved to lift her into the air, to carrying her to their bed, to take her as he had every night for months. As he pulled back a bit, the sound of the door startled him from his trance. He pulled away quickly from her embrace. Though many of his soldiers and brakbarks knew about his growing relationship with Tawni, he went to great pains to hide it. He walked back to his throne, leaving Tawni alone. As he reached the great wooden chair, a soldier stepped into the light of the chamber. At first he stood frozen at the edge of sight, waiting for permission to enter. Rikard waved his great arm, beckoning the young man closer.

"My Vessel, I bear news of the animal city. Digging is to begin in the morning. Brakbark Karnus feels that the few pale skins left in the woods will soon fall to the beasts. He feels that there is no more to fear from them, My Lord." The soldier bowed low and waited for his king to respond. It was not Rikard's voice that he heard, but Tawni's silken tones that answered him. Her voice moved across the room as it came to him. For fear of his king, he stayed bent low.

"Tell your commander that his diligence has been noted but that we expect no more caravans to be attacked in his region. If he is certain that it won't, then so be it,

but he will be held responsible in the future. Am I clear?"
The soldier looked up just as Tawni was lowering her
thin, curvy body into the small throne beside his king. The
soldier stared in confusion for a moment.

"My Lord..." Before he could utter another syllable
Rikard's face grew stern. The soldier silenced himself,
turned and rushed out of the room.

"They do not obey me, My Lord, as well they
shouldn't." Her words stung him.

"They will, or I will lay them dead at your feet." The
rage returned to his voice. Tawni touched his hand,
rubbing her fingers between his.

"My Lord I am not their queen, they owe no
allegiance to me." She kept her eyes low. For months, she
had been planting the seed in his mind. For months, she
had been trying to push him to make her his queen.
Tonight it would work.

"Then my queen you shall be. Tomorrow we will
begin preparations for our wedding. No longer will they
insult you." In one motion he stood from his throne, lifted
her into his arms and kissed her. His passion mixed with
his anger, making his need for her insatiable. As the kiss
deepened and the need for her flesh returned to his body,
he began to move. Away from the thrones, he carried her.
They moved to the stairs that led to their chambers. Still
embraced in their passionate kiss, he climbed the spiral
stone steps to his bed chamber. She would be his tonight,
and every night hence.

DECEIT

It was still dark when Tawni's eyes opened. Rikard's heavy arm lay across her naked body. She slid slowly from under his weight to the edge of the bed. Carefully, she lowered his arm to the bed and moved across the room to find her dressing gown. She had an appointment to keep. Closing the door silently behind her, she moved through the dark hallway to her chambers and slid inside. Once safely out of view, she went for the small table beside the bed. Her hands moved quickly in the dark, as if she could see what she was doing. They found the crystal and dropped it into the ornately carved cylinder. Instantly the room became bathed is soft bluish light. She rushed to her wardrobe, letting her dressing gown fall to the floor as she moved. She moved the gowns and elegant dresses, hung gingerly inside, out of the way, until she found what she sought. Pinned to the back of the cabinet was her old soldier's uniform. It was small and black, and fit her body well. It was perfect for sneaking about unnoticed, which she desperately needed.

After dressing, she slid the crystal from the cylinder and left her room, careful to close the door behind her. She moved down the servant's stairs without a sound. After pausing only moments for the guard to moved out of sight on his rounds, she slipped through the expansive kitchen and out into the night. She moved with haste through the empty streets, making sure to avoid windows and open areas where she might be seen. While she was certain Rikard needed her, any betrayal could still end her life. His anger was quick; and she knew she was not safe from it, not yet. After nearly thirty minutes of silent travel, she reached her destination. The small house stood at the end of a narrow and dark alley. It was the only building so far to have a light still burning within, and Tawni knew why. She was expected.

She opened the door and rushed inside, closing it behind her. "You are late." The voice startled her a moment. She turned to see the oldest woman, indeed the oldest citizen, of their race, sitting at the table in front of a burning hearth. Eldreth sat, silhouetted by the flames, her unkempt hair and jagged features were magnified by the glow of the fire. In the light she looked like what one would expect a demon to, waiting patiently for a soul to devour. Tawni took a few tentative steps into the light. As her face came into view, the old woman turned in her seat a bit, cascading light onto her own face. "Did you bring my payment?" Tawni reached to her belt and pulled the small pouch free. As she tossed it onto the table it opened a bit, allowing some of the jewels inside to spill across the table. Eldreth's greedy hands lashed at each of the free jewels, scooping them back into the bag and then pulling the bag from the table. She dropped it down the front of her ragged dress and rose from the table. She moved slowly to the cabinet behind her and began removing the ingredients for the concoction for which she had just been paid.

Rikard had spared Eldreth during the culling because of her ability as a healer and an apothecary. She mended the wounds of training and crafted the poisons that adorned their blades. But despite her importance, she was a cast-out. Rikard had spared her life, but made no provisions for her care. She had had to find her own food as none of the rations were hers. Once her work on the poison for the blades was finished, what little attention she had gotten all but vanished. She began trading her craft for food, bits of clothing, or objects of value she could trade for what she needed. From that moment, she had expected death. Every day they prepared the ships for the crossing, she had waited for Rikard to snap her neck, to free her of life, but it did not come. She had been given a place on the ships, had been placed inside one of the transports and brought over the great cliff. She had been left inside its belly to listen to the bloodshed as they took the City of Light that first night. And when the fighting was finished, she had been given this small dwelling. Then life returned to normal, only now people had better things to offer as trade, though no one brought her more than Tawni. Everyone bought her silence as well as her craft when they came to her, and no one needed it more than Tawni. What she asked Eldreth to do would surely be her death if discovered.

Eldreth worked quickly, portioning out the herbs and powders she gathered from the wild areas outside of town and those precious ones she brought with her from their homeland. Tawni watched carefully as she always did. This was the third time she had bought the woman's craft, and each time she had watched and memorized each step, each ingredient. She had begun to acquire the ingredients that could be found here, but the few that only came from her homeland were her downfall. Eldreth had a large stock of them hidden away, but she kept them guarded at all times. As the old woman began to mix the solution she spoke. "Does Rikard know you have me end his children?"

"What? How do you..." The shock in Tawni's voice was palpable. She stared in utter horrified astonishment as Eldreth stirred and smiled at her. She had gone to great pains not to identify herself, and Eldreth had never asked. She had felt safe that her secret was hers alone.

"Come now child, even someone as forgotten as I, sees things. Like the fact that the jewels you bring me could only have come from that dead queen. I have heard men speak of the woman who turns our king's head and sits by his side. I am no fool." Eldreth continued to stir. Her smile curled even higher, spreading across her entire face. Fear gripped Tawni. She had thought she was being so careful, coming only to the old woman at night, never wearing her fancy dresses, only her soldier's uniform. She had even given her a false name on her first meeting. To find out that this extortionist knew her terrible secret, a secret that could end her for good, meant only one thing.

"How much more do you want?" Tawni's voice had gone cold. All the silken softness she carried in the presence of others was gone and she stood exposed, like a raw nerve for Eldreth to pluck at her leisure.

"What I don't have my dear, comfort. I want to move into a warmer home, have food whenever I am hungry, new clothes that do not wreak of soil and rot. I want to be seen again." The old woman's smile revealed her teeth. Several were missing and the rest had a strange greenish yellow tint to them. For the first time Tawni really looked at her. She noticed now that Eldreth's face was sunken and gaunt, that her body was shriveled and puny, that her lips were cracked and peeling. The woman looked half-starved and smelled like one of the refuse heaps at the end of alleys like this one all over town. As Tawni studied the old woman she began to realize that she would never be free of her. She wanted for so much. Tawni had spent nearly a month gathering the jewels necessary to pay her. Each time she had waited for the sickness to come before she had sought out the old woman. Rikard was a viral man, she would not be free of her need for the old woman's gifts until she was ready to bear him a son.

"And how am I to do those things? Look at you. I cannot petition our Vessel on your behalf, he would wonder why I had any cause to know you." The disgust and fear in Tawni's voice was unmistakable. Eldreth's smile vanished. She stopped stirring and looked up from her work.

"Perhaps I could go to him myself, tell him how the woman sharing his bed has been killing his children. He would kill me too, to be sure, but I should have died years ago. Your death, on the other hand, would be slow and painful I should think. After all, our Vessel is not known for his compassion or forgiveness, is he?" Eldreth's voice was cold and cruel, but she spoke the truth. Tawni's eyes darted around the room. Her mind raced. Surely there was something she could do, something she could say to save her from this extortion.

"You must understand, I did all of it for him!" Eldreth snorted in amusement to this feeble revelation. "No, it's true! If I were to bear Rikard a son now, in sixteen years Rikard would be stripped of his powers. I do not believe that he will have finished his glorious war by then, it would be the end to all his dreams. I would defeat our people. I cannot do this terrible thing. Don't you see? I must end it, or I would end him!" For a moment Eldreth studied her. She watched as tears rolled down Tawni's cheeks, saw the conviction and heard the truth in her voice.

"You truly believe that, don't you? Then why hide what you do? Why not tell him, beseech him as you have just done me? Surely he would see the wisdom in it." Eldreth waited for Tawni's answer. But it did not come. "He would not agree with you." Her answer to her own question brought the smile back to her face. She returned to her work, content that Tawni was now completely in her debt.

Tawni sat in stunned silence and watched as the filthy woman worked on in front of her. How could she? Eldreth had heard her heart felt plea and scoffed at it. Tawni's mind raced. She couldn't afford to give Eldreth what she wanted, not without raising suspicion within Rikard. And what would happen if Eldreth ever wanted more? What if she could no longer pay? Fear gave way to rage. It coursed within her as she watched the woman add powders and leaves to the bowl in front of her. Tawni's eyes began to dart about the room as she fought her fears. She could kill her, right here in her own home. The thought brought hope.

Tawni struggled with the "how" in her new plan. She could prick her with the pin holding her long hair in place. The poison of her blade was also on the needle sharp accessory. But what if Eldreth had an antidote, or the poison took too long to kill her? She would surely go to Rikard and tell him of Tawni's deceit. No, poison was too risky. She could simply slit her throat and spill her blood on the floor, watch as she drained dry and left in secret. No, she thought. Even a life as useless as hers would be investigated, especially if her death were violent. She did serve a purpose and would be missed if she just disappeared. With each new idea conjured and then dismissed, Tawni began to lose confidence. She could see no future for herself, save a life of debt to this haggard old woman. Lost in thought, she did not notice Eldreth rise from her seat and draw close to her, the vial of medicine in her bony fingers. When the old woman laid a hand on her shoulder; Tawni jerked from her thoughts. Eldreth held the vial out for her, and Tawni grabbed it and hurriedly drank it down. As she held the bottle up right, waiting for the last drop to fall, Eldreth spoke again.

"Now then, child, I expect you have much to do. I look forward to seeing you again soon. I will be packed and ready for my move!" Eldreth's voice trailed into laughter. Tawni swallowed again. She watched, enraged, as the old woman's face twisted in amusement at her expense. She felt the vial slip from her fingers. Heard it shatter on the stone floor. She saw her hands fly at Eldreth's slender neck. As her fingers tightened around the woman's wind pipe, the laughter ceased. Eldreth's hands failed against her, tugging at her clothes and hair, but Tawni could not feel it. Her eyes were focused on Eldreth's. She fell on top of her, squeezing with all her might. Tawni watched as the life drained from Eldreth's eyes, felt the tension in her body loosen under her weight. She held her grip long after the old woman had stopped moving, only releasing the elderly woman's dead neck when her own hands began to ache from the strain.

Tawni rose to her feet. The small room danced with the light of the fire. In an instant, she bent back over the dead woman's body and fished the small pouch of jewels out of her chest. She moved about the room, first to find a sack then to the cabinet. She fished from it all the ingredients for the medicine she needed, leaving as much of the other things as she could. Then she set about searching the rest of the small dwelling. She found most of the jewels she had paid on her other visits stashed away in Eldreth's filthy bed chamber. As she was about to leave, Tawni paused. She let the bag fall to the ground and returned to the body. Lifting the old woman's small frame in her arms, she carried her into her bedroom. She lowered her into her bed and pulled the covers up around her. The last thing she did was run her hand down her face, closing Eldreth's eyes and mouth, obliterating any sign of the terror the old woman had felt at the time of her violent death. For a moment, she stood looking down at the old woman, who now looked as if she was sound asleep; and then she turned and hurried from the house. Back to the castle she raced with her pilfered goods. With any luck, no one would find her for days. Tawni slid back into her own chambers and hid the bag of herbs in the back of her wardrobe. She stripped off her uniform and began washing down her body. The smell of the old woman's filth clung to her. When she finished, she slipped down the hall, and back into Rikard's bed. As she pulled his heavy arm back over her naked body, she smiled to herself. Now, no one could stop her from being his queen of all Plaettan, not even another of his children.

CHAPTER 14
IN PLAIN SIGHT

Maga dipped the ends of her fingers in the soft brown mud. Scooping just a bit onto the tips, she smeared it across Kai's face. Kai sat very still in the oversized chair, allowing her mother to cover her face, neck, ears, arms and legs in the soft sweet, smelling mud. After Maga had covered every inch of the bright white skin, she scrapped the remaining mud off her fingers and back into the bowl. "Now, don't move until it's dry, okay, sweetheart?" Maga smiled down at the little girl in front of her. Kai's little legs couldn't reach the ground, so she swung them freely from the edge of the seat, but other than that small fidget, she sat perfectly still. She was beyond obedient, the perfect daughter. At only six, Kai was helpful and smart. She helped Maga cook the family meals and clean the house. She dressed herself every morning and picked flowers for her mother every day. As Maga stared down at the pretty little girl covered in mud, a thought crossed her mind. The thought furrowed her brow and brought tears to her eyes. For a moment, Maga remembered the woman who brought Kai into their lives, remembered the harrowing tale from her letter, remembered Kai's true name and birth right.

Maga shook her head and cleared her throat. One day they would have to tell Kai of her true heritage, but that day was not today. She pulled back from the table, pushing the wheels of her chair. A gift from Brannon, the chair had been presented to her before they left Antlerbrooke. They had stayed nearly a month, discussing Kai, the Great Lift, the wall and that mysterious army on the other side. In that time, Brannon had insisted that his healers look after Maga. It was then that it was decided, for her health, she should never walk again. Brannon commissioned a new chair for her, comfortable and mobile, so that she could get around her home. When they returned to their village of Gatewood, the people marveled over the invention. Soon there were replicas in town carrying the elderly and infirm. After the Merins returned home, several things about their humble abode had to change. The doors were widened and the counters and tables were lowered a bit so that Maga could work around the house. Another room was added for Kai, though she only began sleeping in it in the last year or so.

Shortly after they returned, several new people moved into town and the surrounding country side. The rumors of war began to spread. When the call went out for soldiers to volunteer, many of the young men in town answered the call. With Maga confined to the chair, and two small children to care for, most did not wonder why Alon failed to volunteer. Each year on the anniversary of their visit to the capital, a visitor would arrive at dusk delivering a small gift for the little girl, a birthday present, from Brannon. At first it was money and fine fabric for clothes and care, but after a few years, the fabric gifts lessened and she began receiving things that would help her live here in Forrenfar, the chief of which was this mud. It came by the barrelful with instructions on its application. If applied correctly it would tint her skin, allowing her to venture into town whenever the family wanted without raising suspicions. Her hair they simply bound in fabric, which was quite fashionable. Her eyes became her only novelty, which rumor quickly contributed to Maga's mixed heritage.

Since then, each year they received the mud among other gifts. Maga lifted the small bowl into her lap and moved toward the door. She could hear the sounds of her husband preparing the wagon. They were headed into Antlerbrooke today because she needed a few things before the royal wedding, which was in a week's time. Brannon was taking a new bride. It had been seven years since his first bride had fallen to an illness and Maga and Alon had received special invitations. Reaching the door, Maga shouted out to her husband, "Alon, I've finished. Could you return this for me?" She had to wait only a second before hearing the sound of footsteps. She pulled back from the door just before it opened, revealing her beautiful son. Duncan was perfect, nine years old, and strong. He was the spitting image of his father with a few small attributes from her like darker hair and a thinner frame. He smiled as he came into the house. Kai always looked so funny covered in her mud. Despite the fact that Duncan loved her dearly, he could never pass up the chance to tease her. "Oh, mother, why did you let the little piggy back out of her pin?" Heartily, he laughed at his own joke. Kai began to laugh, too; she never seemed to get upset at Duncan, no matter what he did.

Maga turned and sternly said, "Now stop moving, child, I don't want to have to start over. Duncan, stop making your sister laugh; it's bad enough she has to go through this without you making her ruin it and do it over." Duncan forced himself to stop laughing and placed a finger across his lips at Kai. She obediently stifled her laughter, too. "Good, now, could you be a dear and return this to the cellar for me, sweetheart?" Maga held out the bowl with the small amount of leftover mud in it. Duncan nodded, took the bowl from his mother, and quickly went back through the door. Maga turned back to the table where Kai was sitting. The little girl still sat very still. She was wrapped around the middle in a small towel, with every inch of her skin, that wasn't covered by the brown terry cloth, covered in the tan mud. Her jet black hair was pinned sloppily to the top of her hair with no less than ten small clips. At once, Maga found herself giggling at the sight. She indeed looked like one of their pigs, covered in mud, sitting in the chair. Maga did her best to silence her laughter as she drew herself closer to the child. With her hand, she probed the thin layer of mud on Kai's arm. It was cracking, and as she touched it bits began to flake off.

"Good, it's almost done." Maga pulled away from her little girl again and crossed the room. She placed a tray with a bowl of warm water and several pieces of cloth on to her lap. Returning to the child, she dipped a piece of cloth into the water and began washing the mud off. Very slowly, she worked in the same order it had been applied. As the last bits of mud were washed from Kai's face, Maga smiled. Kai's brilliant white skin had been transformed into the tan of her father. "Okay, go get dressed, I'll do your hair on the way." Kai hopped down from the chair and ran to her room.

As Maga put the bowl of murky water and the soiled pieces of cloth away, she heard Alon enter the room. He seemed tired already, though it was barely morning. "Are we ready?" He spoke as he moved, crossing the room and laying a light kiss on his wife's forehead.

"Almost, she's getting dressed right now." Maga touched Alon's fingers as they rested on her shoulder. Alon knelt down beside her chair and gazed into her eyes. He wanted so badly to return the joy he saw there, but he felt a pang of fear.

"Dear, have you prepared yourself for what might happen?" Alon held his breath. He knew Maga and he knew her temper, especially when the subject of losing Kai was brought up.

"It won't happen, Alon; it can't. For her sake, he wouldn't. She's not old enough to understand yet. Besides, his new bride will be working on her own soon. You and I know full well how hard it is to try and have a baby with a small child in the house." A forced smile crossed her lips briefly before vanishing again into the look of sadness that Alon's question had brought her. Of course she had thought about it. She couldn't stop thinking about it. The only reason that Brannon had sent Kai to live with them, to raise as their own, was because he had no wife to look after her and a war to plan himself. Now that he was taking a wife those reasons no longer prevented him from raising Kai in the busy and safe castle in the center of Antlerbrooke. She knew somewhere deep down that it would probably be best, that it was what the king and queen of Lylunir wanted for their newborn baby, but she didn't care. She had nursed her, loved her and cared for her for six years now. Until it was time for Kai to take her rightful place as a Vessel, she wanted to continue to be her mother. Surely Brannon would respect that....surely.

Maga pulled herself from her sad thoughts and squeezed Alon's hand. "Get the bags, dear, she will be out in a second; and we need to get started if we want to join the caravan." Alon obeyed, leaving Maga's side and entering their room. He returned seconds later with large sacks of clothes and left through the front door. Maga pulled her chair around the table toward the front door as Kai emerged, lovely as ever, from her room. Once dressed, no one would be able to tell that she wasn't naturally tan. She carried with her the scarf for her hair that matched the dress she was wearing and her hair brush. She crossed the room and climbed into her mother's lap, handing her armload over. Alon entered, went one at a time to the children's rooms and left carrying the bags filled with their clothes. A few seconds later, he returned for his wife. Propping the door open, he pushed the chair out into the light of the newly started day. The sun had just managed to crest the horizon, and even the birds were still sleeping. Alon wheeled his two lovely ladies to the back of the large wagon cart in which they had returned from Brannon six years ago. Opening the door, he lifted Kai to the ground and Maga into his arms. He carried her inside and placed her onto the bench bed at the back. After making sure that his fragile wife was comfortable, he came back out and grabbed the chair. Though it was a struggle every time, he managed to force it through the door and set it on the floor of the wagon, securing it with ties to the wall. When his feet hit the ground, Kai rushed past him into the wagon and climbed onto the bench next to her mother. As Alon started to call for him, Duncan came around the side of the wagon. He was supposed to ride in the back with his mother, but he hesitated. "Dad, can I ride with you? It's always so girly in the back with them, and the smell of Kai's mud makes me sick to my stomach on long rides." Duncan looked sincerely at his father. Alon smiled and nodded, then closed the wagon door. Duncan excitedly ran to the front and climbed up onto the bench next to his father's seat. After securing the door to the house, Alon took his place in the driver's seat, and, with a quick look back at his homestead, he hitched his team forward.

IN PLAIN SIGHT

Inside the wagon, Maga was busy brushing, coiling and pinning Kai's abundance of black hair so that she could hide it in her scarf, but in the driver's seat there was little more than staring taking place. Soon they were out on the road. Several other wagons were in sight ahead and behind them, as people from all over the kingdom were traveling toward Antlerbrooke to witness the marriage of their Vessel. Alon looked at the drivers of the wagons that passed him or that he passed by, each happy and anxious. He thought to himself how jealous they would be if they knew how he and his family would be treated when they arrived. How they would be spirited inside the castle and cared for by the Vessel's servants. If only they knew how frightening this day was to him. In spite of the kindness and care that awaited them, they might be bringing their beloved daughter on a one-way trip. Duncan, next to him, talked about what he wanted to see and what he hoped it would be like. He had been old enough to remember the trip the last time they visited a few years ago, and he loved every minute they spent with the Vessel. Brannon showed him things, like Wolvari puppies, and taught him things, like bird calls, that his father simply couldn't. Alon listened to his son, agreeing or nodding whenever the opportunity presented itself. He even managed a smile or a light laugh occasionally. They rode on, toward what he feared was the end of their little happy family.

CHAPTER 15
THE WEDDING

Kai woke in her room; at least, while they stayed with their Vessel, it was hers. It was larger than her entire house back home, but she always felt cold in it. She slid out of bed and rushed to the fluffy little shoes they gave her for wearing around the castle. Pulling on her little robe, she opened her door and flew down the hall. Duncan's room was past her parents'. When she reached his door, she knocked once, then twice more, and then once again. For three days now they had been playing this game, but this time nothing happened. With the corner of her mouth, she blew the lose strand of hair from her face and tried again, but this time she made sure the knocks were loud. On the other side of the door she heard scrambling. Something fell over, and Duncan's voice could be heard groaning. A few seconds later, he pulled his door open. Kai covered her mouth with her hand to hide her smile. His hair was a tousled mess on top of his head, and his night clothes were twisted and bunched in strange places. He was also hopping on one foot, clutching his big toe and his face was contorted by pain.

THE WEDDING

Behind him a chair was knocked over, and Kai realized that he had been sound asleep. In his hurry to open the door, he must have run into the chair. Picturing the clumsy scene in her head, she laughed out loud a little.

Duncan realized at once that his sister was laughing at his misfortune, misfortune she had caused, and growled at her, "If you're going to laugh at me, you can just go back to bed!" As he started to close the door on her, he caught sight of her face. He had never snapped at her before, and large tears were welling up in her amethyst eyes. "Oh, don't cry, Kai. I'm sorry, it just hurt is all. Come on in." As if the past exchange had never happened, a big smile spread across her face as she rushed past her brother. She jumped up onto his bed and pulled his blankets over her cold legs.

""Why aren't you up and dressed? We are supposed to see the monsters today, remember?" Kai's excitement was contagious, and Duncan remembered Brannon's promise to them. When they had arrived at the castle two days ago, the first thing Duncan had asked the Vessel was if they could see the Wolvari puppies again. Brannon had laughed, not expecting Duncan to remember. He promised that he would show them the puppies one morning before the wedding. He was very busy with the wedding and could not call them yet. He explained that the Wolvari lived in the forests, and he had not summoned them, but, since the children wanted to see them, he would bring them back. The children were promised that as soon as they arrived, he would take them to see the monstrous dogs. Last night at dinner, Brannon received word that two young Wolvari had arrived in the stable. The children naturally wanted to rush out that instant, but Maga had insisted it was too late and too cold for such things. Brannon agreed, but promised that first thing in the morning they would go. Here it was, morning, and Duncan was not ready.

Duncan laughed at Kai. "You're not dressed either!" He eyed the night gown she wore under her robe and the fluffy bedroom shoes on her feet. "Mother will never let you go out like that."

"What's wrong with what I'm wearing?" Kai looked down at her outfit, quite contented with it.

"Come on. I'll pick you out something, then I'll get dressed; and we'll go down together." When Duncan held out his hand, Kai scrambled down off the bed and rushed to take it. With her fingers gripped tightly, he led her back down the hallway to her room. He rummaged through her clothes and pulled her riding outfit from the pile. It was simple and boring, but warm enough. They would be getting dolled up soon enough for the rehearsal later today anyway; it didn't seem to matter what she wore that morning. After he laid out her clothes he left her to dress, pulling her door closed behind him, and hurrying down the hall to his own room. As he passed his parent's room, he heard voices. For a moment, he stood at the door deciding whether to go in and tell them that he and Kai were getting dressed. As he stood there deciding, he began to listen to what they were saying. He heard something about Kai and not coming home. His heart leapt into his throat, and he decided to get a better listen. Moving closer to the door, he pressed his ear to the wood. His mother and father were arguing about whether Brannon was going to let Kai return home with them. Duncan couldn't understand any of it. Kai was their daughter! Why would Brannon want to take her away? As he listened, his mother's voice became thick and heavy. Duncan knew that she must be crying. She began telling Alon about Kai's dreams, about a woman with dark black skin that sings to her at night, about the far off kingdom where everyone has white skin like hers. Duncan listened as Maga sang the soft and sweet Lylunirian lullaby that Kai had taught her. Alon was quiet for a moment before dismissing it as memories.

Their footsteps now moved about the room, and Duncan began to fear he would be discovered. He pulled his ear from the door and rushed to his own room. He dressed quickly, his mind consumed by the strange argument he had just heard between his parents. The description of the woman from Kai's dream plagued him. He had seen her in his dreams too. She did not sing to him, or show him things like she did Kai, but he had seen her, over and over again in his sleep. Each time it was the same. She was leaning against a rock, covered in dirt. She did not move or speak to him, but in the dream Duncan could hear a baby crying. As he pulled his trousers up and began to fasten them, his mind lost in thought; he didn't hear Kai come in again. She was fully dressed and seemed genuinely shocked that she had beaten him. She had to ask him if he was ready three times before he heard her. Yanked from his thoughts by his sister, he decided that he had to have heard them wrong. Brannon would never take Kai away; that wouldn't make any sense. He pulled his shoes on quickly and grabbed Kai's hand, leading her down stairs to the room where they ate breakfast. Brannon was waiting on them, along with his bride.

She was a lovely creature. Her name was Alexa. When they had first arrived, Maga had called her by name. Apparently the first time they had come here, Alexa had been one of the healers Brannon had asked to care for her. It was a jolly reunion, and they spent hours chatting away as the kids played and Alon and Brannon discussed the war effort. The two of them made a lovely pair, sitting at the table in plain clothes enjoying a simple breakfast of bread and eggs. Places for the two children had already been set, and after breakfast, Brannon kept his word. He took them to see the Wolvari in the stable. Duncan had met one six years ago and was astonished to learn that the creature, now bigger than a deer, was the same one from his youth. It was a deep chestnut color now. Its tusks had not grown in yet, and its ridge spikes were still forming. It seemed to remember him, crouching at his feet to let him pet it. As Duncan ran his hand through the thick, soft fur atop its head, his hand touched a spot behind its right ear. The creature let out a whimper and pushed his head harder into Duncan's hand. Duncan instinctively went to pull his hand back but was stopped by Brannon. "No, no, he likes it. He wants you to scratch him there, that's all." Duncan returned his hand and began to scratch. The Wolvari began to moan and shake all over. His great tongue hung from his mouth and his short bushy tail wagged furiously. Duncan scratched harder and harder, and with each increase the worg's enjoyment seemed to grow to match.

The other Wolvari puppy was different. She was solemn and sweet. Her mane was a bright white while her ears, face and back were a deep, dark brown. She was a little smaller than the one Duncan petted. Kai had not hesitated at all. Though this creature towered over her, she did not seem at all afraid of it. She had rushed forward and buried her face it is soft fur. Even Brannon had seemed surprised by this. Kai stroked the worg's fur and the worg in turn nuzzled her face into Kai's side. For nearly an hour, the children played with the massive dogs. Brannon would tell them what the Wolvari wanted and what they were thinking. That was, after all, his gift. He was the Vessel of Forreniah, the tender of the beasts. His new bride laughed and cheered as the children climbed on the animals and chased them around the courtyard. It wasn't until Maga and Alon appeared in the door way, looking sullen and worried, that Brannon called the revelry to a close. They had much to do for the rehearsal and only a few days to get everything ready. The children hugged the gentle giants, then Kai turned and rushed off to her mother. Before Duncan ran toward her as well, he looked up at Brannon and asked the simplest of questions, but one that caught Brannon completely off guard. "You're not going to take Kai away, are you?" Brannon looked at the boy in stunned silence. His face softened a bit and he shook his head. Duncan's face widened into a great smile, before he turned and ran for his parents.

The day had come. Kai sat once again wrapped in a towel and covered in mud. The mud lasted for several days, but her mother had insisted on this ritual every day they were at the castle. Her lovely purple dress lay on the bed in front of her. It was covered in lace and pearls and was the most beautiful thing she had ever seen. Maga was busily brushing her hair mumbling to herself about how much she had to do and how she didn't know how she was going to get it all done. As she finished brushing out Kai's long, pitch dark hair, a maid entered the room carrying the rags and water for removing the mud. After some slight argument, Maga consented to letting the maid wash Kai clean while she dressed herself and checked on the boys in her life. She left Kai in the maid's gentle care and rushed off. Two maids helped Maga into her gown, also of a purple and just as lovely. She had not time to admire herself though. Shouts and scuffling sounds coming from down the hall meant Duncan was fighting the servant sent to dress him.

"I'm not wearing it!" His suit, something he had never worn in his life, was of a deep emerald green. While a lovely color, it was not Duncan's favorite. "Why couldn't it be brown or black or something like that? Why does it have to be green? I'll look like a berry bush!" He had the maid cornered across from him on the other side of the bed. If she moved, he moved, maintaining their distance. Maga had heard the commotion and come to investigate. Pushing the door open with her chair, what she saw brought tears of laughter to her tired eyes. Duncan was in his long underwear. His hair was combed and nicely styled and he was wearing his socks and dress shoes. His dress shirt was pulled onto his body, but was not buttoned, and flapped like a cape behind him as he moved. She watched from the door for a moment before she interceded.

"Duncan, you put that suit on right this minute." Duncan turned to protest but at seeing how lovely and radiant his mother looked, he held his tongue. The deep violet of her dress would look well with the dark green of his suit and, realizing that his family was meant to match in this way, he stopped resisting. The maid, who had spent the better part of ten minutes chasing the young man with a pair of pants, found no gentleness in her touch as she dressed him. As soon as the last button was fastened and the cravat tied, she fled from the room. Kai came through the door only moments later. She looked exquisite in her dress, only slightly lighter than her mother's. She kissed her mother on the cheek and sat gently in a free chair nearby, careful not to wrinkle her dress. The three of them sat waiting for word to head down to the ceremony. Maga listened as Kai talked about the dress that Alexa had shown her and how it had pretty blue gems all over it, except around the middle which is where the red and purple gems were. She and Duncan listened patiently to how Kai wanted her wedding dress to look, which was suspiciously similar to the dress she was currently wearing, only with more pretty pearls and purple gems. After a bit, several maids and the butler arrived to escort them down stairs. Alon had been down for some time now, helping Brannon and leading people to their seats in Brannon's throne room, now transformed into a massive chapel for the wedding.

Alon's suit matched Duncan's; and, once he was standing with his father, he felt more comfortable in his clothes. Their seats were very close to the bride and groom. In fact, they were seated in the front row next to Brannon's parents. The former king and queen had retired to the northern mountains after Brannon had married the first time. Duncan seemed amazed at how old they looked. He knew that Brannon was many years older than he; but he reasoned that when he was Brannon's age, his parents would not look as old as the couple sitting beside his father. He sat between his father and Kai, while Maga's chair was pushed up to the end of the row. Brannon stood nervously tapping his toes on the platform that normally held his throne. Behind him, stood a strange looking man. His flesh and hair were a bizarre gray color. His back was arched a bit and his robe, though a fine fabric, was worn and a bit dirty around the bottom. His eyes, however, were anything but dull. They were a clear, crisp blue, like the sky on a clear summer day. Against his dark, muted flesh, they seemed to glow. Alon leaned down to Duncan and whispered, "He's a Morgathian, a priest, I should think. They live far to the south, beyond Akiliree." Duncan wanted to know more, but Alon sat up straight and returned to silence. The music began to play; and the entire hall, hundreds of guests and well-wishers, stood and turned to see Alexa enter. Kai, in her excitement and admiration, had not done the gown justice. The bride sparkled like a field of stars shining against the pale blue of a spring morning. Brannon almost looked as if he would faint when he saw her. Maga began to cry as she saw the bride climb the small steps to join him on the platform. They listened as the vows were exchanged. The old man's voice was clear and clean, unlike his person, as he issued a prayer to each of the six in the common tongue, and then in the tongue of the gods. When he finished, he motioned for the bride and groom to turn and face the crowd. Their eyes were filled with tears as they gazed down at the hundreds of faces, joyfully watching their great day.

All at once, the hall became a whirlwind of music, laughter, food and dancing, starting with a great cheer that forced Kai to cover her ears. The throne room was quickly cleared of chairs, and everyone began to mingle. Kai and Duncan were introduced as niece and nephew, twice removed, to the Vessel. While not exactly true, it explained, well enough for everyone in attendance, their special treatment. Kai danced with Brannon and Duncan with Alexa, then Alon danced with Alexa as well. At the feast, Brannon insisted that Kai sit next to him; and he cut her antelox steak for her. The party came complete with gifts galore for the new couple. They received hand carved trinkets and heavy fur coats and fruits and foods from all over the kingdom. Kai marveled at the variety of, not only food, but, people too. All the people she had ever seen were like her father, a medium tan, the color of the wood aged by years of exposure. Her mother and, of course, she, were the only different people she had ever met. But here, she saw people from the mountains whose skin was the deep brown of a bear's fur, and people from the coast whose skin was as fair as a deer's light coat and every shade in between. She marveled at the hair of the coastal region. To her it was the yellow of buttercups, the daffodils that grew in their front yard back home. The hair of the mountain people was even darker than Duncan's, though nowhere near the deep black of her own. She whispered in Brannon's ear that among these people she almost felt as if she could have gone without the mud. While he shook his head at her, his smile was warm.

As the feast wound down, and the time for the new king and queen to depart for their trip to the coast drew near, Brannon began presenting his guests with gifts, each more interesting than the last. Many were pets, exotic animals and birds, ordered to be loyal and obedient to their new masters. Others were objects of such quality as not be believed were made by human hands. To Maga and Alon, he gifted a new team of red wine-colored horses for their wagon, said to have a gate so smooth that even in a run you could not feel it. The last to receive presents were the children. Duncan and Kai stood waiting nervously for Brannon's gift. Deep down, Duncan hoped that it would be the wolvari puppies they had played with days before, but instead, two giant horses were brought forward. Larger than any horse they have ever seen, there was a jet black stallion and a silver mare with black hair for her mane and tail. Brannon motioned, and the horses moved forward without being led. They bent low and bowed to Kai and Duncan. Brannon knelt down in front of the children so that he could be heard over the cheers of the crowd behind him. "These horses are special. They are of an ancient race that now only exists here at the palace. They will take good care of you, and protect you. Their saddles are very special. Take good care of them for I feel one day you will find another use for them. The black one is yours, Duncan, his name is Shadow. He is headstrong, but steady. For you, Kai, I present Whisper. She is gentle and swift. May they serve you well." As he rose to his feet, he met Alon and Maga's stunned gaze. "May these gifts see your family home safely! Until we meet again!" With these final words he turned, took his new wife by the arm, and climbed into the carriage waiting at the gate. With a final wave out of the window, a team of those ancient, enormous horses began to move, without the need of a driver. As the carriage disappeared, Alon and Maga rushed to their children. Tears of joy and relief streamed down their faces. Their family would go home, complete and unbroken.

CHAPTER 16

COLLAPSE

The soldiers had never paid the park much attention. Decorative trees and flower bushes were not exactly seen as a threat. Because of this they had hey completely overlooked the secret entrance at the base of the large statue which occupied the center. An antelox stood perched on a fallen tree with Wolvari circled around the base of its legs. Giant birds with wings outstretched stood atop its massive antlers. The statue stood nearly four stories tall and had come to symbolize what Forrenfar meant to the people of Lylunir. But its true purpose was far more practical. After the last great disaster, a monumental storm that leveled half the kingdom, emergency shelters and escape tunnels were constructed in each of the cities. After decades of disuse, they had fallen out of memory or had been boarded or bricked up due to the cold damp air that emanated from the deep tunnels. Several entrances, like this one, were spared but hidden to prevent children from getting lost inside. In the wee hours of the morning, the camp fires in the tent-covered park were all but embers. No lights were lit as the hooded figures slunk out of the small bush at the base of the statue. Silent as the night, the ten figures moved between the tents to the far side of the park. They moved together down the side streets toward the fenced-off section of the city where the slaves suffered in squalor. The man in front, young and strong, threw back his hood as he crouched down at the corner of a building. His pale skin seemed to glow in the soft light of the moon. The man behind him motioned for him to return his hood.

"Look around. There are no guards to see us. It is as I have said. They have grown lazy and inattentive. There is no need to fear the eyes of our enemy if they are all closed." His voice was calm and clear. His eyes flashed as he moved quickly out into the open. As he drew nearer to the fence figures on the other side began to move as well. For a moment his party stopped, frozen in the street. Then, in the soft glow of the moon, he saw that pale flesh in the distance. He rushed forward and gripped the wire. On the other side, hands of all sizes reached for him. Dozens of his people, slaves now, were grouped on their side of the fence. They were thin, beyond reason, and filthy. Their clothes were torn and soiled, and the smell of captivity reminded him of the garbage piles that used to exist in the far corners of this once vibrant city. He waved his hand and four of the men behind him fanned out and began cutting the wire. The leader placed a single finger to his lips. The dozens of refugees instantly fell completely silent. As the four men continued to cut, he turned to them. "Get as many out as you can. We will meet you in the tunnel after it's done." He turned back to the huddled crowd on the wrong side of the fence and squeezed one of the hands that poked through the wire. He watched as a tear rolled down the face of the woman to whom the small hand belonged.

"May Luniah bless you." She whispered as he released her hand. He turned and disappeared again between the buildings, followed by three of the men. They moved quickly through the dark streets. As they neared the tunnel dig site, one of the men spoke.

"Baron, put your hood back up. There are sure to be guards here." The leader stopped, nodded and pulled his hood back onto his head. As the shadow fell across his face, he moved into the open, staying close to the debris that was scattered around the site. His friend had been right. Baron counted no less than ten guards patrolling around the site. But he was right as well. They were spread out, and the distances between the patrols were uneven. He watched for a few minutes learning their movement patterns before he returned to the cover of the alley where his companions waited for him.

"There are ten of them." His voice was soft, so as not to carry.

"Ten! How are we going to get past that many? And even if we do, how will we get out again?" The youngest member of their team did not even attempt to hide his fear. He had only volunteered to come on this expedition to free his parents. They had been taken in the siege and had spent nearly ten years as slaves. Though Baron was barely twenty, he had been their leader for nearly half their life. The day of the siege he had appeared, as if possessed. He had gathered as many as he could find and led them to the secret places that many had forgotten. Trip after trip he had made into the city, each time returning with more lost souls he had saved from captivity. When he realized he could save no more, he led them through the tunnels and out of the city. Deep into the wilds, they traveled. He had been the one to find a hidden place for them to set up camp. It was he that had convinced them to keep on the move. He led the raids on the poorly guarded supply caravans that passed by. Strong and serious, it was as if he had never really been a child. He told the young ones stories of hope, of how their princess had escaped over the wall, of how he believed one day she would return and throw down the monster that had displaced them. Baron alone provided them with hope that their lives would get better.

"Calm yourself, Marc. I have a plan. The patrols are as I thought—slow and uneven. They only patrol the entrance. If we can get into the tunnel, we will find no one else. Once inside, we will set the charges. You three will get out of city, and I will stay behind to light the fuse." Baron saw the looks of fear on the faces of his friends. "Don't worry. I do not intend to be a martyr. I know of another way out. I used it many years ago to get my mother out of danger and it's not far from here. In the confusion the blast will cause, I will make my way. Alone, I can move faster and be more hidden from sight.

COLLAPSE

Are we ready?" He searched the faces of the three men huddled around him. Though terror was painted in their eyes, they nodded. Quietly they moved through the darkness.

Just as Baron had said, the patrols were few and spaced irregularly. He waited until the largest gap presented itself and sent two of the men through. They ducked inside the opening of the tunnel only seconds before the next patrol came into view. When the gap came around again, Baron and his remaining rebel companion rushed across the opening and into the dark of the tunnel. Afraid to use light, they used the tunnel walls to guide them. About half way down the tunnel, Baron gave the signal. The four men fanned out. Each produced a small sack from inside their cloaks. The sacks were filled with a special powder that the miners of Tunaeshir had brought for trade into Lylunir. They had used it for generations to open new mine shafts in their quest for gems and precious metals. Several months ago, a band of refugees from the City of Gems had been found wandering aimlessly in the forests to the north and they had brought with them their knowledge. In that moment Baron had formed his plan. Three days ago, on one of his spy missions into the city, he had heard the celebration. The guards were yelling that they had made it, that the tunnel was finished. All it needed was an opening. Baron had realized they had to act fast.

Now he was here. In the black of the dark cave, each man did his duty. They placed their charges against the support pillars and ran their fuses back toward the opening. Just a few feet shy of the mouth of the tunnel, Baron braided the fuses together as the men took turns shooting the patrol gap back across the site. Once all three were out of sight, Baron began to count. He had to give them time to get back to the park, back through the secret opening. After nearly twenty minutes of quiet waiting, he decided it was time. Pulling a small flint stone from his pocket, he bent low over the fuse bundle at his feet. Finding a rock on the ground he began striking. The sparks, hidden behind his crouched frame, showered over the fuses. After a few tries, the fuse lit. Sparks flew from the end in a shower of light. The flame move quickly along the braided rope into the darkness of the tunnel. Pulling his cloak tight around him, he ducked out of the tunnel entrance and began to slink his way along the side of the wall.

He was almost past the view of the patrols when a voice rang out behind him. "You there! Halt!" He could hear the swift steps of his pursuer. He lowered his hood and turned to face his foe. The guard stopped for a moment, astonished by the glow of the man's flesh in the moonlight, by the smirk that bent his lips, and by the revenge that burned in his violet eyes. Before he could speak again, a horrendous explosion shook the ground. Baron did not stagger, but the guard did. Stunned, he turned to see the source of the earth rattling boom. Dust and debris billowed from the mouth of the tunnel. Baron did not hesitate, pulling his hood back into place, he turned and disappeared into the dark. In every house he passed, lights began appearing in the windows. As he neared his boy hood home, he found the building had burned to the ground. A pang or sorrow hit him as he bounded into the wreckage of his shattered childhood, and began digging in the rubble for the opening. It wasn't until the point of the sword touched his back that he realized he was not alone.

"Stand you cur, and turn round. I don't stab people in the back, even rebel trash like you deserves to see the face of his killer." Baron turned to see one of the Hadrian soldiers. He must have come from one of the nearby houses, heard the ruckus Baron had been causing, and decided to investigate. He looked no older than Baron himself. Baron lifted his hands. The soldier took the end of his sword and pushed the hood off of Baron's face. His breath caught in his throat. The man that stood before him was proud and strong, nothing like the broken slaves. He had never seen a Lylunirian that looked as this one did. His momentary shock was all Baron needed. He spun on his heels. In a single motion, he stripped the blade from the young soldier's hand and plunged it into his chest. The young Hadrian sputtered as if to scream, but no sound left his lips. His body crumpled to the ground, lifeless. For a moment, Baron stood over his body. He imagined a different time when perhaps they might have lived, separate and happy, if only their kind had never come here.

Leaving the body where it lay, Baron decided he

could not use his tunnel. Pulling his hood back up, he raced into the darkness toward another entrance along the city wall. Occasionally, he was passed by soldiers. Each time, he would crouch down into the shadows. They were so panicked by the explosion, most never even looked up from their footsteps to see him. As he rounded the last corner, Just steps from reaching his destination, he found a sight he had not expected. There, a short distance ahead of him, was a general of this retched army. Though he wore no insignia of his command, there was no question of his leadership. He stood over one of the guards from the tunnel, his face gnarled in rage. In his hands, he held one of their blades. Its point poised against the soft flesh of the man's neck. His voice was booming and fierce as he screamed at the man who struggled to hold his neck still. His shouts were rambling questions to which he obviously wished no answers. He asked things like 'How could you be so foolish?' and 'How could you let this happen?' Baron smiled. He slid through the shadows away from the deteriorating scene. Finding his passage, he slid into the tunnel and rushed to join his people, victorious.

CHAPTER 17

THE FURY OF RIKARD

The groan of the war machine as it lumbered down the road grated on his nerves. It had been ten years since he had ridden in one of the infernal contraptions and time had not eased his discomfort. The machine's belly was cramped and dark. He had grown to love the open space of his throne room, the soft blue glow of the illuminators that lit his castle home. He enjoyed his daily strolls through the streets of his capital city where he saw young ones play fighting and trade down every side street. It had been good news that had brought his caravan out onto the road. His call had gone out to all soldiers not needed to maintain digging in the other cities to meet him in the City of Beasts. Three days ago a messenger brought him news that digging on the Forrenfar tunnel had stopped. Not because of the rebel raids, which were becoming more than a nuisance, but because with the next few pick falls that tunnel would crash open into Forrenfar. They were through. For ten years they had dug; well the slaves had dug, into the dark cliff wall, the unnatural barrier between the kingdoms of Plaettan. Rikard supposed it was fate that the first wall to be pierced would be Forrenfar's. He had taken Lylunir, the central kingdom, first because she, Luniah, was his god's first sibling. Forreniah was next in line. To Rikard, it seemed destiny was on his side.

He had called for soldiers and the machines, most of which had fallen out of use and needed to be oiled and repaired, to gather at once for their next great siege. He now sped with all the haste he could manage toward the next great war of his life, and he was certain this one would indeed be a battle, unlike the last. His conquest of Lylunir had been almost effortless. The rebel bands that raided caravans and ambushed patrols had proven to be more difficult than the initial siege had been. He had taken the entire kingdom in less than a week, enslaved its people, and butchered its royalty. At least, that is what his people believed. Next to him in the cramped, dark machine lay his queen. Tawni's small frame lay sleeping, her head resting on his shoulder. He stopped listening to the groan of the machine on the road and started listening to her breathing. Though she had brought him great happiness and comfort over the nine years since their marriage, she had yet to conceive a child for him. He feared her small frame and frail nature could not support the seed which he would plant. For nearly a year now, he had been fighting the desire to take another, larger woman to bed, just to have his heir. After all, he would need an heir if his beloved Hadriah's shantir was to inhabit his next Vessel. As he listened to Tawni's breathing, he decided that she, as his queen, his wife, his love; would bear his child.

After nearly a day inside the belly of the metal beast, he was beginning to go mad. Twice since departing he had ordered the machine stopped so that he could stretch his body. As he sat there, in the dim stillness, he again felt the need to stop. With his massive fist, he pounded on the side of the machine. His fist falls created a loud bong sound that reverberated around the inside of the machine, like being inside a giant bell as it is struck on the hour. Tawni's head jumped from his shoulder, and her body seemed to jerk awake with such force that he wrapped his arm around her, to steady her. Immediately the machined ground to a stop and the large door along the side opened. As the hatch touched down on the ground, Rikard stood to leave. Before he could take a step toward the door a head popped through it. The head belonged to his driver, a smart and strong man who had helped build the war machines so long ago. "My Lord?" His eyes seemed tinged with anxiousness. Rikard stopped moving and looked at his driver.

"Ah, Tomlen, I need to stop. This infernal machine is suffocating me. I can ride no longer." Rikard moved toward the hatch.

As Rikard's head emerged from the opening, Tomlen began to smile, as he backed away from the opening, he said, "You need ride no more, my Lord, we have arrived." Rikard looked past Tomlen. Just ahead of them lay a large stone bridge, and beyond, the gates of the City of Beasts. Rikard had been here before. Nearly ten years ago, he had come for the interrogation of an old man. It was here he had learned that the infant princess was dead and gone, that his purge of Luniah's Shantir from Plaettan had been successful. To look at it now was not to know it. Though the gate was broken, and most of the houses had been touched by flames, the city itself had been quite a wondrous sight. Ten years ago, Rikard had walked the streets and marveled at the statues of beasts that marked every street corner. The trees had been heavy with blooms, and the sun had been shining. Even with the smell of death and battle in the air, the city had been remarkable. Now it looked as if a war had just been fought. The massive rock walls that surrounded the city were covered in metal spikes and plates. The gates were of an ugly make, too quickly hewn, and assembled with little care. The trees surrounding the city, that had once been green and full of fruit, were dead and brown. Many had been felled or burned in place. The air was acrid with smoke from nonexistent fires. Rikard sighed. His people had taken something beautiful and turned it into their homeland. The same thing had begun to happen to the City of Light, the seat of his new empire; but he had stopped it, had prevented the gnarled metal from adorning every wall and stopped his people from scaring the land. He had not been here to stop this. For a moment that thought that all of the great and wonderful cities of Lylunir suffered this fate crossed his mind. He had toured each of them in turn after they were taken. Each had offered him wonders, save the City of the Dead. He recalled fondly the jewels of Tunaeshir, the poetry of Zailia, the wondrous bread of Akiliree; it pained him to think they, too, had been marred by the ugliness of his home land. He had come here to escape their cold lifeless island, but it seemed his people did not share his love for this new land.

Pushing the sad thoughts aside, he stepped from the machine and began to stretch his enormous body back to its natural size. Tomlen bowed and disappeared around the side of the vehicle to fetch the Vessel's things. Tawni emerged from the belly behind him, her crown slightly askew. He smiled at her, and, with a finger, shifted it back atop her head. She smiled back at him; then, walking together, they crossed the bridge and drew closer to the city. As they drew near, Rikard heard the bustle of soldiers on the other side. When the gates to the city lifted, Rikard found fear where he should have found excitement. The soldiers were ragged and looked as if they had not slept in days. Dirt and mud covered their clothes and faces. Rikard's chest fell as he walked between the lines of beaten down soldiers. The men and women of his army seemed defeated and they had yet to start fighting. Reaching the end of the line, Karnus was there to greet him. His chief Brakbark, Karnus, had been placed in charge of the City of Beasts before its siege.

"My Lord, I..How was your journey? I trust the trip was pleasant." As he spoke, he bowed low before his king. His voice was shaking and dripped with terror. Tawni moved up from behind Rikard to stand at his side.

As Karnus rose from his bow he caught sight of his queen. Again he bowed, "My queen, I did not know you would be coming as well." His words to her were hollow, and she scoffed in her throat at his meaningless gesture.

"No, it was uncomfortable and long. We rode through the night, and I could not manage a wink of sleep. Tell me, is the tunnel ready for troop deployment? Our siege of Forrenfar has waited ten years; it cannot stand to wait another day!" Rikard's words seemed to pierce Karnus like a knife. He did not answer his king, but instead seemed to search the ground with his eyes. Rikard spoke again, "The journey has left me in foul spirits. Do not deny me the answers I seek, Karnus. It would be unwise. Have the troops I sent ahead arrived?" Karnus still did not look up from the ground.

"Yes, My Lord. They began arriving yesterday. They now number in the thousands, so many that we have run out of space to house them all. The park in the center of town is filled with tents." Karnus reluctantly lifted his eyes to his king. Rikard immediately recognized the look spread across his face. It was the look he had seen on the face of every soldier who had ever brought his bad news. Karnus shifted nervously under his Vessel's gaze. "My Lord...I...I have bad news."

"What?" Rikard tried to prepare himself, but it was not enough for the blow Karnus was about to deliver.

"It's the tunnel, my Lord. It's collapsed." Karnus' eyes filled with terror as he watched the vein on his king's forehead begin to throb. His bronze skin took on the color

179

of fiery blood as he fumed silently before him.

"WHAT! HOW!!" Rikard's voice shook the ground. The soldiers standing around them fell to their knees. Karnus stood quaking before his Vessel.

"Rebels, my Lord. They came in the night. They used some unknown force to explode the tunnel. It caused over half of the passage to cave in on itself." His voice broke as he finished. He bowed his head and waited for death, but the blow did not come. After several seconds he lifted his head. His king still stood before him. The rage was still written on his face, but he had fallen silent.

Tawni broke the silence. "Is that all of your news?" Her tone was cold and condescending. She had never like Karnus. She had warned him once that they did not wish to hear any further news of rebel attacks, and they hadn't. It was now quite clear that they had not heard because Karnus was not sending word. The attacks had not stopped, but were being hidden from them. A smirk crossed her cold, lovely face as she thought of asking for Karnus' head for this failure.

"N..no, my queen. Many of the slaves escaped in the night as well. We can't seem to find them. But the gate was locked and guarded. They can't have left the city. There is a search underway as we speak." Rikard stood silent; his rage held his tongue, and shock stayed his hand. For ten years, he had waited for this day. For ten years he had tended the flame of his god's revenge, and now that he had gotten so close to fanning the flame with the blood of Forrenfar, his plans were dashed, by slaves no less.

Tawni's voice was shrill with laughter as she yelled at Karnus. "You incompetent fool! Of course they are gone! If the rebels could get through your precious gate and your impressive walls, it seems perfectly believable that they could get out again, wouldn't you agree?" Her bitter and cruel smile signaled his death. Rikard's arm swung swiftly, his powerful backhand striking him across his shoulder. His body flew backward several feet, sliding to a stop against the corner of a nearby building. His arm was shattered, and his shoulder was dislocated. He prepared himself for the final blow. Rikard took two quick, heavy steps toward the broken brakbark who had failed him so miserably. As he lifted his leg to stomp the breath from Karnus' body, Tawni's small hand on his shoulder cause his to pause. Lowering his foot to the ground he turned to her.

"Why? Why not kill the man who has so utterly failed me?" His voice growled at her, soaked with rage.

"He is a symptom, my Lord, not the cause; and his death would not cure the plague of which he is a part. Look at these men, my Lord. They have grown soft and overweight. They no longer represent the fire with which you forged your army all those years ago. They have lost their fight, and only you can give it back to them. This slothful illness must be cured before the war can continue." Her words seemed to touch him. Rikard looked at the men, kneeling in fear around them. As he searched their ranks he saw the truth of Tawni's words. They had grown weak, soft. They had lost the will to fight that they had once had.

Stepping forward, he cleared his throat. In his loudest voice he issued the most important command he had ever given. "My people! What has happened to you? You are no longer my beautiful soldiers. But that changes now. From this day, we will become what we once were. Messengers, prepare yourselves to deliver this decree. There is to be another harrowing. All men and women over the age of forty-five are to be killed unless they can prove themselves strong. Training is to resume. Any man found lacking the strength or determination of purpose to fill a place in my army is to be killed on the spot. The other cities are to send slaves. One fifth of their workforce, to resume work on this tunnel. Until it is opened again, no one in this city will rest. You will train until your hearts give out. Mark my words, if ever this happens again, every man in my sight will die by my hands." He turned his face back to Karnus. Reaching down he placed his hand on his chest. Without mercy, he ripped the emblem of the brakbark from his uniform. The man whimpered in pain, wrenched by the action. He fell back to the ground as the fabric torn from him, twisted and writhing in pain. "No one is to care for this man. If he dies, so be it. If he lives, he is no more than a soldier." Turning from the heap on the ground, he walked back toward the gate. Tomlen, who had been standing at the gate holding their bags, turned and disappeared, trotting back to his machine. As Rikard and Tawni walked to the gate, Rikard tossed the torn emblem to one of the men nearest to him. "Do not repeat the errors of your predecessor, or you shall suffer a fate far worse than his." With these words, he disappeared through the gate and climbed into the war machine.

CHAPTER 18
AS FAR AS POSSIBLE

The pounding sounded again through the dark home. Kai's eyes opened. At first she thought perhaps she had dreamed the sound. She had dreamed so many strange things of late. The noise had just pulled her from a terrible dream. The woman with white hair was telling her to run as giant ruddy bronze dogs with golden eyes chased after her. Sweat beaded on her brow. She must have been thrashing in her bed violently, as her blankets had all toppled off the bed into a heap on the floor. She lifted herself up and onto her elbows and listened, but there was no more pounding. As she was about to lower herself back down onto the bed, she heard other sounds, the sound of voices—some loud and frantic—so many voices. Then, she heard her father's. This was not a dream. She clambered quickly from her bed and threw on her dressing gown. Without a thought to her appearance, she burst from her bedroom. As she stepped into the main room of her home, she could see at least three men from the village standing just inside their front door. The one closest to her looked away from her father's face toward the motion. She realized too late that she was not properly prepared to receive guests. Her hair was perfectly straight and her attire was modest enough, but she was not tinted. Her iridescent skin shown in the dark of the room like a star burning in the night sky. The townsman stared for a moment and Kai, frozen in the shock on his face, held fast by his gaze. She had been told all her life that Forrenfarians could not handle the sight of her Lylunirian traits. For the past several years she questioned the need for such measures, the mud, the hair wrap; but this moment confirmed everything for her. Duncan's hands wrapping around her shoulders broke the spell. She hadn't noticed him standing by the hearth, having gotten up only moments before her.

"Come on." He pushed her back into her room. Closing the door behind him, he sighed. "Did you see how he stared at you? Like you were a monster...maybe mom was right. I always doubted." Apparently, he, too, had questioned the need for the mud. She was a Forrenfarian, born to two Forrenfarians, why go to such lengths to hide what was naturally hers? Now, he stood regretting those doubts and questions. He had seen with his own eyes the shock and dismay on that man's face.

"Wasn't that Mr. Brok? And Mr. Garter? Who was the one in the back? I couldn't see him. What are they doing here? What time is it anyway? It's still dark, right?" Kai's nervous questions tumbled from her in panic. Nothing like this had ever happened before. She crawled back onto her bed and lifter the curtain from her window.

AS FAR AS POSSIBLE

The dark of midnight hung on the other side of the glass.

"It's the middle of the night. The other man is Mr. Felix. I don't know what they want here, but I do know why they have come. They are soldiers, guards from Brannon's castle. They are the ones that deliver your birthday gift each year. They moved here after mother and father took you to Brannon when you were just a baby." Duncan's face was calm. He seemed to be lost in deep though as he paced in front of her door. "Get dressed, make it warm and easy to move in, I have a feeling this is not going to end with a conversation." He placed his hand on the door knob.

"Wait! Where are you going?" Kai's small body slid from her bed. At ten years old she was still quite small. Her limbs were long and thin, but she stood only about four feet tall from toes to crown.

"I'm going to learn more about what's going on. Get dressed." With that, he was gone. As the door closed behind him, Kai began to dig through her clothes. Duncan had said 'warm and comfortable.' As she pulled on the last piece of the outfit she had selected, her door opened again. This time Duncan was not alone. Her father was close behind him.

"Come, darling. We need to talk." Alon's voice was weary and tired. As Kai followed them into the main room, he began to speak. "Sit, both of you. There is much I need to tell you. First, the men waiting outside are here to take us somewhere...else. They think that the war may be starting soon, and their orders from Brannon are to get us out as fast as possible." Seeing Duncan about to speak, Alon raised his hand, silencing him. "We are special to the Vessel, and he wants to keep us safe, but your mother is very ill. She can't travel, at least, not the kind of traveling that will need to be done." His words caught in his throat. He had dreaded the inevitability of this conversation since the day Brannon had told them they could raise Kai as their own. He had always known that he would have to tell her and Duncan of their deception one day, but he had never looked forward to it. "Kai...There is something you need to know. Your mother and I aren't..."

"Going to let them spirit us away without breakfast." Maga's voice cut through the room like a cool breeze. The tension and fear that had hung heavy over the house since the pounding on the door seemed to lift. "So, while I cook us a little something, I want you three to start packing. Remember, this isn't a trip; we are moving, so bring everything you absolutely can't stand to lose." Her skin looked so pale in the illuminator light. Her eyes were sunken and her cheeks were thin, but her smile was warm and wide. Alon stared in dismay, as Maga rolled into the room in her chair, flittering her hand at the children. Duncan and Kai exchanged looks and then obediently got up from the table and returned to their rooms. "You will not destroy this family without talking to me first." Her voice was serious, but her eyes were soft. She moved forward and laid a hand on Alon's arm.

"You are far too ill to take this trek. They mean to

take us all the way to the northern coast. That's three weeks journey from here, at least. It would be better to tell her and let them take her to Brannon than risk your life this way. They are old enough now to understand." His eyes searched her face, everywhere were painted signs of sickness, everywhere but her eyes.

"This weak spell will pass, just as all the others have. I will not destroy her life and then send her away over such a small thing as illness. We are a family, and I intend to see it stay that way as long as possible. So...you go into the bedroom and start packing our things. Tell those men out there to get the wagons ready, we will likely need both of them. I am going to fix us some food. Oh, ask them if they want something to eat too." With that, she turned and headed for the hearth. As she began pulling smoked meat and vegetables from the baskets that hung on the walls, Alon stared at her. She was far stronger than he had thought, perhaps they could make it after all. Rising from the table, he did as she had instructed. After ordering the three men to prepare the wagons and teams, he returned to their room and began to pack.

Kai hastily crammed her clothes into the bags that were flung around her room. She also threw in her music box and the few books she had been given. Alon had taught her to read when she was little. At the wedding four years ago, Brannon had found this out. Since then, she received books filled with allegorical fairy tales and lessons on table manners and etiquette. As the books slid down into the sack, her door opened again. Duncan breezed into the room and surveyed her progress. As he looked at the state of her packed bags, he shook his head. "Really? Just crammed it all in there? Kai, really, as neat and clean as you are with everything else..." With that, he grabbed the bag closest to him and turned it upside down on her bed. As he shook it, her wadded clothes and crammed mementos came tumbling out into an unceremonious pile atop her mattress. She started to protest; but, realizing he was right, she simply put down what she was doing and joined him beside the bed. Working together, they sorted her clothing. Duncan knew this trip would be longer than the others, so he took care to fill one bag with her essentials. Her riding clothes and undergarments filled the sack, neatly folded and categorized. Into the next sack, they sorted her fancy dress clothes, of which she had quite a bit. With all her clothes now neatly packed, she had an entire bag for just her belongings. They wrapped the fragile things inside blankets and packed the bag full. Thanks to Duncan, she was able to take almost everything in her room that wasn't a stick of furniture.

With her room packed, Duncan threw the two sacks of clothing over his shoulder. Kai, carrying the bag of precious objects, followed him out of her room, past her mother cooking over the fire, and out into the night. The men had worked fast. Both wagons were sitting, fully hitched, right outside the front door. Kai pulled her arms closer to her body against the night and its cold wind. The darkness had always frightened her. As she followed

Duncan to the wagons, she saw that there were other wagons beyond their gate. These men had packed their homes before coming to the Merin farm for her family. She stared at the wagons for a bit before Duncan's voice brought her back to the moment. The cold pierced her again. She turned to see Duncan standing at the back of their old wagon. "Bring me that bag, Kai. We are packing all the non-essentials in this one so we have more room to ride in the other one." Kai did as she was told. As she handed Duncan the bag, she saw Mr. Brok emerge from the barn leading Shadow and Whisper. They were fully saddled and ready to ride. In the glow of the moon, the strange saddles looked almost like chairs atop the large steeds. Those saddles were indeed different, though Brannon had called them special. They had tall backs, like a chair, and a strange rigidity to them that, at first, had been quite unpleasant. It was quite difficult to get used to because it forced the rider into a very upright, almost forward, posture. Kai and Duncan had taken nearly six months of riding every day to adjust to them. Now, she could not stand the feel of a normal saddle. The strangest thing about them was the line of holes cut into the other side. It ran along the back bone of the horses. Also, the entire saddle underside, except for the holes, was covered with a thick pad. Despite this, they still rode with a saddle blanket. There had never been a reason given for these holes. After months of puzzling and asking, she and her brother had finally given up, deciding it was probably some method of reducing weight or something trivial like that.

Kai smiled as Whisper drew close to her. The horse dipped her head and nuzzled Kai with her silver nose. She, in turn, lovingly stroked Whisper's neck. Shadow drew close to Duncan as he handed the bags into the wagon to one of the men. Shadow pushed into his back with his nose, sending Duncan lunging forward against the back of the wagon. "All right, all right, boy, I see you, too!" Duncan turned and hugged the horse. Shadow and Whisper had lived up to Brannon's words. They were indeed different. They were smart. Each helped Kai and Duncan do their chores around the farm. They brought them tools or helped herd the antelox through the gates. They were also far more affectionate that any other horse on the farm. Fiercely loyal, no other person could ride them. Once, their father had tried. Shadow had stood perfectly still, not budging an inch until Alon had climbed down. The most intriguing thing, though, was their size. They stood nearly a foot taller than even their largest team horse, with thicker, softer, hair covering their entire body. Their hooves were hidden behind heavy tufts of longer hair. They were beautiful and strong, and it was easy to see why they were considered royal steeds.

As Kai clung to Whisper, stoking her mane, Alon appeared in the open door, calling them for food. The horses pulled away and walked to the front of the line of wagons. There they waited for their riders to return while Kai and Duncan ate a quick meal with their parents. As they ate, the men continued to enter the house. Each time, they left with one item or another. All the food that had hung in the kitchen, save the meal currently on the table, was hauled outside. The blankets from their beds and the cookware that wasn't in use was also hauled away. As they finished, their dishes were cleared and hurriedly washed before also finding space in the pack wagon. They went over the house again before departing. In the span of less than an hour, their home had gone from warm and cozy to cold and empty. All their furniture, save the small writing desk that had been Maga's fathers, still stood in the home. Their beds were where they had always been, and the chairs around the table were neatly pushed into place; but all the little things that had made this a home were packed and stacked in the wagon outside. Alon helped Kai on with her coat as Duncan wrapped their mother in her bed quilt. As Kai walked through the door of her house one last time, she shed a tear, so many memories abandoned so quickly.

Once outside, things seemed to move faster. With Maga safely stowed in the newer wagon, Alon climbed into the driver's seat. One of the soldiers climbed onto the driver's bench of the other wagon; his son drove his wagon instead. Duncan climbed into Shadow's saddle and watched as Whisper bowed low for Kai. She wasn't tall enough to reach her stirrups just yet, and the horse seemed to know, helping as best she could. Once everyone was ready, the wagons waiting at the gate began to move. The wagon carrying their mother went next, followed by the one carrying their home. Kai and Duncan filed in last, riding side by side into the darkness of the night. Neither one knew what had caused this sudden evacuation, but it mattered little. They would do as they were told and hope that soon they would be brought in on the secret everyone else seemed to already know.

They had traveled for days before they stopped to make camp. Rest had come to no one since leaving the small ranch. The men traded off driving the wagons as best they could, taking turns grabbing a few hours of sleep now and then. Kai had spent the better part of the trip in the wagon with her mother. Maga was not faring well on the journey. Her fever had returned; and despite her assurances to the contrary, it was clear that she was not improving. Alon tried several times to turn around during the first few days of the trip, but Maga had resisted every attempt; and now, nearly a week into their journey, there seemed to be no point in trying. It was now a race to reach their destination before the trip took Maga's strength completely. It had been Alon that had suggested the rotation of drivers. They had six wagons and eight men, counting Duncan and the three sons of Mr. Garter, the youngest of whom was only eight. They had decided to set up camp when Mr. Garter's oldest son had fallen asleep driving his family's wagon and run them off the road. Luckily, the horses stopped before any damage had been done.

Kai and Duncan helped set up the tents and build the fire. Alon tended to the team horses, and the wife of Mr. Felix, a healer by trade, tended to Maga. Once camp was set, they all ate together. From a distance, their party might have looked like a group of good friends taking a journey together, but the truth was far less pleasant. The wives and children of the men were as confused, and put out, by the sudden evacuation as Kai and Duncan and knew even less about the reasons. All they were told was that it was vital that Kai, and her family, were taken far away. The resentment bred by this caused no end of tension. They stared at her, their eyes cold and cruel. She was the cause of this suffering, and they did not intend to let her forget it. After dinner, the families retreated to their tents for sleep. Kai and Duncan stayed near the warmth of the flames. They sat in silence, close together, listening to the dusk. They were soon joined by Mr. Garter. He sat across the fire from them and, for quite a long while, he said nothing. He had been the one who stared so shockingly at Kai the night they had fled their home. Since then, Kai made sure to use the mud every few days.

Clearing his throat Mr. Garter began to speak. "Has your father told you why?" The two Merin children stared at him. Duncan shook his head, almost afraid to speak. "I suppose there hasn't been time for explanations. I think maybe you need one, or as least as good a reason as I can give. I saw the way our families glared at you. You must forgive them. They don't know why either except that we had to leave to get you out. They blame you, you see, for having to leave. I'm sorry." His eyes began to tear. It hurt him to have his family so angry with him.

"Then why not tell them the reason? Surely they would forgive and forget if they knew the truth?" Duncan's voice was soft and comforting. Kai leaned a little closer to him. He could be so caring when the need presented itself. Lately he had been so cold and mechanical, caring for the horses and helping with the trip. She had barely gotten to spend any time with him.

"If only it were that simple. The truth is, what they think is very near the truth. We are here to protect you. We had to leave because of you, your family. You see, ten years ago Brannon ordered us to move to Gatewood to protect your family. Our instructions, aside from keeping an eye on you, were that at the first sign of trouble from the other side of the wall, we were to evacuate you all to a town along the northern coast called Darksand. It's where Brannon's parents now live. So you see, in a way, it is your fault we had to leave our homes. I have tried to explain, but it doesn't seem to help. I fear they will never forgive you. I'm so sorry." The trails of several tears seemed to sparkle in the fire light. His eyes lowered to the flames, and he sat in silence, watching them dance, for quite some time.

"Why are we so important to Brannon that he would give you such orders?" Kai's voice was heavy. She had wondered this very thing her entire life. The gifts, the special invitations and treatment. She knew they weren't really his cousins. So why? Why had he taken such an interest in them?

After a long, awkward pause, he lowered his eyes and

said, "I don't know that, Miss. I was never told. I reason it's got something to do with you, your looks, I mean. I understand that your mother is a mixed blood, the daughter of a Lylunirian merchant and one of us. Seeing you, it's pretty obvious you take after your granddaddy. Maybe that's why. But, as I said, I don't actually know." As he finished, his wife called from their wagon. He stood from the fire, bowed slightly, and then hurried into the night, never again making eye contact. Kai listened as the door to their wagon closed behind him.

"I guess mother was right. Forrenfarian's are afraid of mixing the blood lines. He must be trying to help hide you. That would explain the mud. To make sure you get a fair chance at life. It's a shame though. I think your skin is really pretty without the mud." Duncan's voice was serious and contemplative as he spoke.

"You do?" Kai had never heard Duncan talk about her unique qualities before, at least not seriously. All her life he had teased her. It had never hurt her feelings, but this was the first time he had ever said something nice about her strange qualities.

"Sure. And your eyes are really pretty too. At least you don't have to hide those. Well, we should get some sleep. Come on." Duncan stood up and reached down a hand to help Kai to her feet. She didn't need it. She leapt from her seat and wrapped her arms around his waist. She squeezed him in the tightest hug she had ever given. Though he had not intended it, he had given her the first compliment regarding her true appearance she had ever received. While Maga and Alon both thought she was the most beautiful creature in the world, with or without the mud, they had never said it. Duncan had been the first, and she loved him for it. Releasing her bear hug, they walked together to their wagon and climbed in for the night.

They were only a week from journey's end when tragedy struck. Since that first camp they had decided to do the same every few days to allow everyone to get a good night's rest and regain their strength. Kai spent the better part of the following weeks in one of two places, the wagon with her mother and the saddle. She and Whisper would join Duncan and Shadow in the woods along the road. For hours, they would ride parallel to the wagons off in the trees. They explored the forests and gathered berries and fruits they found for the group. Duncan had even taken to hunting from the saddle, and they found game to be quite prevalent. As the spoils from the forest grew more necessary with their stores running low, the tension between the families lessened. Though you could not call them friends, they were, at the very least, civil to them now—at least to Duncan and Alon. Kai was still a sore subject to a couple of the wives. The only one that did not appear to bare her any ill will was Mrs. Felix. She had spent far too much time with the sweet girl to hold her any sort of grudge, though caring for Maga was becoming a full-time profession. Several days before she had insisted that they stop. They found a meadow and set up camp, and there they stayed. It had been nearly three days since they pulled off the road when she emerged from the back of the Merin wagon. Her face was wet with tears, and her hands were shaking, as she walked to the fire where everyone else was huddled. Though it was the middle of the day, the tall trees blocked the sun's light, and warmth, from them. She stood staring at Alon, saying nothing.

At first, Alon only stared back at her. Then, noticing her tears, he had gotten to his feet. He ran past her to the wagon, Kai and Duncan fast behind him. Inside they found Maga. Her chin and night gown were covered in blood. She had begun coughing on the day they had made camp and had not yet stopped. The blood had begun to join her coughs late the evening before. Her eyes were growing dim, and her body seemed to have lost all strength. Alon rushed to her side, falling to his knees beside her. He pressed his head into her hand as he cradled it in his. Kai had never seen her father cry, but now he sobbed openly. "My dear husband, stop this now. You are scaring the children." Maga's sunken face formed a weak smile. She pulled her hand from his and held it out to her children. Kai and Duncan drew close. Alon could not bring himself to lift his head from her side. The three of them huddled around her, all crying openly at the sight. "My sweet babes. Know that I have always loved you, will always love you. I will be with you as you grow, as you become who you are meant to be." Her eyes lingered on Kai for a moment. Something caught in her throat. Swallowing, she continued, "No matter what, I want you to take care of each other. Promise me this. Live well. I love you." Her words tailed off into coughing.

They stayed with her, crowded into the small wagon, but not another word did she utter. As the day drew to a close, so did her life. When she had finally slipped away, the people seated close around the fire outside could hear the wailing of sorrow. Then, in the dark of the night, her body was removed. It was cleaned and bound, after which Alon had it placed back in their wagon. Though the men had tried to convince him to bury her, he insisted that she be taken on to their new home and buried there. He wanted her close to him always. After a few days, they could no longer use their wagon to sleep. Though it was cold, it was not cold enough to slow time. Kai and Duncan took to sleeping in their saddles and under the stars. By the time the party reached Darksand, they had not only lost their mother, but their father too. Alon had slipped into a depression from which there seemed no escape.

CHAPTER 19
BAD DREAMS

"Faster!"

"FASTER!"

"He will CATCH YOU!"

Over and over, the dark woman repeated her warnings, the panic in her voice increasing. Kai ran through the unfamiliar trees. Then there were buildings made of strange stone. All the while she ran, the woman with her shouted. Kai never dared to look back. She could feel the earth trembling beneath his footfalls. She could hear the pounding of his heart in the silence of the night. Now she could feel his breath on her back, hot and close. He was catching her. Terrified, she decided to face her attacker. Stopping, she turned, the dark woman screaming wildly for her to move. Pursuing her was not a man, at least, not exactly. It was a sea of men. They all looked the same. Their skin and hair were the color of bricks and their eyes glowed with a yellow fire. Their teeth were bared, and they carried giant rusted swords. They bore down on her. As they fell upon her, they walled her and the dark woman in, her screams now no more than sobs.

Kai stood spinning round and round, trying to find a break in the wall of men. When one started to open, she rushed toward it, only to find it blocked by a hulk of a man. His appearance was the same as the others, but he was easily twice their size. The sword he carried dripped with blood, and his face was twisted into the most disturbing smile. She rushed back into the small ring, away from the massive man. As he drew near to her, he swung his giant sword. Its blade tore into the dark woman's flesh. As she crumpled to the ground, dead, Kai screamed. It felt as if someone very important to her had just been killed before her very eyes. She lunged toward the woman's body, leaving herself acutely exposed. With only a step, the giant man towered over her, his sword was poised, ready to strike. The twisted smile had grown, spread over his entire face, accompanied by a sinister cackle. His evil laughter bellowed within the circle, and the men began to cheer. Kai watched, unable to move, as his sword began to descend slowly toward her body. She watched, helpless, as it pierced her chest. It sank deeper and deeper into her flesh, tearing and ripping her asunder. The pain was unbearable. Kai began to scream and writhe under the blades touch. She could not move, could not escape. Closing her eyes, she screamed again with her dying breath.

"Kai! Kai! Wake up! I'm here, wake up!" Kai's arms lashed against something warm and firm. She felt hands on her shoulders. Forcing herself to open her eyes again, she found that the hulking man was gone. She was in her bed, and Duncan was by her side. Sweat poured from her body. Her limbs shook, and her face was covered in tears. Duncan wrapped her in his arms, trying desperately to hug the nightmare away. This was the third time this month he had awakened to hear Kai screaming in her sleep. "This time you are going to tell me about the dreams. I can't keep waking up to the sound of you screaming like that. I won't. Come on. I'll fix you some tea, and we'll talk about it." Kai nodded. Duncan was truly her best friend. He had been everything to her since the move. Her mother's death had been hard on all of them, but none so much as their father. Alon had barely eaten for the first month. He spent every moment sitting on the bench Duncan had built next to Maga's humble grave. When he wasn't keeping vigil at her grave side, he was hidden away in his rooms. For almost two years, it had been this way. Brannon's offer to move her to Morghath had only made it worse. Less than six months after they had arrived, there had been a tragedy in Darksand. The former king and queen, retired here after Brannon had taken the throne, passed peacefully in the night. As if they had planned it, they died in unison, holding each other in their sleep. Brannon, his queen Alexa, and their four year old son Brakken, had come for the procession to Morghath. All royal dead were carried away to the land of the dead, so that their memories and lives could be chronicled and remembered. For Brannon to offer Maga a spot in the royal processional was a tremendous honor, but Alon could not part with her. As they left, his self-imposed exile grew deeper.

Though the move had cost them their mother, and their father, their new home was not so terribly bad. The house had been built especially for them, and from the look of the dust they had found inside when they arrived, it had been built some time ago. It sat ready for them, atop a small hill, and all the land that you could see from the windows was part of the ranch. Twice the size of their previous home, each person had his own rooms, one just for sleeping and one for anything else. This private living room had large comfortable chairs and a table in its center. Its walls were lined with empty bookshelves and painted images of landscapes, some familiar and some strange. Between their personal rooms, Kai and Duncan shared an indoor privy. It was the first one she had seen beyond Brannon's remarkable castle; but as Duncan soon pointed out, many of the wealthier families had had them for years. The common rooms of the house lay just outside their private ones. There was a large kitchen. It had a table for preparation and three hearth pots suspended over one long, large fire. Through an archway was a dining room, though it had not gotten much use. Alon took all his meals in his rooms, so Duncan and Kai began doing the same, only they ate together. The table was now covered with papers. Duncan had taken over the run of the farm. He had purchased a nice size herd of antelox after they arrived using the money he found on the table, marked for that purpose. Soon, they were doing business with merchants all over town. Duncan had a head for money; and, with their father drowning in sorrow, among other things, he had taken control of the family interests. Now a boy of almost fifteen, he carried with him the respect of many of the elderly merchants in town. He had grown, too. He was almost six feet tall now, fit and strong. His final growth spurt was in full swing, and Kai was having to buy him new pants almost every month for fear of his ankles showing. He would be well over six feet when it all finished, at least that was what she hoped. She had already begun buying his clothes that size and was using a temporary hem for the time being.

As for her, she had hit her final growth spurt. She stood all of five and a half feet and slender. At almost twelve, her womanly features had not developed yet. She was long and straight, so much so that Duncan had taken to calling her "arrow" when the mood suited him. With the town being so close, and business men dropping by at all moments of the day, she had taken to adding a small amount of the mud to her daily bath water. Here on the coast, the people were far lighter than they had been at the wall, and she found the light mauve color this effected was more than adequate. Her raven hair she no longer hid. People seemed amazed by it at first, but the novelty of it wore off after a few months. Her bright amethyst eyes, however, were still the source of much talk. Her mixed heritage had been given as reason; and, though everyone believed it to be the truth, it was still fascinating to see the lilac of her eyes flash like gems in the sun.

Kai pulled her blanket around her and moved into her

sitting room. Duncan left her in one of the padded chairs and went out into the kitchen to put the water on to boil. He maintained the fire in the hearth at all times during the colder months. Winter would soon be in full swing, which meant that in only a few days' time, her annual gift would arrive. Last year it had been a strange one, the mud, of course, and a letter. Their father had taken it, read it, and promptly thrown it in the fire, despite Duncan's protests. They had never learned what the parchment had told him. Over the year since, all manner of ill news came to them about the wall. There had been an evacuation of their small village of Gatewood just days after they had fled. The entire town was now a military site. Thousands of soldiers from all over Forrenfar were stationed there. Mr. Felix, Mr. Brok, and Mr. Garter took homes in and around Darksand. Brannon was apparently providing for them, as none seemed able to find steady work. They never seemed in foul spirits because of it though. Mr. Garter visited the ranch weekly to check on the kids, and each time he brought a bottle of spirits with him for their father. Alon always seemed pleased to see him coming; but as soon as his fingers wrapped around the bottle, he would return to his lair like a wounded animal. Kai wondered sadly if he had heard her screams, if he had laid there in his bed and listened as his daughter cried out in pain—had pulled his pillow around his ears to block out the sound, rather than come to her. In that moment, she felt more pity than anger for him. Maga had been his whole world. She knew he loved her, that he loved Duncan; but without Maga, life was no longer warm for him. The sun no longer shone. He was trapped in darkness, and the drink Garter brought him helped dull the ache, at least for a while.

As Duncan set the tray down in from of her on the table, Kai was pulled from her thoughts. She watched as he poured her a cup, then one for himself. As he settled down into the chair beside her, she took her cup and cradled the warm porcelain in her hands, breathing in the rising steam that curled from its mouth. "Well, tell me about this nightmare. Is it always the same?" Duncan took a sip from his cup, never letting Kai fall from his gaze. For a moment she held eye contact, then, taking a sip from her own cup, she turned her head to focus on some unimportant spec across the room.

"Mostly. There is a woman. Her skin is like charcoal."

Duncan nearly spit out his tea, "Do you mean she is burned?!" The look on his face was horrifying.

"No, just black. All over she is black, as if she is covered in soot, but she's not, all except for a strange mark on her hand, that's red, and her hair. Her hair is white like snow, and it's long, like mine." Kai stopped to take another draw from her cup. She felt Duncan shift nervously beside her and waited for him to say something. When he didn't, she continued. "She is always in my dreams. They used to be nice dreams. She would play with me and sing to me."

"That song you used to sing, the one mother wanted you to teach her?" Duncan seemed genuinely surprised, not by the memory, but by the fact that this had been happening for nearly her whole life; and it was only now that she was sharing it with him.

"Yes, that's the one. She would tell me stories, and we would walk through fruit orchards together. The dreams were always so wonderful, but then everything changed. The night we had to flee, that was the first." Kai took another sip of her tea. Her voice had cracked, and she could feel the tears creeping into her eyes. Taking long slips of the tea, she pulled herself together. Duncan sat beside her, saying nothing. Finally, she started again, "Now, they are terrible dreams. We are running, running through trees and then buildings. The woman is screaming for me to run faster and faster. That *he* will catch me." Kai had to stop. The image of the woman's crumpled body flooded her mind. Clenching her eyes shut, she took another gulp of the hot tea, winching as it scorched a path down her slender throat.

"Who is *he*? Do you ever find out?" There was real fear and concern in Duncan's voice as he probed. She could not stop now. He needed to know. She thought perhaps if he knew that maybe the dreams would stop.

"Not really, I mean, I can see him; but I don't know who he is. He's big, really big, and dark red all over, even his hair. The color of blood. All but his eyes, those are yellow flames." She cleared her throat. "Usually he just chases me, and I wake up just before he catches me; but tonight was different. Tonight there were more of him. Well...not exactly more of him. There were hundreds of other men who were the same as he, only smaller; they were normal size. They caught us. Then *he* came. He killed the dark woman, and then..." Her voice trailed off. With shaking hands she raised the cup to her mouth. She gulped the hot liquid down her throat. It burned again, but not like the red man's blade had. Maybe that would be enough; maybe Duncan would be happy with all she had said so far.

"And then? What happened, Kai? You need to tell me." She met his eyes for the first time since she had started her tale. They were heavy. He seemed to feel the fear she had felt in her dream. He wanted, needed, to know what she was facing.

"He stabbed me. Really slowly, laughing as the blade sliced through me." Her voice fell flat. Without warning, she erupted in tears. Duncan managed to grab her cup before it fell from her hands. Setting both cups on the table, he reached for her, and she reached back for him. He held her and let her cry for hours, stroking her hair and whispering reassurances in her ear.

When her tears finally stopped, it was nearly day. Kai lifted her head from his shoulder. His eyes were tired, but still open. He had not left her. "Thank you, Duncan. Maybe the dreams won't be so bad now." She managed a weak smile which he returned.

"Maybe next time you can dream that I'm there to protect you. Maybe then it will turn out differently." The thought cheered her. She sat there, in her blanket, in her chair, wrapped in his arms, hopeful that the nightmares would plague her no more. Then he said something she did not expect. "What's strange, is that I've seen this dark woman in my dreams, too." Kai's head jerked from his shoulder and her eyes searched his face.

"But how?" The surprise in her voice gave way to fright. "Do you see the same things as I do? Oh, tell me that you don't! Tell me that you haven't been suffering these nightmares alone, too!" Duncan's hand came to rest gently on the side of her face. At the touch of his hand, she fell silent and let him guide her head back to his shoulder.

"No, no, my dreams are nothing like yours. I only see the dark woman. She doesn't speak to me, she doesn't even move. But I see her. She is leaning against a rock in the bright sunlight. Her clothes are torn and dirty, and the only sound I can hear is a soft baby's cry. Then I wake up. I don't have the dream every night, but occasionally it comes back around. It will linger for a few days, and then disappear again. I just think it's strange that we dream about the same woman, that's all." Duncan sat quietly for a while, just holding her. Then he thought of something. "Maybe we met her! Or knew her when we were very, very young. We weren't old enough to remember her normally, but somehow she stayed with us. That would explain how we are both seeing her. I'll ask Father. Today is Garter's visit, so he should be in a talkative mood, for a while at least."

CHAPTER 20

THE GIFT OF KNOWLEDGE

The day was warmer than usual as Duncan fixed breakfast. Usually Kai did the cooking; but after her nightmare, and the hours of crying that followed it, she had been too tired. At dawn, he had left her to get a little more sleep. After doing the chores on the ranch, he decided to fix their morning meal himself. He was nearly done when Kai emerged from her room, fully dressed and looking rather better than he had expected. He smiled at her as she stretched. She moved through the archway into the dining room and then beyond into their main room. Though they used it only for company, it was warm and cozy. The large windows let in tons of warm sunlight; and the chairs, made of antelox hide, were soft. Flopping lazily across one of the chairs, she shouted into the kitchen to Duncan.

"Did you get any more sleep? I think I have never slept as soundly as I did this morning." Footsteps came through the arch behind her. Duncan had come to join her. On the tray he had used to bring her tea in the wee hours of the morning, was now set a humble breakfast. She loved him dearly, but Duncan was not a chef.

"Sorry for this," he said, as he placed the tray on the small table in front of them and took a seat on the couch. "It won't be nearly as good as yours, and no; but I feel fine. All the chores are already done so we have the whole day to rest, at least till old Garter gets here." Duncan felt himself sink into the comfortable seat. He spent little time in this room, choosing instead his sitting room, or Kai's, to relax in. At this moment, he wondered why. The sun made the whole room light up. It was as if he were seeing it for the first time and he decided to try and spend more time here, at least on sunny days. He picked up his plate and began to eat. He wasn't lying about the food. While edible, it was nothing compared to the delicacies Kai prepared for him each meal. She had learned to cook with his mother, and it showed. He watched as Kai politely, and quickly, tried to choke down the contents of her plate. He laughed to himself as he watched her try to hide the faces brought on by the strange flavors or poor textures within his concoction. Finally, he couldn't take it anymore.

"All right, all right, that's enough. You don't have to eat any more. I'm man enough to admit this is horrible." Laughing he took her plate from her, returned them both to the tray and then to the kitchen. Passing back through the dining room, headed to rejoin Kai, he was stopped by his father. Alon had emerged from his rooms. His face was covered in a week's worth of beard growth, and his eyes were red and sunken. Despite having spent days at a time in his bed chamber, he looked as if he hadn't slept in weeks, even months.

"Father! Uh, good morning. There's some food in the kitchen, but it's not very good." The shock in Duncan's voice seemed to affect Alon. He straightened his back, standing to his full height.

"Kai's food is always good. Is she ill?" Duncan staggered a bit at the real concern in Alon's voice. For months he had seemed to have no interest in the lives of his children, for good or bad.

"She's fine. She didn't sleep well last night so I let her sleep late this morning. I cooked breakfast instead. She's in the living room if you wish to join us. The sun is bright and warm. It's going to be a lovely day." For a moment Alon seemed interested in the idea. Duncan began to hope that perhaps today would be the day he escaped his self-imposed exile and took his place as the head of their little family again. Sadly, it was not to be. After a moment of thought, Duncan watched as Alon's shoulders sagged again.

"No, that's all right. I...well, I...just tell me when Garter gets here, will you?" With that, Alon shuffled past his son into the kitchen. Duncan waited for him to return, observing sadly as he passed him by once more carrying a small plate of food and disappeared back into his rooms. As the door closed behind him, Duncan shook his head. He simply didn't, couldn't, understand how his father could lose himself in his sorrow. Duncan had loved Maga, too; after all she was his mother. Every day he thought of her, missed her and mourned her, but life had to go on. It was as if Alon was dead with her. He seemed trapped in his body, longing for release. With a sigh, Duncan joined Kai in the living room. They spent the morning, and better part of the afternoon, talking and laughing, enjoying the warmth of the light pouring in on them. The sun didn't leave the room until well after lunch. At about three in the afternoon, there was a knock on the door. Before Duncan could reach it, Alon appeared. He had bathed himself and shaved. His hair was hurriedly combed, and he had apparently put on fresh clothes. Kai smiled at him. He looked almost normal, almost happy. Duncan opened the door and found not just Garter, but Felix as well. Between the two of them, they lugged a large chest and behind them on the ground stood the customary barrel. Kai's gift had arrived. Duncan smiled at the men. Since the move, they had become close. It might be unfair to call them friends, but they were close, none the less.

Opening the door wide, he said, "Please come in, come in! Here, let me help you." With Duncan's help, the men brought in the trunk and barrel. They placed the barrel in the privy Duncan and Kai shared and set the large trunk on the dining room table. Duncan insisted that the men stay a while. His father seemed in especially good spirits, and he was afraid that if the men hurried off, the mood would sombre too quickly. The men agreed, and Kai set about fixing a large meal for the small party. The men sat around the fire place in the living room and shared stories of the goings on in town. Not having a steady job made them magnets for gossip, and they reveled in their new found profession. Alon, having received his usual bottle, stayed to share in the talk, a rare occurrence indeed. Duncan said little. He sat in the far corner chair, or stood in the doorway to the kitchen, and just listened. He had not heard his father's laugh in so long that he had forgotten how charming it was. Kai managed to escape the cooking from time to time and join Duncan. Together, they watched the three men laugh and talk and share stories. Kai's meal was delicious, as usual, and the men promised to stay for dinner every time they came if the food continued to be that good. Duncan had promised them such a meal every week if they wished it. As dark approached, the men said their farewells. After Duncan closed the door behind them, he turned to find his father, still sitting in the chair, watching the flames dance. Deciding that now was the time, he chose the chair next to him and began his carefully worded question.

"Father, I was wondering something. Well, you see, Kai had a dream last night, and there was this woman in it. She's been in some of my dreams too, and we were wondering if maybe we had met her once upon a time." Alon appeared to be listening, so he continued. "She's, well, she's got skin like charcoal, and her hair is white like clouds, and well..." Duncan did not get to finish. Alon shot from his chair. The contentment on his face had turned to rage and fear.

"No, you have never met that woman. She doesn't exist! I don't ever want to hear another word about her!

Do you understand? Not another word!" Duncan sat in stunned silence, staring up at his father's crazed look. Alon opened his mouth to speak again, but no sound escaped. His eyes seemed to soften and returned to watching the fire. Kai appeared in the door behind him.

"What happened? Is everything all right? I heard shouting."

Alon did not look up, but replied flatly, "Everything is fine, dear. So, have you opened your gift yet?" Without looking again at Duncan, Alon moved past Kai into the dining room. Placing the now half-full bottle on the table, he fiddled with the latch on the trunk. After several attempts, he finally managed to open it. Flinging the heavy lid back, he peered down into the dark belly of the box. He reached in and pulled out a long roll of paper. Handing it to Kai, he watched as she unrolled it. There were several large maps, all hand drawn. One was of the entire kingdom of Forrenfar. Special marks indicated, among other things, their home now, their home before, Antlerbrooke, and the Great Gate. Another map was of Antlerbrooke alone. It showed each of the town's many burroughs and districts. Several others depicted the different regions of Forrenfar in greater detail. All in all, the roll contained nine well-made maps. Reaching again into the truck, Alon withdrew a stack of books, and then again, pulling more. When all were removed, no less than ten tomes sat spread across their table. "Apparently, Brannon wishes for you to become a book worm." Alon snickered at his own joke. Sticking out of one of the books was the edge of a letter. Pulling it free of the tome, Kai read its contents quickly.

"He thinks Duncan and I could do with some history. These are all about Forrenfar. Apparently, next year they will all be about Akiliree." Handing the short letter to her father, she and Duncan began looking at the titles on the books. There was one about the line of Vessels and one about the Shantir of Forreniah, what it could do and how it had been used throughout history. There were several about animals. Duncan held one up to show her. *50 Animals Unique to Forrenfar*. They smiled at each other and returned the book to the stack. "Is there anything else?" Kai watched as her father reached into the chest one last time. As he drew his hand up, Duncan saw red velvet cloth slip from something gripped lightly in his fingers. It was amber and translucent, and sharp, very sharp. Alon seemed to realize what the object was and quickly returned it to the box. His face drained of color and he quickly pulled the lid closed on the chest. As he began to lift the trunk, Duncan protested.

"Wait, there was more. What's wrong, father? What's in there?" He took several steps toward his father; but when Alon turned toward him, he stopped. The look on Alon's face frightened him. He dared not push this now. He and Kai watched as their father carried the chest through his chamber door and slammed it behind him. Kai looked at Duncan for answers, but he had none to give. He shrugged and began piling the books in his arms. Kai followed suit, and, together, they carried the load into her sitting room. Once all the books were on the shelves, Duncan sat in the chair he had occupied earlier that morning.

"He's acting strange Kai, well, stranger than usual. I think there were weapons in that chest. Special ones meant for you. And when I asked him about the woman from our dreams, he lost himself in anger." Duncan looked at his sister. He had come to depend on her for guidance, just as she depended on him for strength.

"He's lost, Duncan. I had hoped that he would get past this, but I feel that mother's death has destroyed him. All we can do is care for him and hope. Hope that maybe one day he will come back to us, but we can't push. Every time we try, he pushes back. It's getting us nowhere." The truth of her words rang in Duncan's heart. Their father was truly lost; and if they had any chance to get him back, it would have to start with him. Duncan sat for a while in the chair. He watched as Kai pulled one of the books from the shelf and began reading. Every once in a while, she would share some tid-bit of information with him. He would nod, or make a small sound, but he wasn't really listening. His thoughts were on the strange amber object that he had seen wrapped in red velvet. He had to know what it was.

As the evening grew late, he bid his sister good night. On his way to his room, he detoured through the dining room. Stopping at his father's door, he pressed his ear against the wood. All was silence on the other side. He turned the knob, bracing himself for the possible fight waiting for him. As the door swung open, he found the room dark and empty, except for a foul stench. His father's sitting room smelled of sweat and filth. Duncan had not entered these rooms in months, not since Kai had cleaned it and accidentally knocked over a small perfume bottle of their mothers'. Even though the small bottle had survived the tumble from the self where it had been carefully placed, Alon had lost his temper, and Duncan had been forced come to Kai's rescue. Since that day, neither child had set foot inside. Stepping as lightly as he could, he entered the room. The door along the side wall, which led to Alon's bedroom, was closed. Allowing the dining room door to swing wide open, the kitchen fire provided him just enough light to see. Tucked under the table was the chest. Carefully, he moved the chairs out of the way and eased the chest from its place. Opening it, he removed the bundle and returned the chest. Repositioning the chairs as they had been, he retreated from the dark room. As he pulled the door closed behind him, successful, he sighed. With his bundle held tight against his chest, he moved quickly to his rooms. Once inside he placed the bundle on the table and quickly lit a fire in his fireplace to fight back the chill. With the hearth roaring, he returned to the strange bundle and unwrapped the velvet.

There before him were the amber blades he had glimpsed earlier. There were two of them. Too small to be swords, he reasoned that they were daggers. They were exquisite, almost too beautiful to be considered real. For a moment, he thought perhaps they were simply decorations—something meant to hang on the wall or over a fire place. As he stared at them, he thought of his mother's last words, to protect each other, no matter what. Lifting one of the blades in his hand, he held it up to the light of the fire. Through the blade, he could see the flame dancing. As he watched, it was almost as if the flame within the blade moved independently from the fire behind it. Duncan decided to put the blades away and seek out one of the guards for advice. Perhaps they could help him understand these strange knives, and what he was meant to do with them.

The next day Duncan saddled Shadow and headed into to town. He had stood at his father's door and told him he was going to conduct some business, but there was no reply. Kai had wanted to join him, but today was not a good day for her to come. He indeed had business to do, but it had nothing to do with their ranch. He, instead, asked her to ride the fences. He knew she wouldn't object to this. Any chance she had to ride Whisper for hours on end was a good one. Leaving the ranch, he hurried along the road toward town. The whole way, his mind raced with questions. He had decided to ask Garter. Since he was the man entrusted with delivering Kai's gift each year, perhaps he had taken a look inside and seen the strange amber colored blades. He might know what they were for, or what they were made of. Duncan found him outside the general store, sitting peacefully on a bench, watching the world drift by. Tying Shadow to a rail post, he joined the older man. As he lowered himself onto the bench next to Garter, the older man nodded at him. For a long while they sat in silence. Finally, Duncan, realizing Garter was not going to strike up this conversation, made the first move.

"Garter, you trained in combat, right?" Duncan watched his face as he snorted in derision.

"Of course I did! We all did, not much a guard if you can't fight, now are you?" Garter chuckled in his throat. Duncan's question seemed almost childish to him. His laughter stopped when he noticed the serious look in Duncan's eyes. "What is it boy? What troubles you?"

"Well, did you look in Kai's trunk yesterday, you know, before you delivered it?" Garter seemed taken aback by the question. Realizing he had offended the man, Duncan quickly added to his query, "I mean, did you pack the trunk, or did it come to you that way?" The rewording seemed to settle the old man, and he returned to his relaxed position.

"It came that way. I have *never* looked inside, not my place. Why? Was something inside you didn't expect? Or was something missing that you did?" Duncan could tell by his tone that the old man teetered on the edge. If his next words weren't the right ones, this conversation would be over; and he was sure his father would hear about it.

"There were daggers in it. My father tried to hide them, amber daggers. I was just hoping you knew something about them, like where they came from, what they are made of and what Kai and I are supposed to do with them?" Duncan hoped that Garter would be flattered that he would come to him for help and it worked. The older man's chest puffed a bit.

"I don't know anything about daggers being in that box, but if you're wanting to learn to use them, I can certainly help you with that, and not just daggers. I can train you on lots of weapons." Garter stared straight ahead. Duncan felt his heart leap out of his chest. Secretly, this is what he had hoped for, but he never thought it would be that easy. What would his father, or Kai, say to him learning to wield weapons? Kai he might be able to convince, but his father would never understand.

"But my father, he tried to hide the daggers from us, he would never let me train." Garter turned to face Duncan, smiling slyly at the youth.

Leaning closer to Duncan, he whispered, "What your father doesn't know won't hurt him, or you for that matter. I don't seeing anything wrong with this being our little secret." With a wink, he sat back up straight and returned to watching the people pass by. Duncan wanted to jump for joy. This was perfect. For a long while he sat there with the older man, discussing times and places and cover stories. They would begin the following day. Duncan was to bring nothing with him as Garter had all the weapons they would need. Soon Duncan would know how to use those strange daggers, even if he didn't know anything else about them.

CHAPTER 21
COMING OF AGE

Kai wandered out of the tailor's shop wearing a sad face. For nearly a week now she had been checking in daily, hoping to find her perfect dress waiting for her. Last month Duncan had received his annual invitation to the Match-Makers Ball, the event of the year in Darksand and the surrounding countryside. All blossoming adults at least sixteen years old, that had not yet taken a spouse, were brought together for one elegant, magic filled, night. The older women of the town had found great success rates over the past decades. Most of the invitees from the past few years being the result of relationships started at this very event. Duncan had refused to attend each year, every time giving the same reasons. He was far too busy, and still had his sister to take care of. This year he was going. The change had to do with the fact that in with his invitation had been one for Kai. She would turn sixteen less than a week from the ball, and the women organizing it did not see the need to wait for her age to be official. Duncan had planned to refuse again until he began laying awake at night imagining Kai being swept off her feet by some of the less than savory men he knew in town.

When he changed his mind, Kai had sprung into action. She took his measurements and her own down to the tailor. Duncan was now nearly six and a half feet tall and well built, strong and lean. The tailor had made his suit in no time. It was a lovely, deep, dark blue. At first, Kai had thought it was black. She had been so disappointed that the tailor ruined his own surprise. It seemed no one could resist making Kai happy. He pulled her into the back room, where the sun was held at bay, and lit a set of tiny illuminator lights, like those used for the ball. In the splattered light, the suit took on an entirely different look. The blue shown in the reflective thread that patterned the entire garment, as if it coursed with energy. Kai's face lit up when she saw it. She had rushed the suit home to show Duncan but, before she could, he had made several statements to the effect of how glad he was it was simple. Fearing that if he knew the truth about the suit he wouldn't wear it, she decided to keep it a secret. She tucked it away in her closet, reasoning that she took far better care of her clothes than he did and that there she could guarantee its clean and safe keeping. As Duncan was not really looking forward to the event, he saw no need to protest. Seeing the suit hanging in his closet would have only served as a daily reminder of the uncomfortable and awkward night that lay ahead of him.

Kai's dress, on the other hand, was nowhere to be found. The tailor claimed that a woman in town had agreed to help him with its construction, and all Kai had given him was her measurements. She had made no suggestions or requests and, therefore, had no idea what the dress would look like. With each passing day, she grew more and more anxious. The ball was only days away, and she didn't even know what color it would be. She couldn't even plan her accessories. Day after day, she checked in with the tailor. Each time he would look up to see her enter the store, her face bright with anticipation. He would smile sadly at her and simply shake his head. Her smile would fade into a simple, understanding one, and she would turn and walk out again.

Soon, the ball was upon her. Tomorrow, she would be dancing under the stars of a cold autumn evening; but only if her dress arrived soon enough for her to be able to go. She left the tailor's shop and headed for home. Another restless night lay before her, filled with dreams of showing up the ball in rags, or worse, a hideous gown she could do nothing to change. She had wondered if she could wear one of her older dresses instead, but none of the beautiful dresses from her youth could fit her any more. Even the simple dress she had received three years ago could no longer be worn, and with her mother dead, she had not the desire nor the energy to create one for herself. In the last year, her body had changed so much that whole new patterns would need to be made. While she had gotten no taller, her womanly curves and features had grown in. Though she did not seem to care, the boys in town held a very different opinion. So much so that Duncan had ended up in a fight several months ago with the cobbler's son over a comment he made as Kai passed him by on the street. It had taken Kai and Mr. Garter several moments to pull Duncan free of the lad, who looked as if his face had been trampled by antelox. Thanks to Mr. Garter, no punishment was handed down to Duncan. It was reasoned that the boy's statement, which was heard by several people, was so offensive that Duncan was justified in his anger. Since that day, she was not to go into town without an escort. Today, she was joined by her father.

Alon was doing much better of late. He spent less and less time in his rooms or at Maga's graveside. He had started helping out on the farm and even handling some of Duncan's business dealings, though he was quite happy to let Duncan remain in charge. His change had come slowly. It had started with the advent of their weekly meal. The dinner Kai had served Garter and Felix, who brought her annual gift four years ago, had been so well received they had begun coming back each week for another. Soon the two men were joined by the third, Mr. Brok, and then their wives and children. For the last several years, Kai was fixing dinner for no less that sixteen people once a week. They would eat, talk, laugh and tell stories well into the night. Alon had started eating with them and soon started helping prepare for the meal. Before long, he would emerge the day before to help prepare the house and the day after for the cleanup that was necessary. Each week his spirits raised. And for the first time since coming to Darksand, the Merin family seemed to have found a bit of happiness.

Every year she fixed an especially good meal on the night of her gift delivery. They would eat and be merry; and only after the men and their families had left, would they open her chest. Each year, it had been the same. After Forrenfar, she received books and maps concerning Akiliree, then knowledge on Tunaeshir. Last year, several tomes, dusty and well worn, arrived concerning Morghath. Only one parchment map had accompanied these books. On one side was a simple map of the kingdom, and the other had a detailed map of the capital. This year she had two possible kingdoms to learn about. While she knew nothing about Zailia other than its Vessel held the power to heal, she desperately wanted Lylunir to be next. Between the war and her heritage, she felt that she was most closely connected to the Kingdom of Light and Shadow, as it was referred to in every book she had received so far.

She had read every book she had been given, even the really boring ones. The same could not be said for Duncan. If a book was boring, he, stating that he was far too busy to read it just now, would ask her to mark the important information. Then he would peruse the book for her marks and read only the highlights. She had learned so much. She knew now that Akiliree had very few trees. Its houses were built from mud and grass or stone. She learned that Morghath had the smallest population of people and that, unlike all the other kingdoms, the Shantir, or god spirit, did not transfer to an heir at sixteen, but at the Vessel's death to a worthy monk. The Vessel of Morghath did not marry and was never to have children. The book had attempted to explain this, but Kai had not understood how anyone would want to go through life alone. The Tunaeshir books had provided her with the most enjoyment. Many spoke of their Vessel's ability to travel in the blink of an eye, and the gems and precious metals they would pull from the ground, but it was the book on their people that struck her fancy. She had lain awake at night imagining them. The book described them as small, half the size of a Forrenfarian, with pale yellow skin and black eyes. She imagined that they looked like small golden toys, scurrying through their brightly lit tunnels carrying sacks, overflowing with beautiful things.

The book on the rare animals of Forrenfar was her all-time favorite. She had read it many times on wakeful nights. It was this book that she and Duncan had taken turns reading aloud to each other so many years ago and it was in these pages that they discovered the true nature of Whisper and Shadow. They had known the horses were special, but they had never thought they weren't really horses. According to the book, they were a species called Equinox. They were a race of exceptionally large horse-like creatures that had the intelligence of a person, fully capable of completing complicated sets of instructions. They were stronger and faster than normal horses and lived to be nearly one hundred years old, if properly cared for. For centuries, they had pulled the carriage of the Vessel and, according to the book, the remainder of their race could only be found in the royal stables. Duncan had snickered when he read this. Seizing the quill from the table, he had written in the margin, with a careful hand, 'and the Merin ranch.' He and Kai had apologized to their steeds after reading about their true nature and ability. From that moment on, they spoke to them as if they were people. The equinoi became more than steeds. They had become friends and helpers, capable of herding the antelox without a rider, and providing comfort and support when adversity would come, as it always does, on a farm.

As Kai awoke the next morning, terror filled her. Today was the day and she still had no dress. She had barely slept. How could she attend a ball with no ball gown? She pulled herself from her bed and headed for the kitchen. Despite her restless night, she had her responsibilities. As she moved through her rooms and into the dining room, she imagined how happy Duncan would be when she had to give up and agree not to go. As she walked through her door, she caught sight of Duncan sitting with Mrs. Brok at their dining room table. Pulling her robe tighter around herself, and running her hands over her hair, she moved to join them. As she engaged in the customary pleasantries with their visitor, she noticed a large bundle on the edge of the table, wrapped in simple brown paper and tied with twine. Noticing her attention drift away, Mrs. Brok smiled and cleared her throat, waking Kai from her distraction.

"Ah, yes, the package. I'm sorry it took me so long.

The fabric turned out to be more tedious that I had believed. But I just know you'll love it." Kai's face erupted in a wide smile.

"You?! You're the woman whom the tailor spoke of? The one who insisted on making my dress? Why, thank you, Mrs. Brok! I was starting to worry it would not make it in time!" Tears peeked at the corner of Kai's amethyst eyes, and her cheeks flushed a vibrant pink. So much excitement had left her giddy, and a little dizzy. She rushed around the table, intending to tear into the package, like a child would. Reaching the large bundle, she slowed her frenzied fingers and began slowly trying to untie the knotted sting.

Laughing at the delicacy with which Kai was attempting to open the package she so desperately wanted to rip into, Mrs. Brok said, "Child, there is no need for niceties. Tear into it, I want to see your face when you see it. And for the last time, call me Amelia!" Kai found her warm smile reassuring. Foregoing polite composure, she tore into the paper. With each swipe, more of the violet fabric was revealed. As the iridescent cloth came into the light, Kai's eyes began to sparkle. Lifting the gown from the remains of the paper, she held it high in the air. The tears that had clung to the corners of her eyes now flowed freely down her cheeks in joy. It was beautiful, more beautiful than she could have ever imagined. Holding the dress to her, she spun in a circle, watching as the light bounced off and through the fabric. When she stopped, she rushed to Amelia and threw her arms about her neck.

Her hug was long and warm. When Kai finally released her, she found Amelia in tears as well. Duncan, realizing that he was no longer part of the conversation, stood from the table. Smiling at the joy this had brought to Kai, he left the room to start his morning chores.

"Please sit! I want to hear all about how you made it! It's simply breathtaking. How clever you are to have guessed my favorite color! I never wear it." Kai placed the dress carefully on the end of the table, wiped her face free of tears, and then joined Amelia.

"I didn't need to guess, Duncan told me. He even helped me find the perfect fabric. The ball starts at dusk; I was hoping you would let me help you prepare. I only have boys, and I would love to know what it feels like to prepare a daughter for her coming of age, just once. If you'll allow me?" Kai could barely believe her ears. Amelia had always seemed so cold to her. It was she, after all, that had glared so cruelly across the campfire at her when they were forced from their homes six years ago. To find that the woman cared so much for her left her speechless.

"Of..of course! I would love that, Mrs. Br..I mean, Amelia!" Kai hugged her again. They sat at the table for the better part of an hour discussing what Amelia would need to bring with her when she returned that afternoon, and what Kai would need to do in the meantime. After cementing their plans, Amelia departed with the exchange of one last warm hug. Kai was floating as she laid the dress gingerly on her bed. She had so much to do. After fixing her family a quick and sparse breakfast, she began working down her list. The first was to take a short nap. Amelia had seen the sleepless night on her face and insisted that she get at least two hours of real rest. Kai had thought it would be impossible to sleep after the excitement of the morning but was happily mistaken. Lying in Duncan's bed, she had fallen asleep in seconds. Duncan had to wake her nearly three hours later. Frantic that she was running late, she insisted he cook lunch as she prepared her bath. Amelia arrived as she was drying her hair and the two of them retreated into her rooms almost immediately. Only once did the door open. Amelia emerged to hand Duncan his garment, insisting that he get dressed quickly so that she could inspect him. She then, promptly, disappeared back into Kai's rooms.

When at last it was time for them to leave, Duncan stood uncomfortably in their dining room. Twice he had shouted to them that they would be late if they took any longer. Looking to the door, about to shout again, he watched it open. Through the door, Kai appeared, draped in the iridescent lavender dress. It was off the shoulders, with small capped sleeves. The torso was bodiced and tight, accentuating her new, curvy, adult body. The skirt had a slight flare, but, unlike most of the dresses seen in town of late, was not enormous. The dress fit her slight frame perfectly and her pale skin seemed to glow through the tint she had applied in her bath. Her hair was piled atop her head in a cascade of ebony curls and braids, with a small waterfall of curls trickling down her neck onto her back. Her face was not painted, as Duncan had feared. Amelia had added a slight tint of lavender to her eye lids, accenting the amethyst of her eyes, and a little rose to her cheeks. Kai's lips were the pale pink they carried every day. The only jewelry that she wore were simple feather earrings, dyed the same color as the dress. Duncan staggered. He knew his sister was lovely, but this was more than he had prepared himself for. She was gorgeous, breathtaking. Suddenly, fear over took him. How was he to protect her if she was the center of attention? Kai walked toward him, smiling the way she always did for him.

"Well? Do you like it?" As she spoke, she twirled in place. The skirt that had seemed so simple, flared around her, glimmering in the light of the ending day. Duncan found himself unable to speak. How could he tell her how beautiful she was when he could not bring himself to speak?

"You...you look amazing...beautiful..." His voice trailed off into silence as he looked into her smiling face. He watched as tears of joy began to peek in her eyes.

"No tears! I worked too hard to have you spoil it with tears!" Amelia's voice was proud, as well it should be. She had done her best to help Kai shine. Kai turned to her and gave her a light hug, afraid to ruffle the dress.

"I can't thank you enough, Amelia!" From behind her, Kai heard the front door open. Turning, she watched her father come into the house.

"The carriage is ready, whenever your sister is re..."

Alon's words left him as he caught sight of the woman that was his daughter. Unable to speak, he crossed the room and placed a gentle kiss in her cheek. Turning to Duncan, he said, "Take good care of her." Fighting tears, he bowed to them, tipped his hat to Amelia, and adjourned to his rooms.

"Where are our coats?" Kai asked, as she, Duncan and Amelia made their way to the door.

"We won't need them. I think the six enjoy watching this ball each year, its unnaturally warm tonight." Duncan smiled at his sister. Placing his hand on the small of her back, he led her through the door.

The three people left the house, and Duncan help Kai into the wagon. He offered to drive Amelia home, but she insisted that they go on without her. Duncan climbed into the wagon next to Kai, taking in her beauty one last time, before he hitched the team forward toward the ball. Every young man in town was going to descend on his sister tonight. One of them would surely sway her affections. As he steered the team toward the ball grounds, he fought with the sadness that losing Kai from his daily life would bring him.

CHAPTER 22
THE MATCHMAKER'S BALL

Duncan helped Kai down from the carriage. Extending his elbow, she slid her arm into his and, together, they started down the boardwalk to the pier market. Normally, this area was covered with small, tented carts overflowing with the day's catch. Merchants peddled their fish and other items in the late afternoon light, all over the square. Tonight, you would never know it. All of the small booths and carts had been removed, or hidden from view. Small illuminator lights had been hung from every imaginable place, dangling from the trees like thousands of stars, hung in their low lying branches. They were not just of the pale yellow of Forrenfar either. They were acquired by the women's council, the proprietors of this annual event, years before the mysterious, and alarming, burning of the lift, some sixteen years ago. There was white, blue, aqua, green and pink pale light emanating from the different crystals glowing above their heads. Duncan felt Kai's grip on his arm tighten as she marveled at them. Of course she had read about them, one of the multitude of seemingly useless facts contained in the collection of books she had read over the last few years; but she had never actually seen them. She gazed into the trees, her mouth open a bit in wonder, trying to walk without falling. Duncan looked down at her and laughed a little in his throat. It must have pulled her from her trance, as she looked at him and smiled. They had reached the entrance to the market, transformed, as it was, into an outdoor ballroom.

The older woman at the table asked to see their invitations. As Duncan handed her the envelope in which they had remained in since the day they arrived, the woman commented on how lovely the two of them looked. Duncan watched as Kai blushed, proud of her humility. The woman marked something on a sheet of paper on the table, and fetched two of the many flowers placed next to her in even lines. There were two different colors. Most were white, like the ones she had picked out for Kai and Duncan, but there were also several pink ones. Before Duncan had a chance to ask, the woman began to speak.

"This flower symbolizes that the wearer is looking to meet someone here tonight. When you think you have found someone, and no longer wish to be approached, simply pull the petals off the flower, but leave it pinned to you. If for some reason you do not find anyone, and decide you no longer want to be bothered, though I can't imagine that ever happening, you just remove the flower entirely. If you see someone wearing a pink flower, it means that they are only spectators at this event, either they not old enough to be pursued, or are courting someone and are only here for the festivities. Is everything clear to you?" She looked up from them with a smile. In the course of her explanation, she had pinned one of the small white flowers to Duncan's lapel and to the top edge of Kai's bodice. She stood calmly, waiting for a reply. Finally, Duncan nodded. The woman then bustled out of the way and motioned for them to pass.

The market square was similar to the boardwalk leading up to it. All signs of the daily business and bustle that carried on here were gone, except for the slight aroma of fish clinging persistently to certain areas. The same small illuminator lights decorated this area as well. They hung from the branches of the trees around the outside and in the center of the large market; where there were no tree limbs to speak of, they had been strung up on lines that came together at the top of a pole placed in the center. Around it, several benches and flowering plants had been placed to offset its necessity. And on the far side, was set up a small stage. Musicians were placed there and currently playing music for dancing. Before them, there was a large expanse of floor designated for dancing, where several couples were already engaged in the activity. The pair stood at the bottom of the ramp, taking in the scene. There were already nearly one hundred guests, boys and girls, crowded into small groups. Kai and Duncan stood awkwardly frozen, still linked together with their arms, until the woman who had pinned the flowers touched them on the shoulders.

"Perhaps it would be best if you mingled separately. Siblings tend to off put possible suitors, and we don't want that, now do we?" She gave a small, though somewhat forced, laugh and gently pried the two Merin children apart. "There you go, now, go mingle with anyone but each other. Go on." Her gentle prodding was accompanied by a directional nudge, Kai in one direction, and Duncan in the other. Obediently, they waded into the sea of possible suitors, alone.

Duncan decided, disinterested in the prospect of finding a mate in this sort of environment, that he would take up a post on the far side of the square. With his height far exceeding any of the other boys in attendance so far, he could keep an eye on Kai from there. As he stepped out into the crowd, he found crossing the square more difficult than he had thought. Almost immediately, he found several girls following him, stepping in front of him to ask questions, and touching his arm, trying to tug him onto the dance floor. Smiling politely at each of them, he sidestepped them and gently tugged himself free until he reached the post he had picked out. Undaunted, the young women followed him to his perch, and continuing their chatter. Duncan was only half listening to them as he scanned the sea for Kai. Once he found her, he was surprised he hadn't sooner. She stood out from the rest like a light in the darkness. Her dress shimmered in the light, as did the clips and jeweled pins in her hair, though he didn't remember seeing them at the house. Her dress was quite different from the ones worn by the other girls. Their skirts seemed to have a large ring fastened at the bottom, and as they jostled for position around him, he could feel the rings bumping and rubbing against his ankles. Several times, he had to shift his feet to keep from being knocked over by the pressure of one, or more, of the girls trying too hard to draw near to him.

For quite a long time, he listened as they talked around him. Some tried to talk to him, while others began talking to each other about him. It wasn't until one of them ran her hand down the length of his folded arm, that his focus left Kai. He looked down to find a pretty girl stroking his coat sleeve and muttering something about how lovely it was. For the first time since he had been shown the suit some weeks ago, he looked at it closely. Though he remembered distinctly that it was black, here in the shimmering lights of the tiny illuminators, the suit seemed to course with blue energy. Small strands of reflective blue thread had been worked delicately throughout the fabric into swirled and curvy patterns. In the light, he seemed to glitter a dark blue. At first he felt a bit angry, surely Kai had known and simply chosen not to tell him, but this quickly turned to amusement. He realized that he never would have worn it if he had known, and, all things considered, he kind of liked it. It was subtle. Most of the other young men in attendance wore the most outrageous colors. He could see clearly several in a pale orange, about a dozen in a light blue, approximating the color of the sea he imagined, and a multitude in shades of green ranging from very pale to almost black. By comparison, he felt quite pleased with his attire.

He politely answered the girl's question and tried to pull his arm from her touch, unwittingly opening the flood gates. He had not yet spoken to any of the young women crowded around him, until now. All at once, they began asking him all sorts of questions. Questions like 'What's your name', 'who is your father', 'where are you from', 'are you wealthy', 'what business are you in', and more flooded him from all sides. After his eyes found Kai again, he began politely answering each question he could clearly hear over the din of the others. Kai had also been swarmed by suitors. At first, she seemed to be handling it just fine, but now she looked a bit put out. Duncan watched, helplessly, as she would turn and try to move away only to have her path blocked, once again, by the crowd of young men. Duncan tried to move toward her, to escape his captors in order to free Kai from hers, only to realize that he, too, was trapped.

Question after question he answered while trying to wade through the sea of hooped skirts and inane chatter. As he was about to lose his temper, he watched a young girl wade into the crowd of boys and free Kai. Duncan was far too far away to hear what she had said to the crowd of young men, but as she freed Kai from her mob, the mob seemed not to follow. Looks of disappointment and frustration crossed their faces as they reluctantly found other girls to banter with. Duncan envied Kai at that moment, as he still found himself trapped. Relaxing a bit, now that Kai was freed from captivity, he allowed himself to focus on the flood of questions washing over him from all sides.

Kai held the small girls hand tightly as she led her to freedom. At first, the young men's interest in her was flattering. So many wanted to know so much about her. Each complimented her and fawned over her beauty. She had considered each one as they had made their case to her. While each boy seemed nice and interesting, none seemed to be what she was looking for. She had thought perhaps her standards were too high, and then she saw Duncan. He was watching her, surrounded with girls, as she had been surrounded by boys. For a brief moment, she had been hurt by the image. It was then that she realized Duncan was the standard by which any suitor would forever be measured. He meant the world to her. It was also at that moment that the crowd became a mob. She was no longer interested in the faces that shoved themselves in upon her. She had tried to escape, only to have her attempts thwarted by the very thing she was trying to flee. Very near a panic, she had made eye contact with a slightly younger girl at the food table. Apparently the girl could read the fear on her face, because she set down her plate of food and came rushing over.

Nudging her way into the heap of men she said very loudly, "Ah, dear girl, there you are! I have been looking all over for you! My brother, you know the one you promised to meet here this evening, has just arrived and is simply dying to meet you! Boys, if you don't mind, she is spoken for. Excuse us." With that, the stunned crowd of men parted; and the girl, taking Kai by the hand, pulled her free from the maelstrom that threatened to pull her under. The young one led Kai across the crowded floor to the safety of the distant food table, where she had left her plate. When they finally came to a stop, Kai pulled herself upright and tried to regain her composure. The young girl spoke again. "I've never seen them do that before. I mean, sure, they crowd up a bit sometimes, but that was downright scary. Are you all right, girl?" Kai looked down at the small girl's kind face, unable, just yet, to speak. Sensing this, the girl continued. "My name is Rebecca, though most people just call me Becca. I have a pink flower this year cause I just turned fifteen. My mother, she's one of the women on the council, won't let me wear a white flower till I'm old enough, not that I'd want to. At least this year I'm not serving punch or carrying a tray. That's usually what I have to do at these things. So, what's your name again?" Kai laughed at Becca. Despite her unusually small stature, she had an enormous personality. She seemed to be full of energy and mirth, despite the crowd and her age.

"Kai, Kai Merin. I...well, I want to thank you for what you just did for me. I was beginning to panic. Any longer, and I would have screamed." Becca handed Kai a small glass of punch, which she hurriedly drank and held out for a refill. "So, your mother puts this on each year? Is it always this crowded?" Kai took another, slower, drink from her punch glass as Becca answered.

"Oh no, it's usually a lot more crowded. So many of the older men have gone off to the south with the army. My mother only sent invitations to the boys and girls between the ages of sixteen and twenty, as all the men older would be gone." Once Becca had finished answering Kai's question, she returned to her plate of food.

"How are there so many? We have lived in this town for six years now, and I have never met, nor even seen, most of the people here." Kai reached for a grape dangling from one of the trays set in front of her. Her eyes scanned the sea of unfamiliar faces stretching out before her.

Swallowing her mouth full, Becca replied, "Oh, that's because most of them don't live here. They come from all over, some a hundred miles, just for this. The invitations go all over the whole region." Again, she took a bite. Kai watched as a small drip of orange jelly slipped from the pastry Becca was eating and landed on her dress. Becca looked down at it, scrapped it onto her finger, and promptly licked it off before returning to her food. Kai laughed a little, remembering a time when she would have done the same thing. Just then, a hand landed on her shoulder. Fear struck, she reluctantly turned to face what would surely be one of the men from the crowd who had decided to continue the pursuit. Instead, she found herself looking up into Duncan's handsome face. He had managed to free himself from the sea of girls and, despite their instructions at the start, had found his way to her. Relieved, she took the arm that he extended and followed him onto the dance floor. Together, they danced for several songs. At first they didn't speak, but then they began to recount the harrowing tales of their captivity, comparing war stories. Kai recounted Becca's brave rescue, and Duncan vowed that he owed her a dance for such heroism. They laughed and talked as they moved about the dance floor together, completely unaware of the jealous eyes that watched them from every corner of the market. As he held her, Kai realized how comfortable she felt in his arms. Duncan was strong and smart, kind and brave. He was everything she wanted in a suitor. All at once, she blushed with shame. For a brief second, she had allowed herself to forget that he was her brother and strange feelings had flooded her senses. Her body began to tingle where his hands were resting against her skin, and heat began to spread in odd placed beneath her gown. When she looked into his face again, she saw that he, too, seemed to be disturbed by something. At that moment, as if she willed it, the music stopped. The band was taking a break. Without words, the pair separated. Duncan turned and walked toward the small park that joined the market and Kai hurried back to Becca, who still stood eating next to the table where she had left her. Her face felt as if it was on fire. Reaching the table she grabbed for her punch glass. She drank and refilled it three times before the burning in her cheeks subsided.

"Who was that? He's beautiful! I'm surprised your

flower still had petals! I know that if a man like that asked me to dance, I'd never let him go!" Becca seemed truly amused at Kai's behavior.

Forcing a smile, Kai replied, "That's Duncan, he's my older brother." Becca's face seemed to change a bit, as if she realized something Kai did not.

"Your brother? But you don't look anything alike!" Becca seemed as if she was about to say something else, but Kai cut her off.

"Let's take a walk. Maybe down on the beach?" Kai extended her hand and Becca, tossing her plate aside, took it. Kai had to stop her. She had already said too much. It had always been a fascination of Kai's that she and Duncan shared very few common characteristics; and now, with the feelings she had just subdued fresh on her mind, this was no time to revisit them. She and Becca left the party deck and headed down to the water's edge. Here there were torches lined up along the rock edge, but no illuminator canopy. The stars themselves twinkled over their heads as they walked in the sand chatting about life and childhood. Kai discovered that Becca lived right there in town, though they had never met. She also learned that aside from their opinions on sibling resemblance, they had quite a bit in common. By the end of the evening, when Duncan appeared, without his flower, to fetch Kai for the ride home, they had become fast friends.

Kai and Duncan rode home in an awkward silence. Something had happened to them. There was no laughter, or recounting of suitors. No tales of embarrassing moments or admirations over the decorations and lights were shared. Just still, deafening silence rode between them in the dark of the night. As they arrived home, Alon emerged from the house to welcome them home. He insisted that they tell him all about it. They took turns telling him about the evening. Neither of them mentioned the dance that they had shared, though they both wanted to. When Alon had had his fill of stories, he allowed them to go to bed. They didn't even say goodnight to each other, only exchanging a timid nod and forced smile as they entered their respective rooms. Kai readied for bed afraid that things between her and her brother, the most important person in her life, would be forever strained. She dreaded the morning. Would he be her brother again, or would he be the distant and cold man who had ridden wordlessly home beside her in the carriage?

CHAPTER 23

TRAINING

Duncan fell to the ground. Gritting his teeth against the pain, his hand felt for his lip. As he brushed across it, the warm blood that had begun to flow from the fresh cut oozed onto his bruised knuckles. Garter stood over him, extending his hand to help the fallen fighter to his feet. Both men looked worse for the wear. Duncan had been a man on fire today. He always trained hard, but today was different. He almost seemed to be punishing himself. Over the last four years, Garter had begun to train him in all manner of weapons and combat techniques. When it became obvious to him that Duncan was exceeding his ability to train, he brought Brok into the training sessions. At first, Brok had seemed hesitant to help, after all, he would be sworn to secrecy and would not be allowed to mention it to anyone, even Duncan and Garter in the presence of others. The idea of lying to Alon and Kai, not to mention his wife and children, had seemed like far too high a price. This all changed when he saw Duncan practicing. With all that was going on now, the wall, the invaders, the threat of war, and Kai's true identity, he realized, much as Garter had, that training Duncan was a wise decision, even if it meant keeping it a secret. It had been Brok that had brought in Felix, though it took far less to convince him to keep the secret. Felix loved secrets. He hoarded them like a miser would hoard coins, waiting for the day when their worth would be at its greatest before he traded them for what he needed.

Together, the four men had been meeting like this for nearly two years, during which time Duncan had been trained on every weapon they could find. Today he had chosen to practice hand to hand combat. They had spared many times before, but not like this. Duncan had insisted that he face all three at once. Despite the bloodied lip and the bruises beginning to darken around his middle, Duncan had done a fair job of holding his own. The three men, who at first were holding back, were now fighting him as hard as he was fighting them, and they were losing. Duncan seemed to be in a rage today. Every spill, every punch, seemed to be filled with guilt and anger. After nearly an hour and a half of this self-punishment, the three men had had enough. Deciding to put him down, forcing him to stop for the day, they had come up with a plan. So far they had failed to complete it. Duncan had taken every punch and slid from every hold. Impressed as they were at his prowess, they had decided enough was enough.

As Garter helped the lad up Brok bellowed, "Enough, Merin. You're out to kill yourself, or one of us, and I've had all I shall stand for today. Now, if you'll excuse me,

TRAINING

I'm going to clean myself up before my wife sees me and tells everyone I've been mauled by wolvari." With that, Brok turned and walked away. Felix, who had so far seemed to be enjoying himself, shrugged and joined him in his retreat.

"Where are they going? I can keep fighting, it's not that bad. I'm not ready to stop yet." Duncan looked after the men, who now disappeared into the trees surrounding the hollow they used for training practice.

"Ah, lad, you can continue, but they are done. You have utterly thrashed the three of us. We are not the youngling that you are, not any more. Besides, you keep going like this; and someone, most likely one of us, is likely to get hurt." Duncan reluctantly nodded and freed himself from the support of Garter's hands. Walking to the stump where he left his things, he tossed his shirt aside and reached for the towel. He had started bringing a small bag of medical supplies with him. Kai had found him treating a busted lip nearly a year ago, and he thought he would never hear the end of it. Now he did his best to treat and conceal each small cut and bruise, though today it did not appear he would be successful. Blood rushed from the inside of his lip. Applying more pressure with the towel he turned and sat down on the stump. He watched as Garter picked up the broken, wooden practice weapons they had started out with. For weeks now, Duncan had been trying to convince him to train with real weapons. Today, he was glad Garter had continually said no. In his fury, he might well have seriously hurt someone. No matter how hard he hit, or how hard he was hit, nothing seemed to be enough to punish the guilt and shame eating away at his insides.

Garter returned the shattered tools to his cart and joined Duncan by the stump. "So, you going to tell me what all of this was about?" Duncan stared at Garter, who stared right back.

Looking at the ground, Duncan pulled the blood soaked towel from his lip and mumbled, "I don't know what you mean." His bleeding had slowed. He began to dust himself off, careful not to make eye contact with Garter again.

"Son, anyone who punishes himself the way you just did is definitely feeling something, and it can't be good. If I could keep this a secret for all these years, surely you trust me enough by now to tell me what's eating you up inside? You look like you spit on your mother's grave and hate yourself for it." While the thought of doing such a terrible thing disgusted him, Duncan realized that what he had felt was perhaps just as disturbing. Realizing that Garter was probably the only person he trusted as much as Kai, he gave in.

"It's about Kai."

Garter seemed to tense. "What about Kai? What have you heard?" There was a strange panic in Garter's voice that Duncan didn't understand. Looking up from his pants, Duncan saw Garter trying desperately to conceal his anxiousness.

"At the dance, something ...happened. I'm not sure

what to do about it; and ever since I can't talk to her, can't even look at her, without feeling it all over again." The anguish in Duncan's voice seemed offset by the relief on Garter's face.

Pulling himself back to a serious demeanor, Garter prodded, "What happened? Did you hit someone? Did she?"

"No, nothing like that." Duncan couldn't help but smile a little at the thought of Kai punching each of the boys that had crowded around her.

"Did she kiss someone you don't like? What, boy? What could possibly have happened at a *dance* that has gotten you so riled up?" His question had merit. Girding himself, Duncan began.

"Well, you see, there were all these boys that wanted to court her, and all these girls that wanted to talk to me, but we managed to give them the slip. Then, I asked her to dance and for a while everything was fine, and then...everything changed. For a second, and I mean a split second, I forgot she was my sister. She was just this beautiful girl in my arms and...I...well, it's hard to explain." His eyes filled with shame as he dropped them from Garter's gaze to the ground. Garter stood for a moment in stunned silence, realizing that Duncan had experienced what he and the other men had expected him to discover years ago. Kai was a hauntingly beautiful girl and, armed with the knowledge that she and Duncan were not really brother and sister, the men had guessed that he had to feel attraction towards her. It had not happened yet, at least not so far as they knew, and when they discussed the day it would happen, they never looked at it from Duncan's point of view. They never considered how disturbing it would be to feel that way for someone who, as far as you knew, *was* your sister.

Clearing his throat, Garter did his best to comfort the disturbed young man. "I think it's only natural. I mean at a dance like that, her looking the way I'm sure she did, and with all the confusion and such, it was just a momentary slip of reality that's all. No need to feel so guilty over it. I'm sure it meant nothing and was over in a flash." He patted Duncan on the back, trying his best to cheer his spirits. When Duncan looked up at him again, the tears welling in his eyes told him he had failed.

"That's just it. Now, every time I look at her, I feel it again. I can't stop feeling it. I can't sleep because I see us dancing again, feel her in my arms! I'm a monster!" Duncan let the tears roll. He had not cried since his mother had died, not really. Now he stood, a man of nearly twenty, sobbing like a child into the shoulder of a grown man who was not his father. Garter felt almost like panicking. He knew that Duncan had nothing to feel guilty about, but he couldn't tell him. He was forbidden from saying even one word. Slowly, it seemed to him that he could lead Duncan to the conclusion without breaking his oath to Brannon. In his head, he chose the words carefully.

"You know, I grew up with a boy who kinda had the same thing happen. He felt really bad about it too, nearly killed himself over it. Then his parents told him a secret, something they hadn't told anyone. His sister wasn't really his sister." Duncan's head shot up from Garter's shoulder.

"What? What's that got to do with me?" Garter could hear the anger starting to rise in Duncan's voice. Despite his disgust at himself, he still loved Kai. She was his sister, and that was all he knew for sure in this world.

"Well, you know, it's just that Kai doesn't really look anything like you, or your parents. Just something to think about, maybe..." Garter's voice trailed off as he saw the anger in Duncan's eyes grow red hot. He had crossed the line. No matter how angry or ashamed Duncan might be about his feelings toward his sister, she WAS his sister. Realizing he had gone too far, Garter took a step back. "Sorry, I was just trying to help. I thought that maybe thinking she wasn't your sister might make you feel better. I guess I was wrong."

"Yes, you were. I think we're done for today. In fact, I think we might be done for a while. I'll let you know the next time I feel like training." With that, Duncan grabbed his gear and turned, headed for where Shadow was grazing in the tree line. He did not say goodbye, he didn't even look back. Climbing onto Shadow's awkward saddle, he ordered the equinox into a full run toward home. Garter stood for a moment, watching as the disturbed young man disappeared into the distance. He decided that it was time Alon told the boy the truth, before it ripped him apart on the inside. In two days' time, he would be delivering her annual gift. Now that he had burned his bridge with Duncan, possibly forever, that would be his only viable way into the Merin household. He would get Alon alone and convince him, force him if need be, to tell his son the truth, before it was too late.

CHAPTER 24
THROUGH

Rikard moved through the soldiers training in the streets. As he walked past the sparring pairs and weapons training areas, he saw his people as they once were. When he had set out across the ocean, they had been strong, tough and full of rage and desire. Years here in this place of fruit and ale had left them fat and content, but he had fixed that. He was ready, they were ready, it only needed to happen. For nearly two months now, he had called this dark and abused city home. The City of Beasts, once strong and bright, was now filled with gloom and danger. Soon the wall would open, and his people would flood into Forrenfar, like a dam giving way to a lake of blood. But until then, they would train, and the slaves would dig. He had ordered slaves sent from the other three cities digging tunnels, after the rebels had managed to free nearly all of the slaves digging here. Only the extremely old and infirm were left behind, though he was sure it was not their intention to leave anyone. In his rage, those slaves left were made to suffer. Tortured, not for information, but for spite. His rage had to be used for something; and Tawni would not allow him to kill Karnus, though he had desperately wanted to. Any man who fails as soundly as Karnus, deserved to die a most horrid death. Now he was a reminder to all the other soldiers just how cruel Rikard could be. Karnus had been left, after Rikard had arrived to find the tunnel collapsed, with several broken ribs, which healed, and a shattered arm, which didn't. His right arm now hung lifelessly at his side, strapped to his torso, for all the world to see. He had learned to wield a blade with his left hand and, gimped as he was, could best almost any man in Rikard's army. This seemed to enrage Rikard even more, though no further harm would come to Karnus.

With the last remaining slaves tortured into oblivion, and only a few coming from the other districts to replace the ones he had lost, Rikard began a tour of his new lands. He was surprised and disappointed to see that the other cities were nowhere near the tunnel depth that Forrenfar had been. While the City of Beasts needed help to regain its former progress, the others were only just over half way through. Again, Karnus presented evidence that he was far better than Rikard wanted to admit. It was then that he decided Forrenfar was his next target, at any cost. Ordering all but a few slaves to the City of Beasts, digging there would resume at breakneck speed. For nearly six years, he had waited for word that they were close to completion. When it came, he had sounded the rally call for war. He had come here, along with every soldier that his new kingdom could spare, training for the moment it would finally begin again. Part of him missed his throne room, with its colored glass windows and its strange crystal lights. Those types of things were nowhere to be found here; his people had destroyed nearly everything in their conquest. But within him, the fire of Hadriah began to burn again. He, too, began training. His strength had not left him, in fact, to most he seemed to have grown more intimidating over the last decade and a half. Tawni was his only joy. She had come with him and spent every night in his bed, relieving the tension of the previous day and brightening his hopes for the next.

He leaned against the ruined pedestal, of what he was sure had been one of the animal statues, to watch two soldiers engaging in sword play. He watched as their feet and bodies moved in reaction to one another. Swing after swing, they circled one another, waiting for their moment. Lost in thought, he did not hear the sound of the horn. The sound he had not heard since the return of the men in the boat, so long ago. Now, he barely remembered the noise. Only when the men he was watching stopped their dance and stood straight, did he hear it. A clear blast echoed through the soot covered buildings and empty streets. Running like hell was at his heels, Rikard leaped every fence and crashed through every obstacle to reach the mouth of the tunnel. There, he found Karnus' replacement, Malek, a strong, if somewhat conceited man, waiting for him. On his face, he bore a twisted smile.

"My lord, we are almost through. There are cracks where light can be seen, and the rush of fresh air fills the tunnel." He bowed low as he spoke, but Rikard paid him no mind. Striding past him, Rikard ventured into the mouth of the tunnel. From the darkness ahead, a seemingly never-ending blackness, tiny specks of light began to grow. At first, he through them to be glow bugs, a new discovery in this land; but upon closer inspection, he could see the forms of tiny people holding the lights. They were torches. Realizing just how long this tunnel was, and how tall it had been made to accommodate even their largest siege machine, a new understanding for the time it had taken came to him. As the slaves and guards came closer into view, he turned to the Brakbark still holding his ridiculous bow.

"Gather the men, and prepare for battle. We go now." Rikard began to walk away when the man spoke again.

"My lord, it is late afternoon. Even if they were prepared to march now, it would be nearly night fall before we broke through. Perhaps we should wait for morning?" The man's voice showed weakness. Any other day might have seen his head crushed in Rikard's hands, but today was far too important, and it was slipping away from him by the second.

"Not if we use the vehicles. Besides, I do not intend to wait for the rebels to try another collapse, do you?" With that, Rikard turned and disappeared among the buildings. All was chaos in the streets. Men were packing the war machines and sharpening their weapons. The poison on their blades had not been refreshed in a decade, but before Rikard could order a batch made, a large barrel came into view. Carried by two men, and followed by his queen, the barrel was being paraded through the bustling streets. As the men set it down, he drew nearer to them. The soldiers on either side would rush over and dip their swords and daggers into the barrel, withdrawing them coated in the rust red concoction. Then the barrel would be lifted and moved forward again. Reaching the barrel, he looked in and sniffed the tar like red substance it held. Convinced that it was indeed their poison, he looked to Tawni with questions in his eyes. She merely smiled at him.

"My lord, it is the least I can do to contribute to our war, now that you will not allow me to fight. Your armor is ready for you. I will be waiting at the tunnel; there are many more blades that need to be made deadly between here and there." As she finished, she made to move past him and continue on in the same fashion. As she drew beside him, he seized her. Drawing her into him, he kissed her. Long and passionate, it was the first time he had shown her any type of affection in front of his men. After nearly a minute, he drew his mouth from hers. Gazing at her for a moment, his eyes told her all she needed to know. She smiled sweetly at him and brushed her hand across his cheek. Lowering her back to the ground, he released her. She immediately returned to her trek through the frantic streets. Rikard stood and watched her until she rounded a corner out of sight, then he, too, went back to his own devices.

He found his armor waiting for him in the house they

were using for their own. He strapped it onto his body, piece by piece, counting the seconds until he would break through the wall and continue his purpose. The only piece left was his helmet. It was not the one he had worn so many years ago. That one had been destroyed in a cave-in as he crashed through a building on his way to the castle gates. This new one bore atop it a crown, shaped from the helm itself. The peaks were dipped in the poison Tawni now couriered through the streets, and the face guard bore his likeness. For a moment he stood and stared at himself. Deciding that he did not need it yet, nor did he really like it; he left for the tunnel, the helm riding under his arm. Tawni must have ordered it made, though he was not sure why. He was nigh indestructible, with skin like stone wrapped in steel. The armor was to make him look more like one of his soldiers; perhaps that was the purpose of the helm as well, though seeing his face etched into the metal of the mask disturbed him.

At the tunnel, he found machine after machine loaded with soldiers and ready to go. His men and women seemed eager to fight with him once again. Giving the order, the machines started down the long dark of the passage. It was dank inside the lead machine carrying him and his queen, despite his best attempt at ordering her to stay. The light of one illuminator was all they had. The sounds of stones falling onto the top of the machine and the crunch of tools and loose rocks crushed beneath its tracks was all they could hear for nearly an hour, then they came to a halt. A small hatch opened at the top. The head of Tomlen, Rikard's driver, popped through. He was covered in dirt; and in the dim light, Rikard could see blood oozing from under the side of his helmet.

"What has happened?" Rikard could not contain his concern, not for Tomlen, but for the tunnel. He feared that some other force had blocked their path or caused yet another cave in.

"My lord?" Tomlen looked puzzled for a second, then, raising his hand to the rivulet of blood flowing down the side of his face, he seemed to understand. "Oh this, it's nothing, my King, just some falling rocks. We have reached the end, sire. They are about to break through. I thought you might like to know." He waited for Rikard to nod, then lifted back through the opening. No sooner it was closed, than the sound of a great crash was heard from ahead of them. The ground beneath the behemoth that held them shook, and the rain of debris on the roof sounded like the hail that would accompany a particularly vicious storm off the sea. When it was all over, Tomlen's head appeared through the hatch once again. He looked even worse than before; and from the way he held his shoulder and arm, Rikard reasoned it was most likely broken.

"We are through, my lord." With that, he disappeared again, closing the hatch behind him. A second later, they were moving again. The ground they rolled over now was much less even and cleared. The great machine rocked and rattled over the new stones and boulders in their path. Then it was over. Light flooded in through the slits in the sides, and fresh air rushed in from everywhere. It smelled cold and clean. Once stopped, the great doors opened wide, allowing Rikard to exit. Though he could not stop his bride from coming through the tunnel, he did prevent her from leaving the machine. Ordering Tomlen to close the door, he sealed her inside until he knew she would be safe.

Around him, hundreds of his men flooded from the machines that had been behind him. They now formed into ranks behind him, the carriers spilling their bellies full of soldiers on the ground. Rikard looked around. For the first time in his life, he was seeing Forrenfar. He was facing a great forest. Trees, tall as mountains, stood like a wall before him. His machines could roll over the small and fragile fruit trees of Lylunir, but these were different. He would be forced to stick to the roads here. Around him were the remnants of what had been a town. Empty store fronts and merchant stalls stood decaying on all sides. As he studied them, he decided they had been abandoned some years ago, probably in fear of this very day. So they did know he was coming.

No sooner had he decided that this was the case, than a shout came from the front line. Wading through his men, he found his way to the head of the crowd. There at the edge of the trees, blocking the wide stone paved road on which he stood, were man-made barricades. Behind them movement could be seen. The thirst for battle and victory welled up inside him. He would show these Forrenfar soldiers what it meant to stand against him.

THROUGH

Giving a cry, he placed his helm on his head and drew his blade. Looking at the men flanking him, he took several steps forward. They followed. His pace quickened, and then theirs. Soon he was running, head long into the barricaded army, his men at his heels, all screaming and shouting for battle and blood.

CHAPTER 25

DORMANT NO LONGER

The knock on the door nearly made her drop the heavy pan in her fingers. Carefully, she placed in on the cool side of the fire and turned to answer the door. The gloom of the Merin household had become suffocating, and Kai had hoped that a blackberry pie, her mother's favorite, might ease the cloud that had settled over them. It had been nearly a week since she and Duncan had said more than hello to each other, and it was killing her. She knew why it had been strained, the feelings that still rose in her when he would enter the room were unnatural and foul. She wanted to talk to him about it, clear the air. She thought maybe if she told him and they got it out in the open and reasoned their way through it, like they had every problem in the past, this one would go away as the others had. Sadly, it was clear that Duncan was not interested in discussing this issue, or any other, with her. His face filled with sorrow each time he would run into her. A brief smile, then sadness, then he would make a hasty retreat. Even now he was out in the cold of the barn, doing whatever small chore he could find to prevent him from coming back into the house where she was.

Alon had been of little comfort. Neither of them could tell him of the horrible moment on the dance floor when everything in their lives went sideways into disgust and shame. He had watched them ignore and avoid each other for nearly a week now and had said nothing, not even to ask what was wrong. As she passed his door on the way to the front, he emerged from his room, summoned by the same sound. As he stepped into the dining room, his face brightened at the smell wafting in from the kitchen. Kai could almost hear him drooling as she passed him.

"I'll get the door, don't worry. Oh, and don't touch that pie. It needs to set for a while before it's ready to cut." She did not wait for his reply as she passed into the sitting room and around the chairs to the door. Alon, disappointed at his denial of pie, followed her. Opening the door, she found that Duncan had already come to greet the men standing outside. Between them, she saw the chest and barrel that marked her birthday gift. The four men were deep in discussion as she swung the door wide. Trying hard not to make eye contact with Duncan, she said, "Come in, come in! I have a pie cooling right now, though I didn't expect you until tomorrow. It's come early this year, strange..."

As the men moved past her into the room, Brok spoke, "Surprised us, too. It seems that the tunnel into Lylunir opened yesterday. Brannon has a war to fight now." His voice was solemn and calm, but his face showed real concern. The arrival of the long awaited invaders had come either too soon or too late for his liking.

"Then why have the three of you not left for the wall? Or Antlerbrooke, at least? I would think he needs every soldier he has right now." Alon's voice was weak and shaky as he spoke. He was old, but not beyond fighting years. Kai realized that as he spoke, he must have realized that he, too, could be called to fight.

"What should we do?" Kai asked the question instinctively. She knew that they stood in this room, in this house, in this part of Forrenfar, because of the threat of this event, but she still felt that they could do something.

"You will do nothing, but I think I should go." Duncan's voice was cold and precise. He had been looking for a reason to escape the torment of Kai's beautiful eyes searching him every time he happened upon her, and this was it.

"Sorry, Duncan, we have our orders. We are to protect you and Kai, which means you both stay here. Besides, there are thousands of men already there to fight. It will probably end quickly anyway." Garter forced a laugh as he finished his statement, but everyone in the room knew it to be a lie. Whoever, and whatever, these invaders were, it was clear they were determined and strong. To have tunneled thought the wall was an amazing feat by any reckoning.

"But I can fight!" Duncan's voice was becoming

more intense and urgent with every word. "I can't just stay here and hope that everything works out for the best, that we'll be safe. What about the other people, the people of Gatewood? What about them? Are they going to just sit tight and hope everything works out as the men fight and die right outside their homes?" Duncan's passion flooded his words and Kai had to fight the desire to go to him, to wrap him in a hug for his bravery. Despite all that had happened, he was still the bravest and most noble man she had ever known; and she loved him for it. Duncan's glance fell on Kai. Seeing the tears of admiration and love in her eyes, he felt the feeling rise inside him. Quickly, he broke their gaze. Kai's eyes fell to the floor, too. Perhaps it had been foolish to hope that this would be the thing that brought them back together.

"Orders are orders, lad, and don't worry about Gatewood. It was evacuated, you know that! Just days after we did, no one is left there but soldiers. Besides, you are not quite of age. You have three months till you turn twenty, then you are no longer ours to protect. If you want to run off and fight then, so be it." Kai gasped at the thought, but Duncan responded with force.

"By then, it might be over!" His voice was growing frantic now, filled with anger and desire.

"We can only hope." was all Alon could contribute. For a long while the six of them stood in silence, looking from one to another. Finally, Garter, realizing that this was not over for Duncan, and that distraction was his only course for delaying the foolish decision no doubt rolling around in his head as they spoke, bent down and lifted his side of the chest. Brok, the other part of this task, followed suit. Carrying the heavy box into the dining room, they placed it on the table. Everyone had followed them, leaving the barrel in the sitting room. Once in the dining room, the smell of the pie was intoxicating. Even Duncan began to sniff the heavenly aroma from the air.

After a few more moments of awkward silence, Felix was the first to chime in, "Can we please eat that pie? Its smell is driving me mad!" His lighthearted efforts paid off. The room seemed to erupt in chatter and laughter, and for a while, all that mattered was pie. Kai made some small finger foods and added a few bottles of wine to the pie to make it a meal. Together at the other end of the table, they sat and discussed everything from the invaders to the weather, keeping a firm grasp on the tone of the discussion, lest it again get too serious. When the pie was gone, and the wine drained, Garter rose from his seat, and excused himself for some fresh air. As he made to leave, he invited Alon to join him, pulling the corner of a spirits bottle from his inside coat pocket into view. Alon hastily agreed and joined his friend for a short stroll in the cold.

Once out of the house, Garter began what he had intended to do. Clearing his throat, he turned to Alon and said, "Alon, you know how me and my family feel about you and your kids right? I mean, I love them like they were my own." Alon's face changed. He realized that he had been lured outside and now it was too late to avoid whatever assault he was about to endure. Looking away from Alon's dejected expression, Garter continued. "It's just that, well, there's some things you need to know. For starters, and don't be mad, We've, that is to say, I've been training him for combat, with weapons and the like." Garter paused, anticipating the fury of screams that did not come. Alon's face was washed with anger and dismay, but he remained silent. "He's really good, Alon, best I've ever seen. Strong, too. Just the other day, he took all three of us in hand to hand, it was really something! You would..." Alon's face had begun to turn a terrible shade of red. Garter knew that his time was growing very short now so he halted the one thought and moved on to the next. "And then there's Kai."

Alon could hold his tongue no longer. "DON"T TELL ME YOU'VE BEEN TRAINING HER, TOO?!?" Garter staggered at the forceful rage in Alon's voice. It was bad enough he was teaching his son to fight, but his daughter as well?

"No, no, no! I would never do that! Give me a little credit! ...though it might not be such a bad idea now, things being the way they are..." Realizing he was in eminent danger of getting punched, he again abandoned his thought and switched to another. "No, it's not that, it's how they are starting to feel about each other. That dance, it damaged them." Alon looked truly stunned. The surprise of this cryptic information momentarily pushed the image of his son swinging a sword in battle from his mind and replaced it with images of the two of them dancing. As Garter stood watching, his face changed from one emotion to another, Until Alon slowly came around to the terrible truth Garter had led him towards.

"You mean they...they have *those* feelings? That's impossible, they are brother and sister!" Garter's eyes widened. Surely, Alon had not been pretending for so long that he believed his own lies now.

"You know as well as I that they are not. And they need to know it too! Now, before the feelings they have tear them apart forever, if it's not too late already!" Garter watched Alon's face. At first, he thought the old man would agree with him, that he would nod and return to the house to tell them this instant, then his face hardened.

"I won't. I can't! They are my children, Maga's children! I won't destroy this family for some passing fancy at a ridiculous dance! It will pass, and everything will be as it was." Alon's voice was weak and shaky. His hands had begun to tremble with a mixture of fear and anger.

"She's going to learn soon enough if her Shantir becomes active! You need to tell her now so that she can be trained to use it! She was never meant to stay here forever, she was always meant to take her place in Lylunir, to be a part of this war! You were only meant to keep her secret and safe until she was ready! The time has com..." Garter did not get to finish. Alon's fist found its mark along the side of his face. He staggered back, stunned at the power behind the punch. He had almost regained his bearings when another wild right caught him in the jaw. Losing his balance completely, Garter fell backward onto the ground. Alon took several steps towards the stunned and bleeding man.

"Stay away from my family! Don't ever come around here! NOT EVER AGAIN!" Alon stood panting over him for a few seconds, then turned on his heels and headed with some speed back toward his door. As he pulled it closed behind him, he heard the voices of his son and adopted daughter mingled with those of the other men in the dining room. Fearing that these men were of the same mind as Garter, he stormed into the dining room, uttered some very impolite things to the gentlemen sitting around his table and demanded, in no uncertain terms, that they leave immediately. Before he could see the confusion and indignation on their faces, he turned, entered his room, and slammed the door, hard, behind him.

Felix and Brok, utterly confused and incensed by the strange turn in Alon, said their hasty farewells and departed, retrieving Garter from the ground outside as they left. Behind them, Kai and Duncan stood in their wake, confounded as to what just happened and unable to speak to one another to confer on the shocking turn of events. Kai stared at Duncan for a few moments, hoping he would speak with her. When he didn't so much as look at her, she gathered the plates and glasses from what had been a happy meal and carried them to the kitchen to clean. Duncan stood staring at his father's door, wondering what Garter had told him to make him so angry, wondering if he now knew that he had been training for battle, or that he had felt those terrible feelings about Kai, or both. Deciding that he had to know, he pounded loudly on Alon's door. When he did not answer, he knocked again, more forcefully. Finally, he decided to kick the door down if that was what it took. After the second frame rattling attempt, Alon pulled the splintering door open. Duncan stood in the door way, breathing heavily, staring down at him. Alon had never really noticed how tall Duncan had become. He gazed at his son, now some six inches taller than he and much more strongly built. In his face and features he saw himself and Maga. Every inch of Duncan told the story of their love, and his loss.

"What was that? They are our friends! How could you say those things to them?" Duncan was angry, and Alon knew it. His anger rose in kind. He had just as much, if not more, of a right as Duncan to be angry; after all, it was he that had been deceived for the last few years by Duncan's secret hobby.

"How could you train behind my back! All these years I have tried to protect you from violence, and you go looking for it!" Alon was now matching the tone and volume of Duncan. They stood facing each other, in the doorway to his rooms, fully engaged in their argument.

"What else was I supposed to do? Brannon sent us those weapons; oh yes, I know about the weapons, for us to train and learn how to use them! Mother said I had to protect Kai, and that's what I intend to do!" Duncan was not really thinking any more. His anger and frustration at his father's years of uselessness came flooding forward and everything he had wanted to say for so long jostled in his mind to be next to spring from his lips. "How dare you question my decisions! I kept this family going! I made our money and took care of our farm while you hid in your rooms and drank away mother's memory. If she were alive to see this, she would probably hate you, what you became, what you still are!" Duncan's words did more harm than he expected. For all his pride and anger, Alon was no match for the painful truth springing from his son's heated heart. Alon staggered, trying desperately to bring the argument back into his court, to regain his footing before he fell into disgrace and retreated again to the rooms behind him, lost.

"I'm not the one playing house with his sister!" This blow was far lower than Alon had intended. He knew from Garter that these feelings had been tearing Duncan apart, and as the sentence rolled from his lips, he watched it wash over his son. Like a wave of acid, it seemed to eat him up and leave him destroyed. Duncan turned from his father and leaned on the table behind him. For a long time, neither of them spoke. "Son, I...I didn't mean...it's just..." Alon could not finish his statement. He had done far more damage than he had intended. "What can I do?" He took a step closer to his son, reached for his shoulder, and then pulled his hand back.

"Marry her off." Duncan's voice was cold and distant, as his head hung from his shoulders.

"What?" Alon could not contain his shock. This was not at all what he had expected.

"Find someone for her to marry and have it done with. Then she will be safe and out of my house. I won't have to worry with her any more, and I can get on with my life. It's all I can think to do. Her being here, seeing her, it's killing me. It's the only way." Duncan did not look up, nor did he turn. Alon stood, immobilized by the command of his son, realizing only too late how right Garter had been, and how desperate things had become. Before he could respond, the kitchen door flew open.

Kai, who had been in the other room clearing away the dishes, could not help but hear them. At first, the argument seemed to have little to do with her directly, so she had decided to let them fight it out. Shouting or no, they were talking, seriously, about things that had been festering for years. It wasn't until Duncan declared his desire to be rid of her that the argument had forced her to act. She stood, enraged, in the kitchen door, glaring from one face to the other. Duncan looked as if he was a boy, found with his hand in the cookie jar and crumbs all over his face. Her father looked sad and helpless. She stomped into the room, still looking from one man to the next, unable to decide if she would scream, yell, or simply hit both of them. Finally, tears building up in the corners of her eyes, she took off running for the door. Duncan followed after her, trying to somehow take back what he had said, but it was no use. He watched as she ran to the barn, emerging a minute later riding bareback on Whisper. For a moment she stopped, staring through her tears at the two men in the yard. Her violet eyes lingered longest on Duncan, the most important person in her world, her brother and friend, the man who had just betrayed her. Pulling Whisper's reins, she turned the equinox toward the forest and jolted into a run. Duncan watched helplessly as she disappeared into the trees in the dimming light of late afternoon.

CHAPTER 26
SHANTIR OF LIGHT AND SHADOW

Whisper carried Kai swiftly, deep into the forest. Usually Kai spoke to her, telling her about the goings on at the farm and sharing her dreams, but not today. Kai sat atop Whisper's bare back and wept, her face buried in her mane, her arms wrapped firmly around her neck. Whisper carried her farther into the forest than they would normally go this late in the afternoon. After nearly an hour of running flat out, dodging trees and brush, Whisper slower her pace. Kai lifted her head, her eyes red and puffy from sobbing for so long. As they walked on into the darkening woods, Kai began to share her woes with her companion. Whisper listened, snorting or jerking her head from time to time in agreement or acknowledgment. Sometimes Kai forgot that she was no ordinary horse, that she was far more intelligent and had lived for many years before coming to her. As they rode on, Kai began to regret fleeing as she had. She should have stood her ground, made her own mark on their argument. But she had fled. Her emotions had overwhelmed any semblance of a logical and calm argument she might have mounted, leaving her a throbbing mass of raw nerves.

In silence, she sat atop her companion as she drifted through the sea of trees in the fading light. Realizing how dark it had become, and how far they had to go to get back to the house, she asked Whisper to turn around. They horse began making a very wide left. At first, Kai didn't understand why she simply didn't turn around immediately, until she heard the rush of water. Whisper was in need of a drink. Kai smiled at the head strong animal as she made her way toward the sounds of a stream somewhere beyond the trees. As Kai moved with the motion of her steed, she began to drift in and out of sleep. Leaned against Whisper's strong neck, the emotional strain of the afternoon seemed to suck the life right out of her.

As she was about to drift off completely, Kai was jolted awake by Whisper rearing into the air. Without a saddle, she nearly slid right off her hind end. Frantically she dug her fingers into Whisper's mane, pulling the hair fiercely, trying to stay atop the great animal. Suddenly, she saw it. A pheasant had darted from within the bush directly in Whisper's path. The bird now seemed to hang in midair, flapping its wings wildly in Whisper's face. Kai clung to the beast for dear life, but there seemed to be no end in sight for this confrontation. Whisper kicked at the bird, panicking with every miss. The bird answered in kind with more frenzied flapping and pecking. Kai, having been so close to sleep, and then jerked back so suddenly, was in a full blown panic attack. She clenched her eyes shut tightly, and tried desperately to hold on. Opening them again, she wished with all her heart that the bird would disappear, vanish as if it never existed.

Instantly, and out of nowhere, a spear of pure light coursed through the air. As it impacted the bird, there was a loud crack, like lightning, only it wasn't followed by thunder. Instead, the bird burst, momentarily, into flames and then rained down upon the ground as ash. Kai witnessed the event, that took less than a second, with awe and amazement. For a split second, her grip on Whisper's hair relaxed and she began to slide off the still reared animal's haunches. Snapped out of her daze, she tried to regain her grip, but it was too late. Slipping from her perch, she fell through the air to the ground, a considerable distance, what with Whisper's unnatural size. As her legs and back came down on the rocky ground, her head kicked back, hard, striking the exposed corner of a boulder buried in the earth. Her eyes blinked for a moment, and then closed. With Kai lost to unconsciousness, and the bird no longer a threat, Whisper calmed herself. She moved around beside Kai's limp body and nuzzled her face with her nose, but nothing happened. Pawing at the ground, she tried again, nudging her shoulder and side, trying to rouse her fallen rider. The snap of a twig brought Whisper's head up quickly. Looking around, she caught a glimpse of a man. He was running away at great speed just beyond the creek that had been her goal. Realizing the man was not coming to her aid, Whisper set out as fast as her long slender legs could carry her, back to her farm, back to the people who would care that Kai lay injured in the middle of nowhere.

Duncan fastened his pack tightly. It was quite a journey back to Gatewood, more so if you intended to leave at night, especially if he had to convince Shadow it was the right thing to do. In spite of all Shadow was and meant to him, sometimes, like now, he wished he was simply a horse. He dreaded having to explain himself to his steed and beg him to agree to go with him. If all else failed, he decided he would take a wagon horse, though he wanted desperately for Shadow to agree. After Kai had stormed off, Duncan had realized that he had truly hurt her. He decided that this bridge, that had been so strong for so many years, had fallen down around his ears. After Kai had ridden into the forest, Alon had sighed and sulked back into his cave, leaving Duncan alone to deal with his guilt and remorse. It was then that he had decided to leave. He would go join the fight. Kai was better off without him, especially now. Soon she would move on, and he...well, he would have other things to worry about for a time. He knew in his heart he would never be able to really move on from that moment, when her eyes had filled with tears and she looked away from him in pain.

Throwing the pack over his shoulder, he left his home. As he moved down the hill to the barn, he caught sight of movement in the tree line. Seconds later Whisper could be seen, bolting through the field as if chased by death itself. Duncan stood frozen for a moment as he scanned Whisper for a rider and found none. Two had left, and only one returned. He watched as the horse turned and bolted into the barn. Dropping his pack, he, too, ran for the barn. As he turned into the door, he found both horses trying desperately to bash open Shadow's stall door. The sweat around Whisper's neck and shoulders had turned into a thick foam. He knew that she had run quite some distance, and at an unreasonable pace, to arrive here, meaning only one thing, something had happened to Kai.

As he ran up to her, she kicked wildly at the bolt keeping Shadow pinned. Reaching for her mane, Duncan tried to calm the mad beast. After several attempts, he managed to bring her down a bit. She looked down at him, and he could see the panic scrawled inside her blue eyes. "Kai?" was all Duncan had to say. Whisper began throwing her head up and down frantically. Duncan needed no other motivation. Flinging open what was left of the door to Shadow's stall, he swung himself onto the steed's back as he bolted after Whisper. Following the riderless horse, Duncan and Shadow weaved through the forest toward what was surely a tragic scene. Duncan fought the fear that she was dead, clinging to the hope that it was nothing more than a twisted ankle or an injured animal she could not bear to leave, though neither of these explained the insanity in Whisper's eyes in the barn. As Whisper found her way back to where she had left Kai lying on the ground, Duncan came in sight of her. Unable to control the fear inside him, he slid from Shadow's back. Hitting the ground hard, he found his balance and ran to his sister's side. The blood in her hair, and covering the rock beneath her head, told him all that mattered. Checking her chest, he heard the weak thump of her heart beat and felt the shallow rise and fall of her breathing. Whisper nuzzled her again. Duncan placed his hand on her nose and nudged her back as he lifted Kai's unconscious body into the air. Shadow lowered his body to the rocky ground and Whisper, using her head, helped Duncan seat himself aboard his steed. Once Shadow had righted himself, the four set out for home at a slow pace, careful not to do any more harm to the small body draped across Duncan's arms. In an instant, any thoughts of leaving home, or continuing to avoid Kai, disappeared, vanished, like the bird whose charred feathers were all that remained to say it had ever existed.

Reaching the house well after dark, Duncan carried Kai quickly inside. Despite the late hour, Alon, who had been roused by Duncan's calls for help, made haste for the Felix house. Sarah, Felix's wife, was a healer of some skill, and she would never refuse his call where Kai was concerned, not after losing her mother so tragically on the trek to Darksand six years ago. He returned, nearly an hour later, with Sarah, and the entire Felix clan. They set about preparing the house for their stay, as she never left a patient that was not well alone. She cleaned Kai's wound, and checked her head and neck for any sighs of a break, finding none. Then she set about checking her other bones, finding nothing more than some bruises and a few scrapes from her spill. After several hours she emerged from Kai's bedroom with a grim face.

"I have done all I can. She seems to be sleeping, though I wouldn't really call it that, as she can't be roused. She has quite the bump on her head, and I'd imagine that it knocked her pretty good. She may be out like this for several hours, or even days." Duncan's worried gaze fell on her, and she could not bear to deceive him by omission. "You should know that head injuries like this one are tricky. Sometimes, they wake up just fine, others, their memory or personality aren't what they used to be, and sometimes...well sometimes they don't wake up at all." Her face was grim as she fell silent. Walking past the stunned Duncan, she placed a comforting hand on his shoulder. Looking at her family, she said, "Go home, I'll stay." Her husband and sons nodded and, after sharing their grief and prayers with Alon, slipped out the door and back to town. "I'll stay in the room with her. Can you help pull one of those chairs in for me?" Duncan did not seem to hear her. His eyes were fixed on the door between Kai and him. She squeezed his shoulder slightly, and readied herself to repeat her request, when he spoke.

"I'll stay with her. You can have my room." Duncan's eyes were red, as if he had been crying, but she knew he hadn't. At first she thought to protest, but decided that he would fetch her if anything happened.

Nodding, she retrieved her bag and closed Duncan's door behind her. Alon stood for a moment watching Duncan stare at Kai's door. As he was about to turn and leave, he heard Duncan mumble something. Stopping, he turned. Duncan repeated himself, only louder this time. "It's all my fault. If I hadn't said those things about her getting married, she wouldn't have run off. All of this is my fault." Alon moved to comfort his son, but before he could place his hands on Duncan's slouched shoulders, the boy stood. He didn't turn, or even acknowledge his father, but walked to the door, opened it, and then closed it behind him. Alon stood alone, and cold, in Kai's outer room for a moment before slinking away to his own rooms for the night.

At some point during the night Duncan retrieved one of Kai's chairs. Once brought into the room, he did not leave it, save to bathe and use the privy, for three days. Day and night, he sat by her side. He held her hand and talked softly to her. He apologized to her over and over again. When that did not seem to rouse her, he told her of the training sessions, and the weapons he had learned to use. He told her of his dreams, and how he wished he could help defend Forrenfar. He even confessed to the strange feelings he had experienced on the dance floor, as he held her in his arms. With each confession, he felt lighter. The feelings seemed like such a small meaningless thing now, brought on by the night, and lights, and the strangers. It all seemed so silly now, as he held her small hand and prayed for her to wake up.

Despite how much better the discussions made him feel, nothing seemed to rouse Kai.

At the start of the third day, things even seemed to get worse. Early that morning she had begun to writhe in her bed. It wasn't long before she began to moan and cry out in her sleep as well. Duncan soon realized that the nightmare she had escaped so many years ago had come back for her, and now she had no escape. She would not wake before the yellow-eyed man's sword plunged all the way through her. As the nightmare grew steadily worse, she began to scream. At first they were just sounds, but after some time they became words, and then phrases. He listened, helplessly, as she pleaded for the life of their friends and family, as she begged for his life to be spared, as she wished for her own life to end. When he could take no more, Duncan bent low, his lips nearly touching her ear, and began to whisper to her. He repeated over and over that he was there, with her, and that he would never leave her, never let anything happen to her. Slowly, she seemed to calm. The nightmare subsided, so long as Duncan kept a firm grip on her hand.

On the fourth day, as if by some miracle, Kai's eyes batted open as the morning sun peeked through her window. Her head hurt terribly, and her body felt heavy and sore. As she moved in her covers, she felt Duncan's hand grasped firmly around hers. Looking down, she saw him. He was sitting on the edge of a chair, pulled close to the bed. His arms were crossed on the side of the bed, and his head rested on them. He was sound asleep, still clutching her hand. She stopped moving, afraid she would wake him. For a long while, she watched him sleep, curled up beside her. As the sun moved across the bed, it crept across his face. The light through his eyelids woke him. He sat up, careful not to release Kai's hand, and stretched as best he could. It wasn't until he moved to check on her that he realized she had been awake, and watching him, the whole time. Ecstatic, he leapt to his feet and engulfed her in a tight hug. In spite of her joy at his change toward her, she couldn't help the small whimper of pain that escaped her.

Pulling back, Duncan apologized, "I'm so sorry, are you all right? I have just been so worried, I mean finding you there in the woods like that, and then you didn't wake up. Sarah said you might never wake up, but I didn't believe that, you're too strong for that. I'm just so happy you're awake." He studied the confused look on her face for a moment, trying desperately to tell if she knew who he was, or if she understood anything he had just said to her, remembering Sarah's warnings about the changes that a head injury can bring to someone. "Kai? Are you okay?" The concern, fear, and joy in his voice made her smile.

"Yes, I think so," was all Kai could manage just yet. Her throat was dry and tight, and the pain in her head was making the sunlight hard to bare. "Can I get some water, please?" Duncan nearly fell over himself as he scrambled out of the room. When he returned a few moments later he was accompanied, not only with a glass of water, but

Sarah and their father as well. Once Kai had drank the glass of water, and managed to clear her throat properly, they began asking her all sorts of questions. Some were simple 'how are you feeling,' 'does this hurt' kinds of questions, while others were stranger. Sarah asked her to remember small pieces of information from the last few years of her life, and her father asked her to tell him information she had learned from her books. The one question Duncan managed to ask seemed to be the one she should have had to answer first. What happened?

Straightening herself in her bed, she told them how the bird had startled Whisper, how she had tried to hang on, but couldn't. Then she told them about the light. The three onlookers seemed confused by the last part of her story. Finally, Sarah said she should rest and ushered everyone else out of her room. Once in the living room, she stood for a moment, lost in thought.

"It could be a problem with her memory, caused by the fall, or something else that her mind didn't or couldn't properly process at the time." Sarah sat down in one if the chairs, still lost in her own thoughts on how to explain what Kai had just described.

"Perhaps it was lightning." Alon chimed in shyly. He knew full well that the skies had been clear that night and that she was in the thick cover of the forest, but he had seen, with his own eyes, a bolt of rogue lightning when he was a child.

"Does it really matter?" Duncan's voice cut through the silence that had enveloped the room. "I mean, she is awake, and her mind seems to be fine; do we really care what she saw in those last seconds? Real or imagined?" The logic of his words seemed to hit home for the two other people. Nodding her head, Sarah stood from her seat and excused herself to go and pack her things. With Kai on the mend, she no longer needed to stay here; and she dreaded to see what had become of her home, now that her boys had been without her for nearly four full days. Alon offered to take her home on his way into town. Kai normally did the shopping, and they were now running dangerously low on essentials. As the two of them loaded into the wagon and set off to town, Duncan returned to Kai. They had much to discuss now that she was awake again, namely his apology.

CHAPTER 27
MEANS TO AN END

Four days earlier, Rikard had paced in his tent, unable to spend one moment longer in the belly of his machine. The moment he had broken through the wall and charged the line of defenses ahead was the beginning of this honorable war that in two days had claimed nearly one hundred of his precious men. Though they had taken four of Brannon's for every one of his, he had so many more that Rikard could not match. Rikard found himself in a position he had not planned, at a loss. This would be a war of attrition, and even if he managed to win this one, there were four others that could be just as hard fought. The idea of losing hundreds, if not a thousand, of his own small race would destroy them. He had only around five thousand, or so, in good fighting condition to start with. As he paced in the dim light, Tawni watched his steps.

"My husband, I cannot help you if you do not talk to me." Her voice was silk as she reclined in the crudely constructed chair. Rikard stopped and turned to face her.

"I cannot afford the men necessary to continue this war, not if there are four more to fight. I will have no men left to populate this place." His brow was creased in thought as he turned again to his pacing.

"But we are winning, my lord." Her voice almost purred at the end. He could hear the tinge of amusement in her tone and spun in his heels.

"What's the point of winning if we do not get to enjoy the spoils?" Rikard's tone was both questioning and angry. He needed advice, not patronization.

"My lord could retreat, give your people a few decades to build a war worthy population, sadly you will be gone before they fight again, and then there's no way to be sure they will even wish to fight any more. You've seen what they become in this place without your constant leadership." She was referring to how fatted and content they had become before the tunnel was collapsed. He stood remembering the lazy pace and stretched guts of his men when he had arrived hours too late.

"Hadriah will not wait for a future generation. I was meant to return him, in my life time! I must succeed!"

"Then the war must continue."

"But I can't continue to lose men."

"My lord, we are going in circles. A solution will require more than simply wanting to win and soon, it will require a plan." She stood from her chair and stretched her long, thin frame. Rikard watched, greedily, as she adjusted her dress and moved to him. Her body always soothed his mind and helped him forget his troubles, how he wanted it now. As he reached for her, she gently sloughed off his advancing hands. "Not until a decision has been reached, my lord, otherwise, we will never finish this conversation; it will end the same way each time." Her lips curled in a sly smile as her hand traced the muscled lines of his arm to his shoulder. She pulled him down into a chair and began rubbing the muscles atop his shoulders and his neck.

"Perhaps a diplomatic solution would suffice for now. Allow me to acquire a foothold in this land and the others, a better, stronger, position from which to attack later down the road." He had closed his eyes and was enjoying the caress of her hands. When he finished, Tawni took a step back, her hands sliding from their work. He opened his eyes and turned to face her. Her face had changed, she looked angry. He had never seen her beautiful face twisted with rage before, it alarmed him.

"You are a conqueror, not a diplomat! You are the Vessel of Hadriah, the King and Champion of Hadrir, Usurper of Lylunir! I will not allow you to destroy all that you have worked for by groveling to that man for space in his precious kingdom!" Rikard took a moment to process her words. No one had even spoken to him that way, not since he had come down from the mountain. Anger and admiration swirled in his heart as he looked over his queen. Her supple lips and seductive eyes and been replaced with the gritted teeth, clenched jaw and fiery eyes of a woman possessed with rage.

Standing, he met her anger with his own. "What would you have me do? Continue to bash our men against this wall until it breaks, only to have no strength left for the others?" He towered over her, but she did not back down.

"You speak as if the way we have been fighting is the only way. Why do we not attack at night? Why do we wait from their lines to form before charging onto the battle field? Why do we stop in the evenings to allow for the dead to be retrieved? They are the dead, they no longer have purpose!" His anger rose within him. He raised his hand to strike at her and then quickly spun around. He had sworn to himself that he would never hit her, never lay a hand in anger on the woman he loved. It had been an easy oath to keep when she was pleasing him; but now, with her venomous words and cold heart, it took all he had to stay his hand.

"And you know another? I fight with honor! Brannon fights with honor! What would you have me do!?!" He hung his head, wringing his hands as if trying to squeeze the desire to strike her from his fingertips. Sensing that she was dangerously close to disaster, Tawni's voice changed. Her silky tone returned as she drew her body close to his back, pressing herself against his flesh.

"My lord, does it matter the tactic if it means victory? I can give you a way to win this, and every other kingdom, if you forget honor and strive for victory!" The feel of her body pressed against him began to wash away his rage. As her hands moved on his arms and chest, his head lifted.

"What would you have me do?" His tone was complacent and she knew she had succeeded.

"Kill them, all of them, in their beds." Rikard jumped free of her embrace.

With indignation and astonishment in his voice, he said, "There is no honor in that! How am I to be a honorable king if I kill my enemies in their sleep?" Despite how revolting he found her suggestion, his tone remained calm. As much as he hated the idea, she had a point. Killing his enemies while they were unaware would save hundreds of his men. He had done basically this to Lylunir, and the victory had been swift and resounding, but this was different this time. Brannon knew he was coming. He had set up defenses and gathered and trained an army. "Besides, they have guards and scouts that would see and hear us coming."

"We have archers capable of shooting the eye out of an eagle as it soars overhead. I have a special poison that kills instantly. I have been working on it for quite some time, to perfect it. Arrows and blades dipped in this will dispatch your enemy silently, unlike the days of screaming and madness that follow what they currently drip from their blades...it's far more humane...and honorable, don't you think?" She reached for him again, and this time he did not turn away. She pulled him down to her and kissed him. His arms encircled her small body and pulled her against him. They stood for a long while like this before she pulled back. "My lord, act now. There is no time to waste."

Rikard hesitated to let go of her. She had come to represent peace in his violent world, but he realized that if her plan was to work, he needed to act. He left the tent and ordered his men to rouse, but quietly. He brought together his best men, numbering only one hundred or so. Sitting them together he described his plan. He had thought to see disappointment or disgust on their faces, but instead found agreement and encouragement. His men had grown weary of a head to head fight. Tawni had two of the men fetch another barrel from the machine. She had made both poisons. Rikard wondered for a moment why she hadn't simply provided him the more lethal poison to start with; but as the bustle of preparations swung into high gear, he could not afford the time to puzzle over it.

The archer's arrows found their marks as the guards to the Forrenfar camp fell from their posts. In the cover of night, his soldiers spread out. One by one, they entered tent after tent. Throat after throat they slit. As the sun began to brighten the sky, the call went out to pull back. Rikard's men fled into the woods, out of sight as the few living soldiers rushed from the tents. Despite his command, Tawni had instructed the men to leave some of the soldiers alive. The terror of waking next to a man whose neck had been cut clean through to the spine in the night would be enough to send them running, fleeing from the battle field. She had been right. Rikard's scouts watched as the spared soldiers came running from their tents in a panic. Screams and cries of fear rang out like music from the sea of tents. That morning Rikard lined his army up on the battlefield, but no opposition came. Most of his men knew nothing about the dark deeds perpetrated in the night. Ordering them forward, they made their way into the camp. There was nothing left but dead. The living men had fled. Running from an enemy that could kill silently in the night, running back to their Vessel.

Rikard ordered his men to burn the dead and search for any supplies. They found many weapons and enough food for two armies. Deciding that this would be a good place to prepare for the siege of the capital, he moved his army into the Forrenfar camp. They tended to their wounded and sent scouts to assess the road ahead. In the late afternoon, a soldier came running through the streets. A bird had landed on his tent with a small bit of paper strapped to its leg. The man held the dead bird high in the air as he ran to his king. Reaching him, he fell to his knees and held the bird in the air. Once Rikard had taken it, the soldier turned and ran out of sight.

Rikard turned the bird over and over in his hands. It was larger than most. Its wings were long, spanning several feet when extended. Its feathers were brightly colored, forming stripes of varying hues across the bird's body. Rikard did not know that in his hands he held a Rainbow Wren, one of the fifty species native only to Forrenfar, though all other countries had acquired them for their special skills. They could deliver a message to a specific person. All that needed to be done was to attach the message and say the place and name of the person. Somehow, the bird did the rest. Rikard studied the dead animal for a few moments before removing his message and tossing the carcass aside. As he read the message his face began to change. The calm confidence of victory was replaced with rage and panic. According to the message, the small town of Darksand held rumor of a girl, light of skin and dark of hair, that had vaporized a bird with a very bright light. The note was on its way to a husband stationed in this town, no doubt one of the multitude that were killed in the blood bath of the previous night. Rikard crushed the note in his fingers and started off into the distance. He did not move, just stood, fuming from the revelation the tiny note had brought him. Of all the people to have found it, it had come to him.

Tawni, seeing him standing, staring off into space, joined her king in the road. "My lord, what has you so entranced?" She tried to follow his gaze but found nothing. Puzzled, she scanned his person. There in his hand she saw the note, crumpled in his fingers. "What did it say?"

"It says you are a liar." His voice was calm and cold. In his head he relived the moment from sixteen years ago when she had told him that the girl, the baby, princess to Lylunir, was dead, the last words of a dying old man. "It says that the princess of Lylunir is STILL ALIVE!" In an instant, his hand dropped the note to the ground and seized her by the throat. He lifted her body from the ground as he began to squeeze the life from her. Betrayal was the one thing he could never forgive her. As she began to fade she whispered something. Over and over again she tried desperately to say something through her closing windpipe. Finally the word, please, could be discerned.

As Rikard loosened his grip slightly, she took a deep breath and, in a weak raspy voice, whispered, "I carry your child, please..." Rikard could not believe his ears. It had been so many years that he had given up hope of having a child with her. He had planned to wait until it was done and then take a maid to bed, several if necessary, until one bore him a child. Now his beloved queen, the woman whose lie had allowed the princess to come of age, was carrying his seed. His grip on her neck relaxed, and she slid from his hand. Before she crumpled to the ground, he caught her and lifted her to him.

"Why did you lie to me? Why did you tell me the princess was dead?" He almost pleaded with her for a decent reason. He needed something that would allow him to forgive her.

"He said she was dead, gone. I took him at his word."

"Did he say dead? Or did he say gone?" Rikard watched as her face tinged with panic. He did not need to wait for her answer. Perhaps she had not lied to him. In her haste to endear herself to him, she had heard what she wanted to hear. He lowered her back to the ground and waited for her to steady herself. With a flick of his fingers, he summoned two soldiers to him. "Take the queen back to the capital. See that she is tended to and that her every comfort is provided for. I will return when it is done." He turned to walk away from her. She reached out and caught his arm in her weak hands. He turned to meet her pleading eyes. "The battlefield is no place for you. You will be safe in Lylunir. Perhaps I can forgive you, given enough time." Pulling his arm free of her fingers, he continued his departure. Tawni was ushered into a machine and, within moments, was gone.

Rikard now had to deal with this rumor. Calling a group of men to him, he assigned them the task of finding this girl and bringing her back to him, alive. If she was indeed the princess, he wanted the joy of killing her with his bare hands, a joy that had been denied him by her mother. As the group turned to leave, Karnus rushed forward and fell to one knee.

"Allow me to join them, my lord. At worst, you would lose a soldier you care nothing about, at best I could redeem myself in your eyes." Rikard looked at the man for a moment. Deciding that perhaps he could be of some use, he nodded. Karnus gathered his gear, and the crumpled note from the ground, and joined the ten men in the small machine. Fast as wind, they took off down the only road from the camp, knowing only the name of the town they were to find. Forrenfar had very few sizable towns and detailed sign posts at each crossroads would make finding their destination far easier than they expected.

CHAPTER 28
DARKSAND REACHED

Alon watched Sarah wave as she entered her home. When the door was closed behind her, he flicked the reins and pulled hard to the right, turning the wagon around in the yard. Once he was heading back down the road, he flicked the reins again, speeding up the pace. He had a long list of things to get before he headed back home to his daughter. She had been unconscious for days; and, now that she was awake, he and his son had to play catch-up with their lives. There were three people and two stores he needed to visit on this trip. He drove on, trying to decide the best order in which to take his tasks so he could get home and be with the daughter he feared he had lost. First stop was the market on the boardwalk. There was a merchant there who had been expecting antelox milk for nearly two days now. As Alon pulled his cart to a halt at the end of the path, and climbed over the driver's bench into the back, a voice called out to him. Looking up, he saw Garter jogging toward him from the other side of the street. At first he remembered the anger of their last meeting, but upon seeing the concern and sorrow on his face, his anger faded. Garter and the other men had gotten to know Kai well over the last several years, and it occurred to him that they were probably just as worried about her as he had been.

As Garter drew near, he shouted down to him, "Kai is doing fine." Instantly, relief and joy spread through Grater's features, slowing his pace. As the man continued to draw closer to him, Alon realized that he would need to speak with the man; and in this public setting, he could not lash out as he had outside his home.

"I sure am glad to hear she's all right. Brok told me about the fall and how she wasn't awake yet. That was two days ago now." Alon watched suspiciously as Garter reached the end of the wagon and eyed the crates of bottled milk stacked in the back. Finally, Alon decided it was no use denying the man's devotion to his duties. Alon motioned for Garter to come on up and help. In an instant, the two men were standing side by side lifting boxes of milk bottles into the air. Reaching the end of the wagon they set them down. Together, they jumped to the ground and grabbed the sides of the crates, lifting the milk off the wagon. As they began walking to the start of the boardwalk, Garter cleared his throat.

"Alon, look, I'm sorry if I hit a nerve the other night; it's just that, with Maga gone, all you've got is those kids. I'd hate to see anything happen to them, especially if we could prevent it." Alon felt the anger beginning to bubble inside him again. He couldn't understand why Garter felt the need to bring it up again. Gritting his teeth, he tried to

298

focus on the task at hand. "Has Kai talked about what happened in the woods yet?" At first, Alon didn't register Garter's question; then as it repeated in his head, he found himself thinking about what Kai had told him about the strange light.

"She said that a bird startled Whisper, that's all." Alon's jaws clinched shut when he saw the look on Garter's face. He seemed to know something Alon didn't.

"Nothing about a light or the bird exploding?" Garter's voice dropped low, almost a whisper, as he asked the leading question. Alon nearly dropped the crate between them.

Whispering now too, he asked, "How could you possibly know that? She imagined it!" His voice was becoming more serious as his pace slowed. He and Duncan had agreed that the light was simply a trick of Kai's mind, a remnant of the head injury and nothing more. How could Garter know about his daughter's hallucination?

"She didn't imagine it; Alon, she caused it. Old man Praken saw the whole thing. He was out hunting on your land when he saw Kai on her horse. He's told everyone about how he saw the pheasant pop out of the bush and scare her horse and how she looked at it and bam! A bolt of lightning hit the bird and it was gone! Only, he said it wasn't lightning exactly. It was short, like a spear, and it was bright and hot, like a ray of sunlight. Most people think he's out of his mind, saying a thing like that about sweet little Kai, but we know differently, don't we,

Alon." Alon had listened to the incredible tale Garter had just shared, his heart racing and his mind frozen. At first he wanted to shout that it wasn't true, that Kai couldn't do anything of the sort; but he did know differently. She was the daughter of the Vessel of Luniah, destined to be the Vessel herself; and she had just come of age. The two men stood, unmoving, in the middle of the market entrance. Garter watched as Alon struggled through his own realization of who his daughter really was and what she had become. Finally he gathered his senses enough to speak.

"I wrote them letters," was all he was able to say. Garter waited for more, but none came.

"Letters? What are you talking about?"

"After our fight, I had another one with Duncan. I said some things I shouldn't have and then Kai ran away. I decided that maybe if I wrote down the truth, I could build up the courage to tell them. But then Duncan brought her home hurt, and I just packed the letters away." Alon's eyes met Garter's. He was trapped between sorrow and desperation. His daughter had changed into who she was always meant to be, and he knew that the life he had been trying so desperately to preserve was over, gone forever. Garter smiled sadly as he helped Alon deliver the crates of milk in a strangled silence. After Alon's brief business transaction was completed, they walked back to Alon's cart, still in silence. As Alon climbed into the driver's seat, Garter placed his hands on the reins.

"I know it will be difficult, but you need to tell them. Then we need to take her to Brannon; he will need to see her now, help her figure this out. I will ready the men and meet you at your house this afternoon." He turned to walk away, but Alon called after him.

"Make it tomorrow morning, will you? I want one more night, if she'll allow it, for us to be a family." Garter nodded. He knew how much Alon wanted a different life for his little girl, for his broken family. Giving a comforting smile, Garter turned again and disappeared into the crowd, headed for home. Alon sat on the seat for a long while trying to decide how he was going to tell Kai the truth, how she could possibly forgive him for keeping such a huge secret from her for all these years. Then his thoughts turned to Duncan. How would he handle the truth? After all that had happened in the past weeks, would he leave too, never to return? Deciding that whatever happened, it was time, he set out to finish the most important errands and then return home. He drove the cart to the general store in town and climbed down from the seat. He entered the store and walked to the counter. As he fished in his pocket for the list Duncan had given him, he became aware that strange sounds, screams and shouts, coming from outside. The store clerk had left his post and was headed for the window. Forgetting the slip of paper in his pocket, Alon joined him.

There, in the center of town was a large, strangely built contraption. It was the size of a storage building, and made of a metal he didn't recognize. As his eyes scanned the monstrosity, he saw wheels under it, though he saw nowhere for horses, or any beasts for that matter, to be attached to it. He wondered how it moved. Then, the side of the machine broke open and lowered to the ground, forming a steep ramp up and into it. Out of its belly came eleven strange men. They were like nothing he had ever seen before, though it was clear that where ever the machine had come from, they had come with it. As they piled out, they spread out around the vehicle, stretching and looking at the stunned faces of the crowd. One of the men, whose right arm was strapped to his side, waved a strange looking blade in the air and began shouting at the crowd. At first Alon could not make out what the man was saying, but as his voice grew louder and more impatient, his words could be made out through the glass. He was asking about a girl.

Fear gripped Alon. A flood of conversations washed through his mind. The strangers in Lylunir, the loud crash on the other side of the wall, the lift burning, and finally the news that had accompanied Kai's birthday gift, the war had begun. Alon stared at the men. They were the race that had conquered Lylunir, had killed the king and queen and they were here for a girl. He wondered for a moment how they could possibly have known she was here. It took only a second for the conversation he had just finished with Garter to provide the answer. Praken. He had been telling everyone about what he had seen. Rumors spread fast in Forrenfar, especially from town to town. All it took was a bird. It was quite likely that by now the entire kingdom had heard of her ability. Her ability. He realized suddenly that they were here, most likely, to kill her. After all, her mother and father had been murdered by these strangers, why not a young girl, unable to control her powers, unable to fight back. Deciding that he needed to get Kai out before they found her, he nodded to the clerk, still too engrossed in what was happening outside to notice, and then left. As he exited the general store, he tried to hide his face. He shuffled through the onlookers toward his wagon. Just then, a blood curdling scream forced him to stop. He turned to see a woman being held up by two of the men. Her face was streaming with tears and her jaw quivered in terror. She kicked her legs in the air, trying desperately to break free of their grasp, but they had her.

The man with the dead arm drew his blade close to her throat. Leaning close to her ear he asked again, loud enough for everyone to hear, "Where is the girl who created light in the forest? I will not ask again." The woman stared at the man, cringing as his blade drew even closer to her neck. She began scanning the crowd for anyone that could help her. Lost in panic, her eyes found Alon. As she stared at him, the man with a dead arm followed her gaze. Reading her stare, he ordered Alon seized. Alon raced to his wagon. He was trying to get the horses turned around when the strangers grabbed him. They pulled him roughly from his seat, letting him land hard on his side. The fall had knocked the wind from him. He lay on the ground coughing as the men stood over him.

"Bring him to me." The one armed man motioned and the woman was released. The two men that had pulled him from the wagon, lifted him by his arms and dragged him to their leader. As he was being hauled into the open area of the street, he locked eyes with the terrified woman as she clambered away from her captors on all fours. As their eyes met, he could see the fear in them, mixed with sorrow. The two men that had him lifted him back to his feet. His side hurt from the fall, and he was still coughing, trying to regain his breath.

"Perhaps you know the answers to my question. Where is the girl from the story?" The man stared at him. His golden eyes flashed with rage and hatred. Alon did not answer. "I said, where is the girl?" This time the question was accompanied by a punch to the gut, courtesy of the man holding his left arm. Alon coughed and sputtered at the force of the hit. Hanging his head, he clinched his teeth against the pain that radiated from the spot on his side. The men shifted him in their hands. A third man approached him from behind and seized his head, forcing him to look up at his interrogator. Alon steadied his breathing and tried to suppress the pain.

"I don't know what you are talking about." His voice was labored, but strong. He watched as the anger his answer produced spread across one-arm's brick red face.

"Of course, you don't." The leader nodded; and Alon was struck again, this time by the captor on the right. As the pain washed over his side, he heard the gasps and cries from the crowd. He could feel their eyes on him, begging him to stay strong. "How about now?" Alon clenched his teeth and lifted his own head. He look up at one-arm and forced a laugh.

"I have no idea what you are talking about." He continued his labored laugh until the leader nodded again, and a second punch dug into his left side. As the man's fist impacted his chest, he felt the ribs give way under the force, heard the crack of his own bones. He could not contain the cry of pain. The crowd cried out with him. None of them had ever seen anything like this before. Nothing more than a fist fight between boyhood rivals had ever happened on these streets, nothing like this.

The men holding him shifted him again, forcing his head up to meet another question. This time, the one-armed man removed a scrap of crumpled paper from his pocket. "You mean you don't know about this?" When Alon made no motion, he leaned his sword against his leg and spread the paper between the fingers of his only hand. Clearing his throat, he began to ready the note on the paper. " 'Dearest Aaron, Hope you are well.' By the way, Aaron is most likely dead, we killed a lot of people in that camp, a-hem, 'You won't believe what I heard today. That pale girl, with the black hair, she was seen in the forest conjuring light of all things. At least that's what everyone keeps saying. We always knew she was different.' It prattles on about kids, and other useless matters after that." He wadded the scrap back into a ball and tossed it carelessly to the ground. Alon scanned the crowd for the wife he knew had written the note. After all, there was only one Aaron in town. He found that her face was not among the crowd. At first he wondered where she was, but then he realized that she would be where he is now if she had been here. Knowing that she would not have been able to stand the callous way the one-armed man had joked about her husband most likely being dead. Alon decided that he could not risk anyone but him being the focus of this questioning. He loved Kai enough to protect her, but the others might not feel the same. Setting his jaws together, he stared past his captor, saying nothing.

Over and over again, the one-armed man asked his questions. Each time, Alon held his tongue. Each time a punch landed in his abdomen. With each hit, he could feel the shattered ribs shifting under his skin. Several times he had blacked out from the pain, only to be roused again. After nearly half an hour of torturing him, the one-armed man had had enough.

"Put him on his knees."

"Karnus, what are you planning to do now? It's obvious that he won't talk." The man behind Alon seemed tired of this wasted effort. "Why don't we just kill him and start on another one?" The one-armed man, Karnus, spun to face the soldier. His look was enough to cause silence. Alon was forced onto his knees, his head pulled back so that he could look up at Karnus. With his blade against Alon's upper arm, he asked again. Alon's silence brought movement to the blade. It slid into his flesh as

Karnus drug it away. The sting of the deep cut was quickly replaced by a severe burning. It reached out from the wound to his fingers and the side of his face. Despite his decision to make no sound, he could not contain the cry brought on by the cut. Karnus placed the blade against his other arm and asked again. Without even waiting to see if Alon would answer this time, he dug the blade deep into his tissue. Again, the burning produced another uncontrollable cry. The man holding Alon's head up released him. Then the men holding his shoulders down relinquished their grip. Alon slumped to the ground. As he lay prone, he could hear shouts and cries from all around him, the scuffle of feet. He faded in and out of consciousness as the clamor around him grew louder and more fierce. Most of the crowd had fled, the running of the women and children that had been watching his ordeal died away in the din of fighting. Trying to lift his broken and bleeding body, he caught sight of Garter. He was not alone. Brok and Felix stood beside him. The three men were engaged in a fierce battle with the ten soldiers from the machine. The eleventh, Karnus, stood back, watching the skirmish, as if amused. The three men held their own, matching swing for swing, against the onslaught of the strangers.

Alon looked past the fight to see a small face hidden behind his wagon. Lying on the ground on the other side was a young girl. She had tear trails on her face and was staring at him, not the fight all around him. For a long moment he stared back, wondering who she was. His eyes pleaded with her, to get help, to warn Kai, to do anything she could to stop this nightmare. As if she could hear his prayers, the girl jumped up from the ground and turned to run. Reaching the end of the wagon, she looked one last time at Alon and nodded. Then she was gone. As Alon looked after her, he heard the cry of a wounded man. Turning slightly, he saw Garter fall to his knees, the better part of a foreign blade protruding from the back of his left shoulder. Garter turned his head to look at Alon as the life drained from his eyes. Despite taking one of the invaders with him, he fell to the ground like a stone, lifeless. The other two men fought on, but now, down a man, they soon suffered similar ends. As Brok fell to his knees, a deep sword wound in his side, Karnus, stepped forward and stabbed his blade into his heart. Felix, wounded, tried to take the one-armed man's head into oblivion with him. His swing was wild. He toppled over his own blade, landing flat on his back a few feet from where Alon lay, broken and torn. As he struggled to regain his blade and his feet, Alon watched the point of a sword pierce his neck. As blood rushed from the wound, the body of his friend slid free and crumbled to the ground. Karnus lifted his blood soaked blade and looked at it. A twisted smile pulled at his lips as he took the several steps to where Alon lay, unable to move.

"Find another one. We will kill every one if we have too." Karnus' voice was almost excited at the prospect. Looking down at Alon one last time, he said, "We *will* find her." With those words, he swung his blade, removing Alon's head.

CHAPTER 29
THE WARNING

Kai shifted in bed. Duncan was bringing her a glass of hot tea, and she needed to be ready to take it. The last few hours had been hard on her. Their discussion about the words that had driven her from home, into the forest, was awkward and painful. Duncan had tried to apologize, but after Kai probed a bit, she found that, despite his regret, he actually did feel as if it would be better if they were separated, at least for a while. He couldn't bring himself to discuss the dance. She tried over and over to steer the floundering conversation toward this difficult subject; and each time, Duncan managed to turn it away again. Finally, she had given up. Agreeing that nothing could happen right now, they decided to put it behind them. After a long pause, she had asked for something to drink and Duncan had promised some tea and left the room. When the sounds of movement began to grow from her outer room, she smoothed the blankets across her lap. When he entered carrying the tray, she couldn't help but laugh. He had managed, in his effort to do it properly, to spill the hot water all over the tray. He teetered on his toes, trying desperately to keep the scalding liquid on the tray and not spill it down his chest.

As he moved closer to the bed, Kai called out, "Don't bring it here! Take it back out to the table, I can get up." Her laughter deepened as she gingerly swung her legs over the side of her bed. It had been days since she had stood, and she could feel the muscles' reluctance to carry even her small frame.

"Wait there, I'll help you. Just...let me put this down." Duncan's voice wavered as he tried to balance the tray. With a small thud, she knew that the tray, for better or for worse, was now resting on the table. He returned, slightly wet in front, to help her out of bed. At first, her legs were wobbly under her, and the pain in her back and head were sharp. As she moved about, the ache seemed to dissipate; and her strength began to return to her. Duncan helped her into a chair, then took the one opposite. Doing his best to clean up the tragedy that was their tea, he handed her a half filled glass. Holding the warm cup of hot, brown, liquid, Kai inhaled the steam. Her eyes closed, and she sighed as it flooded her lungs and warmed her heart. Duncan did his best to mop up the loose tea, then, resigning to defeat, seized his own glass and reclined back into his chair.

They sat quietly for a while, nursing their partially filled cups. Kai broke the silence with a simple question. "So, what was in the chest this year?" She took a sip from her cup.

"I don't know. We never opened it. I mean, when you

got hurt, we just forgot about it. It's still sitting out there on the table." For a moment, they sat looking at each other. Then, as if they had planned it, they both stood and began making their way out into the dining room. Duncan moved slower than Kai, just in case she would need his help.

Reaching the chest, she lowered her body down onto the edge of the bench. "You open it."

"All right." Duncan lifted the lid and peered inside. "Looks like...this year is...Zailia." As he finished, he drew one of the maps from the chest and handed it to Kai. There, written by hand on the corner of the rolled parchment, was the word 'Zailia' formed in lovely script.

"Oh. I was hoping for Lylunir. Oh, well, I guess it will come next year." She took the map and unrolled it, revealing one of the most attractive maps she had received yet, it was drawn by a delicate hand. The mountains were formed using a light stroke in a pale ink, while the roads and villages were drawn, and named, in other, darker, tones. From the look of the map, Kai wondered if the villages were actually on the mountain tops. As she studied the beautifully drawn map, Duncan continued to pull maps and then books from inside the chest. He stacked them up on the table, eagerly searching the bottom of the chest. Disappointed, he pulled the lid closed.

"No weapons this year. I guess he sent everything he planned to send." Duncan lifted the chest and slid it under the front of the table. Then, sliding onto the bench across from her, he seized one of the books and flipped quickly through it. Kai watched him, over the edge of the map, as he replaced the book and lifted another, flipping quickly through it as well.

"I doubt any of them have pictures." She snickered. Duncan looked up at her and rolled his eyes, tossing the book back onto the pile.

"Are you hungry?" Kai hadn't thought about until now. Duncan's question rolled around her head like a boulder. Instantly, her stomach began to ache and growl with the hunger of four days of missed meals.

"Famished!" Duncan smiled and got up from the table. As he left the room to fetch something for them to eat, Kai set the map aside and looked through the books. As she read the titles, one caught her eye. The book was thin and bound in black. Silver letters embossed on the cover read *The Dark Race*. Cracking the cover she began to read. A few pages in she let the book slip from her fingers. As if fell from her hands to the table, she screamed for Duncan. She heard him drop whatever hand been in his hands and scramble through the door.

"What!" Duncan studied the shock on Kai's face as she pointed a shaking hand at the book, lying open and face down in front of her. Her mouth hung open and her eyes were wide, as if she had just seen a spirit. He walked to her and lifted the book. As he read, the color drained from his face. Closing the book, he slid down onto the bench next to her.

"It's her! She is a Zailian!" Kai's voice was as shaky

as her hands.

"Why would we be dreaming about a Zailian? It doesn't make any sense...I've never even met someone who has seen one before. How, when, would *we* have met one?" They sat in stunned silence for a moment trying desperately to find the hidden memory that would explain this, but nothing came to them.

"We'll ask father when he gets back; maybe he will remember her." Kai's eyes pleaded with Duncan for reassurance.

"Okay, yeah, he should know." Duncan didn't believe his own words, but they seemed to comfort his sister. He lifted himself off the bench and moved to return to the kitchen. Now, not only did he need to bring her food, but he had a colossal mess to clean up as well. Kai lifted the book and slowly began to read again.

Before Duncan could make it into the kitchen, they heard the front door burst open. Frantic steps pounded through the living room toward them. Turning, they saw the small, terrified face of Becca. She panted and doubled over against the edge of one of the chairs. She seemed to be exhausted, unable to slow her breathing enough to talk. Through her breaths, she managed to blurt out the words 'strangers', 'swords', 'looking for Kai', and 'torturing Alon'. Duncan and Kai exchanged a confused look, and then jumped into action. Kai helped Becca into a seat while Duncan quickly fetched a glass of water for the poor girl. Becca struggled against the help at first, but when presented with the water, she grabbed the glass and guzzled it down greedily. As her breathing slowed and she calmed, tears began to stream down her face. Kai and Duncan listened to her terrible story of the strange men who had come into town inside the belly of a horseless carriage. She told of how their father had been captured and beaten, of how the man in charge had wanted to know where the girl who made light in the woods was. At this, Kai and Duncan exchanged panicked looks. At first, they thought maybe they could rescue Alon from the strangers, but Becca stopped them.

"No! Don't go back there! He wants you, and he knows what you look like! If he catches you he'll kill you, just like he killed them!" Becca was now sobbing, clinging tightly to Kai's night gown.

"Them? Whose them, Becca?" Duncan reached out and captured her small, terrified face in his hands. "Who did he kill, Becca?"

"Mr. Garter, Mr. Brok, and Mr. Felix. They tried to save Alon, but there were too many of them. And...well...I think he killed your father, too. I mean, it looked like he meant to." She watched as Duncan's face grew hard with anger. Knowing what he wanted to do, she spoke again, "You can't help them! You have to get out! Someone will tell them where you are! I know they will! You have no time!" Becca's word were filled with urgency and truth. After a small pause, Duncan stood and began barking orders to the girls.

"Becca, go home. Go through the woods. When you get there, get your family out! Take them to Antlerbrooke, you'll be safe there. If they try to turn you away, tell them I, we, sent you." Becca nodded and got up to leave. As she started to walk away, she paused, ran back and hugged both of them tightly, kissing Kai gently on the cheek. Tears filling her eyes, as she took one last look at her friends, turned and vanished. "Kai, I need you to get dressed and go saddle the horses. I'll pack some supplies. This isn't like last time, only a few essentials; we won't have a way to carry much more than that."

"What about the maps and the books?" At first Duncan thought the idea if weighing down the horses with dozens of books and maps was laughable, but then, realizing that Brannon must have sent them for a reason, he agreed.

"Bring the really important ones and the maps. If you know one really well already, just leave it."

In an instant, they were busy. Kai rushed into her room, emerging only minutes later, hurriedly dressed and carrying an arm load of books and maps. Laying them on the table, she bolted out the door to the barn to start saddling Whisper and Shadow. Duncan emerged from his room with a small bag of clothing. Adding a few pieces of Kai's to it, he began packing the books into the other side of the saddle bag. When that one was filled, he placed the few remaining in the next bag. Staring at the maps, he unrolled each of them. Stacking them atop each other, he rolled them together into one large roll and wrapped that in a thin blanket. As he looked down at the bags, he remembered food. Rushing into the kitchen, he gathered every dry food item he could find, from cured meat to bread, and wrapped them in kitchen cloth. When they were away and safe, he could hunt for anything that they needed. Bringing the small bundle back to the dining room, he tossed it on top of the books. As he prepared to carry the bags out the barn, he remembered the weapons. If ever they needed them, it was now. He barged into Alon's room and over turned the table to reveal the first chest. Flipping open the lid, his eyes met with a hoard of points and blades. Four years' worth of gifted weapons stared at him from the mouth of the chest. He pulled the swords and daggers from the velvet, sliding one of each into his belt, and placing the matching pairs on the floor next to him. The throwing knives were in sets with their own small leather pouches, followed by two small crossbows and quivers. Except for the crossbows, every weapon was made of the same strange amber colored stone.

He had no time to marvel over them. As he gathered his arm load together, he noticed the small envelopes at the bottom of the trunk. Returning the stash to the floor, he reached in after them. There were three envelopes. Two had a name written in his father's hand across the front of them, one for Kai and the other for him. The third envelope looked much older and bore no name. Deciding this could wait, he tucked the letters inside his vest pocket and gathered his load back into his arms. After stowing the weapons in the empty saddle bag, he disappeared into his chambers to get their money. All the profit and income of the farm was stashed away in a drawer in his room. Before he could return to the dining room, he heard Kai's voice calling to him. As he emerged from his room he saw her standing over the saddlebags, the twin to the sword on his hip grasped in her hands. She looked away from the blade to him. She wanted to ask where he had found them, but he stopped her.

"Are the horses ready?"

"Yes, they are just outside. I tied the camping gear to Shadow." Duncan forced a smile despite his panic.

"Good, grab a bag." He ran to the table and pulled the other onto his shoulder. Together, they rushed out the door. After flinging the bags across their horses' back hips and securing them, they flung themselves into the saddles. Taking one last look at yet another home they were being forced to abandon, they rode off across the field and into the forest, not sure how long it would be before the strangers kicked in their door in search of the girl who made light.

They rode for nearly three hours before Kai asked to stop. The anxiety of the day, coupled with her recent fall, and the shocking events, made the journey more than her spirit could bare. Finding a small clearing, and confident that they had managed to escape without being pursued, the two stopped to make camp. Exhaustion set in as they pulled the saddles from Whisper and Shadow and gathered wood for a fire. The equinoi walked out into the clearing to graze as Duncan retrieved a hunk of cured meat for dinner. Using his new dagger, he sliced off a large section and tossed it to Kai before taking his seat across the fire. He watched as she devoured the meat in seconds, remembering how long it had been since she had eaten. As he began to nibble on his, figures erupted from the trees around them. Dark men with horrid faces burst forth, seizing the two frightened and weary travelers. It was no mystery that these were the soldiers that had attacked their town and murdered their friends. The man with one arm emerged from the trees and walked to Kai. Reaching out, he grabbed her face in his hand and studied it.

"There you are, young one. Someone has been looking for you for a long, long time." Looking across the fire to Duncan, struggling against the two men who held him, he said, "Kill that one. He only wants the girl." He turned and began to walk back into the forest. One of the men holding Duncan started to draw his blade. With his grip loosened, Duncan managed to free his arm. Drawing his own blade, he drove it into the belly of the man to his left, then swung in into the man to his right. As the two soldiers fell dead to the ground, Karnus stopped. Without turning back to face Duncan, he nodded toward the other men. Three more rushed forward, flanking Duncan. He fought them well, despite being outnumbered. He had managed to kill another one before the hilt of a blade came down hard on top of his head. The blow rendered him unconscious, and he fell forward to the ground. The two remaining men readied their blades to plunge them deep into his back, but Karnus stopped them. Running his finger along the side of Kai's beautiful face, he decided he needed compensation for the three men Duncan had taken from him, and Duncan would watch as he took it. The men lifted Duncan and bound him. One of the men slapped him hard across the face, bringing him around. Still dazed, Duncan writhed at Karnus as he traced his finger along Kai's flesh. Kai screamed as his hand slid into the front of her blouse. Her eyes, filled with rage and fear, found Duncan's. She had hoped that he would give her strength. His eyes, also filled with fury and hatred for the man at her side, only added fuel to hers. In an instant, the men to either side of Duncan fell to the ground, smoldering holes burned through their chests.

Karnus snatched his hand from her body as the men behind him cried out in fear. Bolts of light had pierced the men holding Duncan. It had burned right through them, leaving nothing but the holes behind. Kai wanted to do it again, to kill all five of the remaining men, but she didn't have the strength. What little she had after the ordeal of the last few days was spent. With the man who was holding her in a panic, she slipped from his grasp and slumped to the ground, fighting to stay awake. As Karnus tried to calm his men, the sound of hooves, beating on the ground, rose in her ears.

CHAPTER 30
WHISPER AND SHADOW

Duncan, still bound, sitting on his knees, heard the crashing behind him. Turning his throbbing head, he could see their equinoi crashing through the underbrush. Shadow and Whisper had heard the commotion from the clearing and were rushing toward the sound of danger. Duncan watched as the horses bound into the scene, positioning themselves in the center of it all, searching for their people. Finding Duncan wounded and bound and Kai on the verge of unconsciousness, the massive creatures focused their attentions on the men responsible. Rearing onto their hind legs, both beasts began lashing at the soldiers with their front hooves. Each potential blow carried behind it the force of hundreds of pounds of muscled weight, and could easily kill or maim whomever it found. For this reason, the already terrified men began to dodge and flee the kicking animals. Karnus tried desperately to regain control of the situation, but the rampaging animals were more than his words could overcome. Slowly, the horses succeeded in driving the men backward, away from the camp and the two weakened Merin children.

Duncan watched the horses striking out at the strangers, then turned his focus to Kai. Her captor was gone, fleeing before the lashing hooves of Whisper. Despite his pounding head and blurred vision, Duncan rose to his knees and crawled toward her, his hands still bound behind his back. As he drew next to her she managed to lift her head. Seeing her brother, the tears came again. Inching closer to him, she buried her face in his chest. Calming a bit, she turned her head to watch the scene unfolding just beyond their small campfire. Whisper and Shadow now stood in a V shape with all five remaining men arched in front of them. Karnus must have found the right words to rally his men because now they seemed to be fighting back. Their swords aloft, the men were swinging as the horses brought their enormous hooves through the air. As Whisper reared especially high in the air, one of the men in front of her rushed forward, holding his sword high in the air. As she descended, the point of the sword was driven deep into her chest. Her hooves came crashing down on the man as his sword sliced its way into her. With a cry of pain, the equinox lost her balance and fell, crushing the man beneath her. His sword was buried into her to the hilt. Duncan and Kai watched in horror as she tried to stand, but found no strength. Two of the men peeled themselves from Shadow to finish her. Driving their swords deep into her neck and shoulders, they stabbed her flesh over and over again. With each successive blow, the horse cried out in pain.

Duncan wanted to cover Kai's eyes, to hide from her this gruesome death; but his hands were still bound behind him. He whispered for her to look away, but it was too late. She had watched it all. With one last cry, Whisper fell silent; her body limp. Backing away from her ravaged corpse, the two men staggered for a moment and then rejoined the effort to bring down the second, massive, horse.

Shadow, enraged by the death of his companion, redoubled his efforts. His kicks became more focused. Alone now, the four remaining men attempted to surround him; but he blocked them as best he could. Duncan watched his steed as he seemed to dance with the evil men. Coming down from a rear, one of Shadow's hooves caught the edge of a blade, knocking it from his owner's hand. Seizing the opportunity, he reared and kicked again. As the hoof made contact, the man screamed in pain. Shadow's hoof dug deep into the man's shoulder, crushing the bones. The man fell to his knees. Another well-placed kick caved in his face. As the bloodied body slumped over dead, one of the soldiers managed to slice at Shadow's back. A long cut opened along the animal's side. Turning quickly, Shadow knocked the man to the ground. Before he could come down on him with a killing blow, Karnus stepped forward and drew his attention. The opening was all it took. The man lying prone on the ground dug his sword into Shadow's leg, slicing tendons and muscles necessary for it to function.

Shadow staggered, trying to gain his balance without

the use of his front leg. Too late, Duncan realized it was all over. He watched as his friend tried and failed to rear again. The three remaining men encircled him. Unable to focus his attentions on one man, the horse was left to hobble in circles, trying to avoid the myriad of swings now bombarding him from all sides. The men seemed to take pleasure in the fight now, making only small slices and shallow jabs into the animal's flesh. Duncan watched, impotent to stop it, as they tortured and tormented his beloved friend. Suddenly, the world seemed to lose all color. Sounds of birds faded into silence. The scene in front of him continued in black and white. Looking down, Kai was still pressed against him. She looked up to meet his eyes, and he found hers, still a vibrant violet. Behind him, he felt his hands released. Reaching down, he felt the dirt of the ground, the leaves, but it was different, as if he could feel them, but not move them. Bringing his hands around, he wrapped Kai into his arms. Trying to bury her face against the violence unfolding before them. The men had all but skinned poor Shadow. He fought on, despite the pain and hopelessness of the situation. Duncan knew that once his horse was dead, they would follow. The one-armed man would turn his attention back to them. Remembering the payment he meant to exact from Kai, he hoped that this time he would simply kill them, so at least she could die in purity and he would not be forced to suffer through watching her violation.

Karnus, tiring of the game, stepped up to the beast and drove his blade into the creature's side. Shadow staggered, but did not fall. The other two men, taking the cue from their leader, followed suit. They drove their blades deep into his guts. Shadow wobbled and then crashed to the ground. Karnus withdrew his sword and ran it across the animal's neck, spilling what little blood still remained on the ground. Shadow was gone. Turning back to the camp, his look of triumph gave way to one of panic.

"Where are they?!" He yelled at his men. "They were right here! Find them!" He and his men rushed toward the camp, shock spread wide on their faces. Duncan watched them, lost in confusion. He and Kai still sat huddled together where she had fallen. They were out in the open and clearly visible. A terrible thought hit him. What if they were dead? If they had become spirits and were watching this scene from the other side? This thought caved under the search the men were engaged in. If they were dead, their bodies would be clearly visible; there would be no need for this frantic searching. One of the men turned and began to move at speed toward them. Duncan tried to stand, but the dizziness from the blow to the head prevented him from finding the strength. As the man bore down on them, he clinched his eyes shut. A strange tingling sensation crossed his entire body. Opening his eyes, he watched in terror and amazement as the man's foot slipped right through him. Turning his head, he saw the man walking, unaware of what had just happened, behind him. The man turned and looked down. Bending at the waist, he lifted the rope that had bound Duncan's hands, still formed in the loops that had slipped from his wrists. He held the rope in the air for Karnus to see.

"That's impossible; they can't just vanish! FIND THEM!!" His golden eyes flashed with rage. The men fanned out, looking up into the trees and kicking leaf piles in search of what was right in front of them. As Duncan watched the men, he noticed something moving in the trees beyond them. Unable to focus just yet, he tried to find it again amid the trunks. Just then, right next to he and Kai, a large beast slinked from the woods. It's footfalls made no sound. The animal had the form of a great dog, though his front shoulders were a considerable bit bigger than its hind. Around its neck was a think mane of hair. It's face was curled in a sneer, revealing rows of razor sharp, enormous teeth, and from the top jaw hung two dagger-like fangs.

As Duncan stared at the creature only feet from him, Kai whispered what he already knew. "Wolvari." His grip around her tightened. The auburn-haired creature began to creep closer and closer to the soldier before it. He was so engrossed in the search, he realized, only too late, that he had become the prey. The wolvari pounced, digging its massive fangs and sharp teeth deep into his flesh. He screamed for a brief second and then fell silent. The momentary scream drew the attention of the other two men, who rushed back toward the campsite. The man in its jaws now dead, the wolvari released him and vanished back into the trees.

Aware that some new enemy had arrived, Karnus and

the remaining soldier drew their swords again. Standing back to back, they began to make their way down the hill to the south, toward their vehicle; still sitting where they left it. After they had received the information they wanted from the unwilling town's people, they had rushed to the Merin farm only to find it abandoned. Following fresh tracks, they took their vehicle into the trees, weaving through the trucks where they could fit. They had almost given up when one of the men had spotted the distant glow of a campfire from the belly of the machine. Karnus could not believe his luck. Now, as he fled some invisible terror with the only remaining member of his team he wished they had not found them. Eight men lay strewn on the ground dead around the camp of two children. Eight of Hadrir's finest had fallen to mere kids and horses, and now this silent death. Catching sight of the machine, Karnus bolted, leaving the soldier at his back stunned and alone. Within seconds, he heard the cries of death from behind. A second wolvari had pounced from the shadows, ripping the throat from the screaming man. As Karnus raced for the vehicle, claws dug into his shoulder. Pulling forward, he could feel the flesh give way to the claws. Too afraid to look back, he quickened his pace. Reaching the door, he pulled himself inside. Before the door could close, the claws lashed at him again, nearly claiming his leg. As the door drew shut, the paw retracted back through it. Breathless and badly wounded, Karnus pulled himself into the driver's seat, started the machine, driving away as fast as he could from the beast that had nearly killed him.

As he disappeared into the dark of the forest, the wolvari returned to the small camp. Sitting themselves down across the fire, they seemed to stare at the two horror-stuck and terrified Merin children. Kai and Duncan stared back, unable to move. As Duncan studied the two animals together, he realized something. They knew these creatures. He pushed Kai up a bit from his chest.

"Kai, I think we know them." Kai followed his eyes and really looked at the pair of worgs.

"The puppies from Brannon's wedding!" Instantly everything changed. Color came back to the world, and Duncan could hear the birds singing. As Kai pulled away to go to the wolvari, Duncan seized her, turning her face to his.

"What was that!" The confusion and fear were thick in his voice. He had just spent nearly ten minutes in a place he had never even imagined, the Shade.

"I'm not really sure. I just wanted to disappear, to go somewhere they couldn't find us. That's when the color went away." As she talked Duncan could hear the faraway tone of her voice. Realizing she was in shock, he decided that this conversation was best left for a time when she was well again. Releasing her, he watched her stand. She walked toward the wolvari but before she reached them, her eyes drifted to the corpse of her beloved Whisper. As if she had just discovered her dead, she flung herself onto the body, sobbing wildly. The black wolvari with the snow-white mane joined her. Resting beside her, she pressed the flat of her face against Kai's sobbing back. Duncan tried to stand, but couldn't. Falling back to the ground, he tried again. The auburn wolvari rose and came to him. As it bent down, Duncan tentatively placed an arm around its neck. Slowly, the animal lifted him to his feet and helped him to where Shadow had fallen, almost as if it knew that he would want to mourn the loss, as Kai did. For quite a while the four of them sat with the two fallen steeds. Kai cried until she had no tears, while Duncan only stared. He wanted to cry, wanted to sob as Kai had; but the tears did not come. Eventually, the wolvari led them back to the fire. Realizing that they could not stay here, surrounded by death, both friend and foe, Duncan began the task of packing away their camp.

Kai watched him load the saddlebags that no longer had horses to carry them. The bags were heavy and she wondered how on earth they would manage them. Leaning against her saddle, she moved her hand through the white, soft mane of the wolvari at her side. As her hand slid out of the mane, to her shoulders, Kai's hand touched something hard and sharp. Pulling her hand away, she looked at the creature. Running down its spine were spikes, bone had grown up through the skin in cone like points from shoulder to tail.

"Well, we won't be riding them. Have you seen their backs?"

Duncan stopped what he was doing and inspected the chestnut wolvari sitting near him. He hadn't noticed the bone spikes before. As he eyes the line of sharp protrusions, something said to him long ago came rushing to the front of his mind. He recalled the memory out loud, "These saddles are different, special, one day you will know why..." Kai watched in confusion as he scrambled to his saddle and turned it over. There, along the underside, was a line of cone shaped holes. Turning to Kai he spoke again, "Yes, we will." The wolvari were very patient as they waited for Duncan to figure out how to strap down the saddles. He secured his own and then Kai's. Realizing they needed reins of some kind, he retrieved the bridles from the bodies of their dead horses and, using his amber dagger, began modifying the leather harness. After several tries, he managed a makeshift halter. Slipping it onto the chestnut worg, he lifted himself into the saddle. The saddle had been difficult to get used to atop a horse, but atop a wolvari, it was heavenly. The high back cradled him like comfy chair, and the angle compensated perfectly for the slope of the creature's back. Sliding from the saddle he quickly modified Kai's bridal and loaded the packed saddlebags.

As they climbed into the saddles, Kai stopped to look again at her dead horse. "Shouldn't we bury them? Or something?" Her eyes began to fill again with tears.

"We have no time. Besides, they are part of the woods now. Their bodies will feed life. It's best we just leave them." Giving one last look at Shadow, he turned his wolvari and spurred him into motion. The wolvari moved fast and quiet through the trees. They seemed to know where they were going and after several failed attempts to change their course, Duncan decided to trust them. As they slipped through the trees, he and Kai sat silently, processing the tragedies this day had brought to them. Their father was dead, their friends gone too. Their home lay behind them. Everything they had had yesterday was lost to them. They were alone and cold, lost in the darkness of the night and the forest.

The wolvari turned and began heading toward a large boulder. As they drew nearer, Duncan could see their destination. At the base of the enormous stone was a small cave-like outcropping. Sure enough, the wolvari made their way straight to it. Sliding from his saddle, he helped Kai down and, for the second time that night, he made camp. Kai had cried herself to sleep almost as soon as the fire had been lit, leaving Duncan to stare hopelessly into the flames. His whole world was shattered. His father, his wonderful father, was lying dead in the streets, and he could not even pay his last respects. The thoughts of his father reminded him of the letters still tucked away in his vest pocket. Pulling them out, he studied the envelopes again. Setting the older, unmarked one and the one addressed to Kai aside, he peeled back the seal on the one meant for him. In the glow of the fire, he read the first line of the letter. Unable to process it, he read it again, and then again. 'Duncan, my son, Kai is not your sister....'

www.ingramcontent.com/pod-product-compliance
Lightning Source LLC
Chambersburg PA
CBHW020905200626
46814CB00001BA/177